MIKE BLACKSTONE
NIS SPECIAL AGENT
ASSIGNMENT: NAPLES, ITALY

A NOVEL

by

LT. WILLIAM CRAIG ELLIOTT
UNITED STATES NAVY- RETIRED

The Mike Blackstone Series, Number 1

DISCLAIMER

This is a work of fiction. Names, characters, businesses, places, events and incidents are either the products of the author's imagination or used in a fictitious manner. Any resemblance to actual persons, living or dead, is purely coincidental.

DEDICATION

To my wife, Patty who never failed in her support for this book.

First printing May 2016
Second Printing August 2016

Printed in the United States of America

ISBN: 978-0-9978989-0-3

ELLIOTT BOOKS
North Carolina
E-Mail: mikeblackstonebycraigelliott@gmail.com

PREFACE

These are the exploits of the fictional character, Naval Investigative Service Special Agent Mike Blackstone. They take place during the 1980's. While fictional names of characters are used in this novel, no attempt is made to correlate them to actual agents or other persons.

Background locations including Naples, Italy as well as other European countries under the jurisdiction of NIS Naples forms the backdrop for these adventures.

The official name of the Naval Investigative Service (NIS) was changed to Naval Criminal Investigative Service (NCIS) and continues in use today. Since this novel predates the name change, NIS will be used in lieu of NCIS.

The actions of Blackstone concentrates mainly on his NIS adventures doing battle with the bad guys. It will also be a trip of discovery for the reader to explore everyday life in the 1980's in Italy, the U.S. and Europe.

CONTENTS

CHAPTER 1
THE EARLY YEARS

The hometown fans were on their feet. Thunderously, the crowd was cheering with wild foot stomping on the metal benches; sounding much like cannon fire. No box seats here – just long metal planks seating around 500. Mike Blackstone was heading for the end zone. He made it and scored the winning touchdown in the final game of his high school football career for the Stoney Creek Hornets against the mighty big city Kiley Black Falcons. The final football game was played and his senior year in high school was almost over. *Now*, he thought, *what should I do with the rest of my life?*

Mike grew up as a typical small town Indiana farm boy who liked to play Cowboys and Indians. He was large for his age and was a good student and well liked in school.

Entering his freshman year of high school in 1963 and wandering the halls one day, he was noticed by the football coach. Mistaking Mike for someone visiting from the nearby college, Coach Jones asked if he could be of any assistance. It was easy for the coach to make that mistake as Mike was 6'3" and weighed 205 pounds. This was a pretty big guy for late 1960's.

"I'm sort of lost. It's my first day of classes." *Oh my*, thought Jones, *have I got a prospect here.* He convinced Mike he should play football for Stoney Creek. Mike would be a busy player as he found himself playing defensive end, offensive tight end and on the kicking teams. His team only had 30 players. The band

1

had 40. This compared to the big city schools like Kiley who had anywhere from 60 to 70 football players. He did have the distinction of being the first player in his high school's history to be a four-year letterman in football.

While in high school he worked odd jobs at gas stations and soon found this would not be his life's vocation. After graduation in 1967 and not knowing what he wanted to do, he enrolled in college at nearby Upper Indiana University (UIU). The school was little known as a basketball school and much less for their football program. The basketball team would later gain national attention when their star Harry Boyd played Clipper Jackson for the national basketball championship in 1979. It was not to be UIU's day and they lost to Wabash State.

Mike was anxious to continue playing football and tried out for the freshman team as a walk-on. Standing in line on equipment day to get his gear a fellow team member from one of the big city power houses remarked, "I played for the Washington Captains and I just don't know how I can play for a bunch of trees." Mike could hardly keep from laughing at the poor misguided fellow and attempted to enlighten him. "You see Sport; Sycamore does not stand for a tree here at UIU but rather for an Indian tribe; like the Sycamore Indians." With that revelation, he was OK doing battle for the Sycamores. Mike made the team as a defensive end.

Suiting up for his first game and proudly donning his blue and white UIU jersey, he was ready. Entering the second quarter of the game, Mike was ready to do gridiron battle against the boys from Central Eastern Illinois University.

2

On the first play from scrimmage, his college football career came to a screeching halt. Their offense ran an end around with the pulling guard drawing a bead on Mike. Blackstone was ready and fended off the initial block from their offensive tight end. He moved across the line to make his first college tackle. Coming straight at him like some guided missile was their huge pulling guard. He wasn't just huge – he was massive. Mike heard a loud 'pop' and the next thing he knew he was flat on his back with a broken ankle.

The injury kept him from continuing in football so he was left with only being an ordinary student. With a heavy heart he tried to concentrate on his studies but he spent too much time shooting pool and cutting classes. Before long he was failing and his student deferment was in jeopardy. He had a decision to make.

This was a critical juncture in his life as this was during the draft for the war in Vietnam. Now what was he to do? Wait to be drafted into the U.S. Army or join the U.S. Navy? Having received a failing grade in an art history class he made his move. Mike headed straight for the local navy recruiting office.

Meeting with a recruiter and being promised an aviation related job, he enlisted. Since he did have some college, he was promoted to the permanent rank of Aviation Apprentice (AA) and allowed to wear the authorized two diagonal green stripes on his uniform once he reported to boot camp. His next stop would be the U.S. Navy Boot Camp located outside Chicago, Illinois in December 1967. A stay in northern Illinois in the winter was something most people would not want to contemplate. Frigid winter weather in boot camp in Great Lakes was something Mike could not have imagined.

Since he was from Indiana and had spent many winters, he thought he was used to cold temperatures. Boy was he wrong – spending months on the Great Lakes gave a new meaning to cold! Mike felt like he was in the Artic rather than a few hundred miles north of his hometown.

Since Mike had joined in December, it would be the first time away from home for Christmas. Lonely would not accurately describe this feeling even though he had 80 fellow recruits in his company to share his misery.

Christmas Eve 1967 was spent in a cold drafty battleship gray drill hall with over 500 other homesick recruits singing 'Silent Night.' Boy, talk about being homesick and he sure would miss his mom's Christmas dinner. Little did Mike know he would spend many a Christmas and other holidays away from loved ones.

Days at boot camp were spent in nautical related classes, monotonous marching, target practice with a rifle and leading his company as he was awarded the designation of Recruit Chief Petty Officer; an impressive title but alas only good while in recruit training.

One of the more challenging evolutions at Great Lakes was laundry day. No washing machines or clothes dryers here; just a bucket, water and a little soap. Yep, Mike would learn the fine art of hand washing his dungarees. The routine would be to head to the barracks' laundry wash room with clothes in a bucket; washy-washy, rinse, wring out – all by hand. Now for the good or bad

4

part depending on one's proclivity for pain.

Putting on his navy issued blue Pea Coat and blue knit watch cap, he went outside with his laundry. Normal temperatures in December were ranging between 10-15 degrees Fahrenheit with blustery wind gusts. The clothes lines were located adjacent to the barracks. Remember, it was winter and cold – no, not just cold but damn sub-freezing cold!

Once outside, Mike and the rest of the wash team were directed to the aforementioned lines. Yep, 10 plus degree weather and he would be tying (no clothes pins) his clothes on modern day drying structures with short pieces of line. When finished, it was time to go back inside to thaw out.

When suitably frozen, the procedure would be reversed and back out into the cold to retrieve his uniforms. They resembled stiff frozen slabs of beef more than any recognizable clothing. Once back inside, they would be taken to a special heated drying room. First his uniforms would defrost which resulted in puddles of water collecting under them. Sometimes it took up to six hours for his clothes to dry out. Such was the life for our 60's sailor in boot camp; hand washing and frozen clothes. It seemed to Mike the navy had some documented scientific evidence that freezing of clothes helped the drying process – go figure!

Time flew by and before he knew it graduation day had arrived. This was a very big moment for Mike and the rest of Company 670. Assembling in a large drill hall festooned with rainbow colored signal flags and spotting his mom and dad in the reviewing stands, he thought his chest might explode. When

5

all recruit companies formed up it was time to pass in review. With the recruit band playing a rousing rendition of John Philipp Sousa's 'Stars and Stripes Forever', it was time to proceed. Drawing his cutlass, as RCPO he was entitled to wear one, he ordered the Guidon to raise the company flag and shouted the command, "Forward March!"

Next stop for AA Blackstone would be Aviation Mechanics School in Millington, Tennessee. Prior to reporting to this first duty station, he would be granted 30 days leave at home with his parents and friends.

Back in his hometown, he enjoyed wearing his wool Dress Blues or Cracker Jacks. The original usage of the term Cracker Jacks must have come from the popcorn candy treat of the same name – you know the one with the sailor on the cover of the box. When dressed our newly minted fleet sailor looked like the spitting image of that sailor with his white Dixie Cup hat, black neck scarf, blue jumper with white piping and the familiar 13-button blue bell bottom trousers. Mike was especially proud of the embroidered sharks on the underside of the cuffs on his jumper. He had those sewed on in Chicago while on liberty. Yes, sir, he definitely thought he could have posed for the box cover.

With his leave up and saying goodbye to his friends and family, it was off to Tennessee for further training.

Arriving at the school he was assigned to a barracks with 50 other aviation mechanic trainees. Days were spent going to classes where all aspects of reciprocating engines were taught with the goal of reaching the final requirement for graduation. One exercise Mike

6

thought was pretty stupid was to push a cannibalized obsolete aircraft around a parking apron. The trick was to get it to move with 10 students behind each wing, grunting and straining their guts out. Successful completion was to move the plane 10-15 yards simulating a re-spot on an aircraft carrier flight deck.

The final graduation practical would require the students to start up a single engine propeller driven aircraft. This would be no walk in the park; there were over 20 steps to master in starting it. Mike wondered, *why do it from memory? They had already practiced the evolution with its flight instruction booklet?*

He answered his own thoughts by remembering the navy logic of freezing clothes made them dry better. He was sure there was some long standing navy experiment that made the memory exercise worthwhile. The aircraft to be used was known as the A-1 Skyraider or SPAD for short. Even though some aviators considered it obsolete, it was still being used in Vietnam.

Nights were spent on liberty and filled with new and exciting experiences for this small town boy. Town liberty meant either Millington or Memphis depending on how much money Mike and his buddies had to spend. Walking into Millington to catch a movie was no problem. The price of admission was in their budget and the popcorn and sodas were cheap. One movie night there was some excitement when a large rat hopped onto Mike's foot. A night on the town in Memphis was always a difficult proposition

Most of his fellow trainees were too poor to afford a car but Fred had one. It was a brand new fire engine red Oldsmobile 442 convertible. His daddy was big in oil back in Oklahoma. As a

7

matter of fact, he was never short of money as his mommy sent him $100.00 every month to get by on. This was in addition to his regular monthly navy pay. He even supplemented that by charging Mike and his buddies $5.00 each to take them into Memphis.

Spending money for Mike and his buddies, except for Mr. Olds 442, was always in short supply. At the time, Mike was receiving the exorbitant sum of $30.00 every two weeks. While an ice cream or a soda was only 10 cents; his pay still did not go that far. By the end of the first week after payday, he would be shaking out his pants looking for any spare change. Small change might get you an ice cream or a candy bar but certainly not a night out on the town in Memphis.

What to do to solve this shortage of coin? Mike would be introduced to the time honored navy system known as Vampire Liberty. This was when one headed to the nearest blood bank and sold blood for an impressive $10.00 a pint. While this provided a ready source of extra income, one could only donate once every couple of months. Now with money in their pockets it was time to go to town and it wouldn't be Millington.

Graduation day finally arrived and with his new designation of ADRAA which meant he was now a designated striker or trainee in the Aviation Machinist Mate Reciprocating rating. After proudly sewing on the white ADR rating propeller atop his two green stripes on the upper sleeve of his jumper, it was off to his new duty assignment in Rota, Spain. This new assignment would be with VQ-2, a reconnaissance squadron. It was used for covert intelligence collection from the air.

Flying into Naval Air Station Rota, Mike was ready for any new and exciting experiences. After checking in with the squadron duty officer, he was driven to his new barracks. Barracks 28, nicknamed the Animal House, would be his new home for the next two years. His new squadron mates were known around the base as the VQ-2 Animals. Little did he realize how soon that moniker would figure largely in his life.

On his first night in the open style barracks, he was awakened in the wee hours of the morning by shouting, laughter and other noises. Jumping up from his rack or bed in civilian terms, which was located in a cubicle measuring no more than 12 feet by 15 feet, he was shocked to see a noisy disturbance in progress at the end of the hallway

Standing transfixed he saw several slightly inebriated guys; no they were definitely drunk and stumbling through the back door. What surprised Mike was that they were carrying a recently dug up 10-foot-tall palm tree, roots and all. Even with the dim lighting he could see the boys were having a difficult time with the tree. The tree crashed to the deck a few times before they managed to get it propped up in the corner. Evidently, the Animals of VQ-2 had arrived.

Still standing at his cubicle wearing only his standard navy white issued boxer shorts and tee shirt, he appeared to be the only person stirred by the commotion. No one else was jolted awake by the ruckus. Apparently, the others in the barracks were numb to these early morning escapades and continued on in dreamland: making their own noises – wheezing, snoring and farting.

The lone exception was a very old salty portly sailor with thinning silver grey hair who seemed to be more than a little pissed off by all the commotion. Dressed in his dress blues and wearing a white web belt with a wooden night stick attached, he looked rather official. In fact, he was the barrack's security watch.

Walking up to Mike, he introduced himself, "Hi, I'm Seaman Bob Jones but everyone calls me Pops and you must be the new guy." With Mike staring at his uniform which seemed to be a plethora of white and red stripes on his left sleeve, Bob explained the three diagonal green stripes denoted a non-designated Seaman (SN) and the six red stripes were for 24 years of service.

Wow! Mike thought to himself; *Bob must be at least 45 and with 24 years in the Navy and only a Seaman (E-3); promotion in this man's navy might just be a little slow.* Since it was only his first night with his new squadron, he would wait to find out more about Pops. With Bob returning to his duties, our new Animal decided to investigate this early morning activity.

Mike, making his way toward this boisterous group of sailors, was approached by one very heavy-set guy. "Hi, I'm Tony Thomas from New York and you must be the new guy." Apparently the whole world or at least the world of VQ-2 knew he was the new guy.

A few more fellows approached and more introductions were made: Pete Taylor was a pint size five-footer; Jimmy Talbot Carter was from New Orleans, Louisiana who the guys called Jimmy T; Gary Race was short and stocky and his strong northern accent marked him coming from New Jersey. Last to be

10

introduced was a very tall slender fellow named Jim Jay – called JJ. This band of brothers would be Mike's inner circle of friends for the next two years and what a wild roller coaster ride it would be compared to his life before joining the navy.

Mike was assigned to the line crew along with his new squadron mates. Disappointed at first that he would not be working on aircraft engines; he would make the best of it. He did have a swell bunch to work with doing all the jobs of a line crewman.

Days were spent washing the squadron's airplanes, fueling them and assisting in take-offs and landings. The inventory of VQ-2's aircraft consisted of propeller driven EC-121 Super Constellations, nicknamed Willy Victors or just Willys and EA-3D's, which were jet propelled and referred to as Whales.

It was routine for two or three-line crewman to deploy with the Whale aboard an aircraft carrier in the Mediterranean. It would be Mike, Gary and Jimmy T who were assigned on the next rotation. On a routine mission one of the squadron's E-A3D was launched from the carrier and got a cold catapult shot from the angled flight deck. It headed over the side of the ship and down into the azure colored sea. Just before it hit the water and sank, the plane captain could be seen climbing out of the top hatch and survived.

This crash was sobering for Mike and the crew of the aircraft carrier. Even though the crash took the lives of only two of the crew instead of three; it must have been small comfort for the families. Sadly, during the deployment, Mike lost his friend Gary when an arresting cable snapped and cut him in half.

The Willy was much different than the squadron's

11

EA-3D's. It was huge and an awesome sight. It was the same type of aircraft seen in old movies of white commercial propeller driven transatlantic planes with the familiar red TWA logo emblazoned on the side. The Super Constellation was still being used by some major airlines. It was initially produced as a luxury transport in the 1930's but was drafted as a military transport in WWII. After the war, several commercial versions were produced.

A unique identifier which made the Willy stand out was the three tails or vertical stabilizers. The big difference between the civilian version and VQ-2's was the addition of a radome on top and a bulbous one on the underside of the aircraft. To make the Super Connie even more menacing was the color scheme: white on top and solid black on the underside of the fuselage. Both the EA-3D and the EC-121 were used for electronic surveillance missions.

VQ-2's operation area was comprised of Eastern European Bloc Countries. It's sister squadron, VQ-1 was homebased in the Pacific and operated in the Far East area. The 60's were a dangerous period with the U.S. pitted against the Warsaw Pact whose chief sponsor was the Soviet Union. To illustrate the point, on some missions VQ-2's aircraft had some close calls from the communist bad guys. On the other hand, VQ-1 had a tragic confrontation when North Korean MIG-21's shot down one of their Willy Victor's with all on board presumed killed.

When not attending to their duties, Mike and the others would retire to the line shack and read comics or play the navy's age old game of Acey-Deucy, which was similar to Backgammon but more difficult and fun.

12

On a rotating basis, Mike and the other Animals would be assigned to night duty; 4:00 PM to 12:00 AM. It would comprise only two men and was pretty quiet unless planes were returning from deployments. It was Mike and Jimmy T's turn at bat. They would eat mid-rats from the galley, usually bologna sandwiches.

The flight line at night was full of hazards not normally encountered on the day watch. Mainly it was launching and recovery of aircraft, especially the Willy Victor. This gigantic black and white beast was huge in the daytime but it seemed even more massive and scarier when seen at night. Danger! – Danger! – Danger! This would be the operative words when working on the flight line at night.

On Mike's first night, the team was informed a Willy would be returning from deployment and arriving around midnight. Since he had numerous night duties under his belt, Jimmy T went over the landing plan. "Mike, you won't see the aircraft at first – you'll just hear it." Mike pondered this and thought, *with the size of this beast, how could one not see it coming in for a landing?* He would soon see the error of that thought.

Mike drove the squadron's yellow gear tow tractor, which was similar to a large civilian tow truck without the crane, to the flight line. Jumping out of the tractor, Mike donned his ear muffs and grabbed his red illumination hand wands; he was ready – he hoped.

"Mike, here it comes," exclaimed Jimmy. Looking around in the direction of the runway Mike said, "I can't see a damn thing except what looks like numerous small fires in the distance."

13

"That's him and he's on final approach. What you are seeing is stack gases being ignited from the exhausts." "Oh Shit! Jimmy it looks like some apocalyptic nightmare with a flying dragon swooping in and spewing fire," shouted Mike.

As the aircraft touched down, not only was it belching the aforementioned fire from its stacks; it was making the most awful screeching sound – the brakes. The sounds from the plane were eerie to say the least; engines making a fluttering sound and brakes sounding like some screaming wounded alley cat every time they were applied.

Mike was getting just a little apprehensive even though he was an old hand at daytime take offs and landings. He thought his first night duty would be pretty routine with only the difference being that, well, it was at night. It was the wrong assumption and answer. "Jimmy, don't forget I haven't done this before." "Mike, don't worry I've got your back."

As the aircraft exited the runway onto the taxiway it headed for the parking apron. Mike and his partner moved into position and prepared to receive it. Taking their positons - they were good to go and Mike said a silent prayer. With the approach of this demon from hell, still emitting orange and blue flames and screaming like the Devil, Mike's buddy began waving his wands in an up and down manner. This alerted the pilot to proceed straight ahead.

With this monster screeching and belching flames, it continued to head straight for Jimmy T so much so that Mike thought the plane's props were about to turn him into hamburger meat. When the aircraft was about 10 yards from him, he pointed his left hand wand towards Mike while continuing to move the right one in an up and down motion with the pilot's understanding that he was to follow the directions to the next set of red wands. Mike standing about 20 yards from Jimmy took over and directed the pilot to continue turning left with motions from his red wands. This procedure would continue with the two line crewmen alternating positions until the plane completed a 270 degree turn and had come to a stop.

Mike, standing in front of the aircraft with his wands crossed indicating to the pilot to keep his brakes deployed, waited for his mate to run under the plane's wings and place large yellow chocks at the main landing gear wheels. With the plane secured, Mike signaled to the pilot to cut his engines – a movement much like the universal signal for cutting one's throat. With all four engines shut down, Mike removed his ear muffs and regaled in the sweet sound of silence.

Mike liked working days better than nights and was getting into the group's standard routine. At quitting time, he and his buddies would head back to the barracks to play Payday Stakes Poker. Payday Stakes meant they would play with poker chips, keep track of winners and losers and settled accounts on payday. Payday for the U.S. Navy was every two weeks.

To break up the routine, the boys would head over to the enlisted club after work and down a few Cuba Libres for $.10 each. In the 1960's, navy bases had a segregated system of clubs: pay grade E-4 and below had the EM Club; E-5's and E-6's the Acey-Deucy Club and finally E-7's (Chief Petty Officers) had the

Chief's Club. When not hitting the EM club and not playing poker, there was always time to go Rota Root-in.

Rota Root-in meant walking into town from the base and drinking up one side of the street and down the other of the main drag. The object wasn't so much to get drunk but to score with the local bar girls.

Trying to date respectable Spanish ladies was out of the question. Just like back in the states in the 60's, these ladies of Spain just did not 'do' sailors. Their opinion of American sailors was much like the sentiment of: 'Dogs and Sailors Keep off the Grass.' This attitude left bar girls as the only viable option for our boys unless they paid for the services of a hooker. Paid sex didn't seem right so the Animals would keep on trying to get a freebie.

Of all the Rota bars, the two most popular were Benny's and the California. Benny's was located right outside the main gate and was the boys bar of choice. All the bar girls who worked there were either English speaking Europeans or American.

Let the games begin! The trick to scoring was to buy the girl copious amounts of drinks at inflated prices, usually only tea, with the hopes of taking her home after the bar closed. It hardly ever worked out for Sammy Sailor. He would usually end up poorer in the peseta (Spanish currency) locker and drunk while she would head home with her steady boyfriend. This age old practice of buying bar girls drinks in hopes of getting laid must have been where the phrase: 'Buy Me One Drink-ee – Love You All Night' originated.

With the days and weeks passing, Mike's efforts to land a

steady girlfriend resulted in one rejection after another. It was about to change one night when he was in Benny's. A pretty American by the name of Susan became interested in him. She had just starting working at the bar so Mike thought he'd give it a go.

Deciding that 'No Balls – No Blue Chips' would reap results and benefits, he made his move. Buying her drink after drink which allowed her to stay and talk to him, the conversation led to a startling revelation. Susan told him she was from a small town in Indiana and had attended Upper Indiana University. Mike was really blown away; her background was similar to his.

What a small world, 3000 miles from home and up popped a girl from his home state and university. If it was a story from a movie, it could not have been improved. Mike and Susan would be a couple for the next two years. She continued to work at the bar getting lonesome sailors to buy her drinks and Mike would take her home at closing time.

Learning of a happening place outside the town limits of Rota, the Animals decided to give it a shot. Mike, Jimmy T and JJ were the only Animals allowed weekend liberty. Grabbing a cab, they were off for a new adventure.

El Patio was nothing more than a rundown cinder block shack with peeling paint on the walls and an outdoor patio. This was where mostly Spanish ladies and gents would go for a good time to dance and listen to American music. Mike paid the entrance fee of 420 pesetas (exchange rate was $1.00 = 70 pesetas) for the group and headed inside. This was the time before 70's disco and it really was a pretty run down place but it was better than sitting in a

17

noisy bar and getting hustled. There was a local band playing some pretty lame tunes. A jukebox might have been a better option. Making their way to the bar and ordering some drinks it was time to find a table and check out the action. With the walls vibrating to the music it was hard for Mike not to jump up and start to dance.

It was definitely the 'in place' for the beautiful people. Mike surveyed the ladies and plenty were drop dead gorgeous. The Animals sure could look but any touching was out of the question. What the hell, the beer was cold and cheap and they came to party.

After a couple of hours and plenty of Cervezas, the lads were getting bored just sitting and ogling the women. They decided to call it a night and head back to the base. Heading for the exit all froze and stared in the direction of the main entrance. A lone Spanish fellow had just entered El Patio.

"Mike, get a load of that guy at the door." Mike turned his attention to where Jimmy T was pointing. As he gave the fellow the once over, he felt he was looking at himself in a mirror. Someone said or wrote something to the effect that everyone had a double somewhere in the world and Mike was looking at proof positive of the theory.

Mike walked up to the gent and with a cheerful "Hola", greeted him. With both standing less than a foot apart and not knowing what to do next, the Spanish Caballero nodded and passed by. This was about all the excitement they could handle so it was really time to head to the base.

While time in Rota was filled with exciting escapades for Mike and his buddies, it was time for the Animals to spread their

18

wings. Next stop would be liberty in Torremolinos, Spain or simply T-Town. This would be the first big road trip for the Mike and the boys. Unfortunately, due to heavy work requirements, only Jimmy T and Mike could get a three-day pass. On blast off day, Jimmy pulled his sharp solid black 1966 Mustang 2+2 up to their barracks and loaded it with their clothes and plenty of beer. Mike jumped in and our dynamic duo headed out of town.

Heading out Rota's main gate in Jimmy's speedster, our liberty hounds were on their way to T-Town. Since highway speed limits were not strictly enforced in Spain; in no time at all, they saw the town looming in the distance.

T-Town was a famous resort city on the coast of Spain, more commonly referred to as the Costa del Sol. Tourists from around the world including our intrepid partygoer's visited for fun in the sun. Having been schooled in the wily ways of bar girls, the two Animals made a pack not to get hustled for drinks at the local bars. They knew from experience the only value received would be to end up with a little temporary company until their money ran out.

The first bar they decided to hit was called Fun City; a noisy fast paced place with many beautiful girls and lots of loud music. Just as they entered, the Beatles, 'Hey Jude' was ending and the Door's, 'Light My Fire' was beginning to blast away on the jukebox. Cruising up to the bar the two ordered a couple of beers.

As Mike and Jimmy surveyed the room, it wasn't long before a couple of babes sauntered over to our boys. The ladies weren't just beautiful they were a pair of gorgeous Spanish honeys. Introducing themselves, they asked to join our boys for some drinks.

19

Mike was quick to say, "Sure, but we aren't buying you any drinks." This had the obvious result and the two left in a huff to continue working the bar.

Feeling pretty smug, the boys continued to enjoy their drinks and were content to watch the action. Their euphoria at not being hustled was short lived. Two fine looking ladies had walked in the bar and Mike and Jimmy surmised they were ordinary tourists. It was clear to our wily sailors these two women were not bar girls out hustling drinks - or so they thought.

Jimmy being more fleet of foot was up off his bar stool looking like he was shot out of a cannon. He made a bee-line for the ladies. With remarkable speed, he looked like some world class sprinter. A short conversation and he strolled back to Mike with the two ladies in tow. He laid claim to the blonde while Blackstone was left with the not too shabby red head. It was party time.

The boys, being proper gentlemen, asked the ladies if they cared for a drink. *No problem here,* Mike thought. These were obviously not bar girls. They had not been in the bar. The two had just walked in much like our boys had done earlier. More importantly the ladies did not come on to Mike and Jimmy in fact it was just the opposite. These ladies appeared to be in their early 20's and politely ordered two very small bottles of a Champagne type drink called a Piccolo, complete with straws.

Conversation was lively but it was soon apparent the duo would not be scoring, so finishing his drink, Mike asked for the bill and what a shock! The bill came to 700 pesetas or $10.00 U.S. While this might seem reasonable to some remember it was the

1960's and Mike and Jimmy's monthly pay was around $90.00 each. A light suddenly came on and Mike realized the truth of their situation - these worldly sailors had been had! A beer was less than $1.00 U.S. which made each 5-oz. Piccolo about $9.00.

Mike cautiously moved from his bar stool to give Jimmy the bad news. "Old buddy, the bill is $10.00 U.S." Not understanding the worried look on Mike's face, Jimmy responded, "What's the problem? I don't think $10.00 for two beers and two drinks for the ladies is all that bad." He was not going to like the explanation but Mike went ahead anyway, "No. It's not together, it's $10.00 for one beer and one Piccolo – we've been had." Sensing the game was up, the girls left. Our boys, with down trodden hearts, reluctantly paid the bill.

OK, this just could not happen; two world wise sailors out on the town could not be had! They would move on and be a little careful as the night progressed. As the two walked the main drag it was time to check out another place. After all, they were getting pretty thirsty again.

Los Lobos was their bar of choice and they would be on high alert. What a surprise for them as they entered but who would be sitting at a secluded table chatting up two older well-dressed portly gentlemen but the ladies from Fun City. It was not hard to mark the men as tourists. Their loud flowered Hawaiian shirts and cowboy hats made them stick out like sore thumbs. Misery loves company so our duo grabbed a couple of barstools and ordered a round of beer.

Watching someone else getting fleeced would take some of

21

the sting out of their recent experience. Our boys decided to do a little math and counted that group's drink total. Counting the number of Piccolos on the table came to a grand total of ten plus the men's drinks. As they watched, two more rounds were ordered. Now in front of the two gentlemen were drinks that totaled around $90.00 for the girls plus the cost of the gents six empty beer bottles.

Sensing this drama was about to get interesting Jimmy ordered two more beers and they both sat back to watch. When the next round came, it looked to Mike like the gentlemen were asking the ladies to pay for the round. The next thing observed was Jimmy and Mike's 'ladies' jumping up and exiting in a not too lady-like fashion: more like feet don't fail me now. The two suckers were left with empty pockets and dreams of what might have been. With shattered hopes, the two signaled for their bill. The bartender approached the men and handed them the tab.

With the two looking at the bill, there appeared to be a pretty good confrontation with the bartender. The next thing our boys saw were two flowered blurs sprinting past them with the bartender in hot pursuit. The Animals weren't having any luck with the ladies but the entertainment was sure worth the drive from Rota.

What seemed like minutes but actually was more like 60 seconds, back came the bartender followed by our heroes and two Guardia Civil policemen. They were not hard to miss dressed in their green uniforms and wearing their easily recognizable famous black shinny leather tri-corn hats flipped up in the back. Jimmy nudged Mike, "Check out the dudes with the funny hats and machine guns." "Jimmy, pipe down! They're the Guardia and we

22

certainly don't want any trouble."

The history of their tri-corn or tricornio (in Spanish) hats dated back to the reign of Queen Isabella II who authorized the unique upward shape of the hat for the Guardia Civil. The smashed hat look would become part of Spanish military folklore. The moss green uniforms were instituted in the same time period as the hat.

During Mike's tour, these police were not to be messed with as they were famous or infamous in Spanish history and used by the dictator, General Francisco Franco for his personal ideas of population law and order. In fact, on one occasion in Rota, they were used to relocate some Gypsies who were squatting on the outskirts of town and causing problems with American sailors and marines. They moved on.

The two men obviously had seen the error in their hasty decision to run out on the bill and were seen emptying their pockets and paying the check. Since there was not going to be anymore fireworks Mike and Jimmy decided the town was a little out of their financial league. It was time to head back to Rota.

On the drive back, the boys decided that they needed a more outrageous story to share with their squadron mates. The story hatched was to embellish their adventures with numerous amorous verbs and adjectives about scoring with the ladies. It just wouldn't do to reveal the truth about how they got hustled.

Time flew by for Mike at VQ-2 with days spent in the same routine of working and playing with his buddies. It never seemed to get boring working on the line, playing poker, drinking and chasing girls. Of significance, Mike had passed his rating exam and was promoted to ADR3. He proudly sewed his rating badge which showed one red chevron, a white eagle and his white propeller between the two.

Orders had arrived at VQ-2 for Mike. He was being transferred to a new assignment in Norfolk, Virginia. His best friend Jimmy T was headed to Vietnam. With a heavy heart he said goodbye to his other shipmates and Susan. Even though he would miss them, he was anxious to report to his new station with VRF-31. Once onboard the aircraft, Mike perused the information packet he had received.

Arriving at the Naval Air Station it was only a short drive to the other side of the base where his new squadron was located. The first thing he noticed was a colorful banner hanging from the hangar's main door emblazoned with Home of the VRF-31 STORKLINERS. He also noticed the absence or near absence of any planes parked on the flight line. This was much different from VQ-2; it had a full complement of EC-121's and EA-3D's. He remembered from his information packet that the mission of this squadron was solely to pick up and deliver various types of aircraft to facilities around the U.S. Well, he figured he would get the whole story on VRF-31 once he checked in.

Entering the hangar, he reported to the duty officer who sent him to see the leading chief petty officer for the squadron, Master Chief Aviation Machinist Mate Reciprocating (ADRCM) Williams. Williams was an imposing figure but what really caught Mike's attention was the aviator wings on his flight jacket. For you see, he was not wearing navy enlisted aircrew wings but rather navy

24

pilot wings. Prior to reporting to VRF-31, the only pilot wings he had ever seen were worn by commissioned officers back in his old squadron.

Mike was in the presence of someone from the history books of naval aviation; an enlisted full-fledged naval pilot. He had to learn more. Seeing the curious look on Mike's face and with him eyeing the wings, the Master Chief volunteered he was in fact the last remaining enlisted pilot in the United States Navy. Williams was qualified to pilot over 10 different types of aircraft including both fixed wing and rotary types. With time running short, ADRCM Williams told Mike that someday he would tell him the story of how he became a naval pilot.

Looking over Mike's service jacket, ADR3 Blackstone was assigned to the line crew and he departed to continue checking in with various departments at the squadron and around the base.

The following day Mike reported to the leading Chief Petty Officer of the line division: Chief Aviation Machinist Mate Jets (ADJC) Richards. The Chief advised their duties were pretty limited since the squadron didn't own any aircraft. His primary job would be mostly assisting in the landing and take-off of aircraft and refueling them. Mike's military duties would include standing barrack's security watches and providing security at the hangar area.

Mike thought his assignment to VRF-31 was going to be pretty boring and tame after the excitement of working and partying with the Animals.

After being assigned to the line for about three months, Mike visited the squadron's aircrew lounge to bring fuel reports for

25

the transient planes on the flight line. In the lounge he ran into ADRCM Williams and decided to ask him to explain the duties of VRF-31 enlisted aircrewmen.

"Mike, aircrewmen act as co-pilots, navigators, radiomen and plane captains. Additionally, they perform pre-flight and post flight inspections of the various aircraft in which they are assigned. The best part was crewmen get to fly all over the U.S. When not flying, off-duty crews hang around the lounge and play Pinochle or Acey-Deucy. Some read and study technical manuals on different types of aircraft."

Mike got to thinking; *this is the job for me but how to get from the line crew to the aircrew?* The answer for Mike was simple, he just had to fill out a Special Request Chit requesting transfer from the line to aircrew duties.

Mike approached Williams and with the Master Chief guessing the real purpose of his visit, helped him fill out the paper work and forward it up the chain of command. While he was waiting for the results, he was told to get a flight physical.

Finally, the big day arrived for Mike and he was called to the aircrew lounge. His chit was approved and now he was on the road to becoming a qualified Special Duty Aircrewman. Searching the aircrew lounge, he found ADRCM Williams. After checking with him, he was instructed to proceed to a scheduled water survival test which included a ride in the Dilbert Dunker.

The Dunker was a type of metal sled resembling an airplane cockpit that traveled from the top of the base swimming pool, entered the water, turned upside down and ended at the bottom of the pool. The object of the exercise was once the sled was at the bottom, the trainee was to extricate himself and swim to the surface.

Strapping in, he readied himself for the ride of his life. The instructor shouted, "Ready?" Mike gave him the thumbs up signal and the sled was released. Plummeting down the track at an impressive speed, it hit the surface of the water with a jolt. It immediately sank to the bottom upside down with Blackstone still strapped in. Mike grabbed the quick release on his harness but it was jammed. Trying not to panic – no easy trick as he was running out of air, the harness released and he swam to the surface.

Once at the surface, Mike climbed out of the pool gasping for air and figured he was finished. "Not so fast, Mr. Blackstone," shouted the swim instructor. There was one more trial he would have to pass – the water survival float test.

The float test was designed to see if a flier could remain floating in the water after a crash landing or parachuting over water from a crippled plane. To receive a passing grade, ADR 3 Blackstone would have to enter the pool fully clothed in flight suit, boots and helmet and remain floating by any means for 20 minutes. Just to make it more difficult, a clock was placed on the wall to remind one and all how much longer they had to float to qualify. At any time, an individual could quit just by swimming to the edge of the pool and announcing – "I quit!" Mike was sure that he would pass since he had always been a good swimmer since childhood.

Jumping into the pool with the other applicants, Mike watched as the clock started. It was readily apparent this was not going to be a leisurely swim as his flight suit and boots quickly filled with water and he started to sink. Thrashing wildly, he rose to the surface and began the laborious task of trying to stay afloat. It would be 20 minutes of pure hell flailing his arms back and forth just to stay in an upright position while treading water and gulping copious amounts of chlorine-laced water.

Totally exhausted after 15 minutes, Mike was ready to throw in the towel. The instructor noticed he was struggling and heading for the side of the pool and shouted, "Mr. Blackstone are you a quitter? There is no room in naval aviation for quitters so come on over and climb out." He just could not go on and finish and would take the instructor's offer. His dream of being a flier was soon to come to an abrupt end.

Mike was almost to the side of the pool when a very senior looking gentleman with silver grey hair swam over; "Son, I'm over 45 years old and if I can make it, so can you." With that encouragement, he reluctantly dog paddled back over to the middle of the pool. The clock struck 20 minutes and a wonderful sounding buzzer blared. One tired but elated soon to be flier had passed.

Returning to the squadron aircrew lounge after having passed all aircrew requirements, he found Williams and gave him the good news. Now, all Mike had to do was sit tight and wait to start flying. The Master Chief gave him a well-earned Bravo Zulu or a Well Done. He was instructed to report to the parachute loft to be issued his flight gear.

Checking in with the petty officer in charge of the parachute loft, Mike was issued a large navy standard green parachute bag. First into his parachute bag went his flight suit, flight helmet, boots,

28

survival harness and other required stuff too numerous to mention but the last and albeit the most important was his parachute. One item would not go into the bag was his brand new leather flight jacket with an American flag patch on one shoulder and the squadron patch on the other. Mike liked the graphic portrayal on the VRF-31 patch of a stork in midair flight. It showed the stork wearing a flight helmet and goggles delivering a plane carried in its beak. He thought it funny that the plane was wrapped in a diaper.

Before leaving, Mike was told he could decorate his helmet in any fashion he desired. Removing the helmet from his bag and with the help of the parachute rigger, he proudly decorated his helmet with fire engine red flames and with his flying nickname HOOSIER emblazoned right on the top. With his bag filled up, he was off to report back to the squadron.

Finding Williams in the ready room, Mike was told he was ready to begin his training and would be a very busy guy. He was only an aircrew trainee and would have to study and master any and all systems related to the fixed and rotary reciprocating aircraft he wanted to be qualified in. In order to receive his coveted naval aircrew wings, he would have to pass all tests related to his chosen planes plus accumulate the required number of flight hours. To his surprise he had been scheduled for his first flight the next day. Wahoo! He was on his way.

Dawn broke bright and sunny with Mike staring at the ceiling in his barracks room. He had laid awake most of the night; he was just too excited to sleep. Giving in, he got up and carefully dressed in his Green NOMEX flight suit and laced up his aviator's brown flight boots. He saved the best for last; his blue ball cap with the gold VRF-31 logo was carefully placed on his head. Looking in the mirror Mike thought he looked like one of the pilots from the movie the 'Flying Leathernecks' starring John Wayne. Musing he reflected, *not too bad for a small town Indiana farm boy.* Grabbing his parachute bag and extra clothes he was off to the hangar.

Since it was a Saturday, the squadron as well as the aircrew lounge was pretty much empty except for another crew that would depart later in the day. To his surprise, he would be flying with ADRCM Williams as the pilot and ADJ2 George Chance as the qualified Aircrewman.

Chance was of average height and weight with nothing noteworthy about his appearance unless you count the very sore looking black eye he was sporting. Inquiring, Mike was told it was just the result of a slight misunderstanding with some lady's husband. Not a very talkative guy, Chance did relate it wasn't half as bad compared to his next encounter with another irate husband. With a puzzled look on his face, Mike inquired, "OK George, so if that shiner wasn't so bad – what could be worse?" "I'll tell you. How about having your new Corvette shot up by another irate husband with a blast from his shotgun."

The story for Mike of the VRF-31 STORKLINERS was just beginning and he was sure there would be more to follow. Mike reflected on Petty Officer Second Class Chance's stories; *maybe this tour with VRF-31 would turn out to be just as interesting as the time in VQ-2.*

With the trio sitting around the navigation table, Williams

went over the flight plan, RON (Remain Over Night) spots, and the ultimate destination of the Bone Yard; a nickname given where old planes went to rest or die. This facility was located at Davis–Monthan Airfield in Tucson, Arizona. With all preparations complete, it was time to depart. Their aircraft would be a S-2F TRACKER, an anti-submarine warfare type aircraft, nicknamed the STOOF which was being sent into storage at the facility.

The S-2F was fixed-winged with twin reciprocating Pratt & Whitney engines. It slightly resembled a smaller version of a WWII B-24 LIBERATOR twin-engine bomber without the Plexiglas navigator/bombardier nose station. After the preflight of the aircraft by Blackstone and Chance and with Williams finishing filing the flight plan, it was time to board. To his surprise, he would be riding in the co-pilot's seat. George would be looking over his shoulder functioning as his trainer for this flight. Boy, talk about life in the fast lane, it was much like when his father threw Mike into the town's lake to teach him to swim. It was sink or swim - no lesson's required.

For those folks, including Mike, that had only ridden in commercial aircraft's passenger area, riding up front would be a wondrous experience, albeit a little scary. He strapped himself in the co-pilot's seat on the right side of the cockpit and contemplated his view of the runway. All systems were in the green and it was time to start the engines. First the left one got off to a rattling start followed by the right which coughed and belched gray smoke. It was time to taxi to the departure apron. With the plane idling at the run up area, the Master Chief called out the final checklist. The engines were run up to maximum RPM's. The aircraft was vibrating with every nut and bolt trying to shake itself loose and the noise way off any decibel meter, it was time to go. ADR3 Blackstone was instructed to depress his set of brake pedals and to place his left hand over Williams' right on the throttles. This was standard procedure for backing up a pilot to insure the throttles didn't back off and the plane lose power as it started its take-off run.

Williams shouted, trying to be heard over the roar of the engines, the command, "Let's Go" into the radio intercom. Now with both engines at full throttle and with the aircraft vibrating like it was about to come apart; the brakes were released.

While this aircraft wasn't no F-4 PHANTOM, it seemed to Mike like they were breaking the sound barrier as the plane headed down the runway. The sound of Clickity-Clack as the wheels made contact with the runway expansion joints reminded him of a runaway railroad train traveling down its tracks. Reaching the end of the runway, the Master Chief violently pulled back on the stick (actually a wheel) and they were airborne. With the order "Wheels Up"; they were on their way to Tucson.

Pretty much the first leg was routine at least to Williams and ADJ2 Chance but to Mike it was another story. As he gazed out his side window at the scenery, it seemed like he was living a dream. With a blast in his ears from his radio headset, Williams brought him back to reality with, "Mike, take it for a while." Not sure of this aviation terminology, answered "Take what?" Williams busted out laughing, "Why, fly the airplane; just keep it level, watch your altitude and steer a compass course of 180 degrees." *Wow,*

Mike thought, *piloting an airplane, who would have thought?*

With Mike at the controls, valiantly trying to keep it level, fly in a more or less straight line and pretty much keep from screwing up, he noticed Chance pull out a little green memo book from his flight suit pocket. The book was pretty small for any important flight information, so what was the book used for? Blackstone decided to try for an answer from George.

"Mike, this is probably the most important book I carry – it's my lady's address book categorized by RON cities." Now that he thought about it, Blackstone had seen other crewmembers with the same book. It seemed that George was not the only one who carried the little green book and a few more of VRF-31's crewmen were geographical bachelor's and carried the same book.

He was actually piloting a U.S. Navy aircraft and would wonders never cease? What seemed like an eternity was over all too soon, Williams took back the controls for their landing at their first RON location: Naval Air Station (NAS) Pensacola in Pensacola, Florida.

With the STOOF secured for the night, it was time for some sleep or so Mike thought. There were three things explained to him by Chance. They each were on $25.00 per day per diem for food and lodging, they never slept on base as VRF-31 personnel were authorized to use civilian accommodations and crewmen always had time for a beer and some fun after a hard flight.

Pooling their per diem, the trio checked into a Holiday Inn and got a triple at a cost of $24.00. Mike was way ahead on the math and figured he already had a quick $17.00 profit. With his normal navy pay, flight pay and now this per diem thing; he never felt so rich. Those early days when he shook his pants for loose change to buy an ice cream seemed like a bad dream. After taking a quick shower, it was out the door for a couple of beers and dinner. Nothing too exciting and with an early take-off scheduled for the morning, the crew headed back to the hotel.

Since it was still early, George listened to some music while Williams was busy catching the Wall Street reports on the TV. With Mike having very limited experience associating with senior enlisted personnel; he sat in a chair and read the S2F flight manual. He was most familiar with hanging out with fellow junior enlisted sailors and focusing on chasing babes and drinking. From time to time he would look up from his publication to see what Williams found so interesting on the tube. "What are you watching on the TV?"

Not used to being someone's tutor on his personnel life, Williams decided to make an exception for Mike. He explained, "Not all enlisted sailors think only of booze and broads; some actually have other interests. I'm interested in the stock market as well as investing in real estate. I actually own a little bit of downtown Norfolk." Mike definitely thought he could learn a lot from this fellow and not just about flying.

Turning the TV over to Mike so he could concentrate on the financial pages of the local newspaper, Blackstone went channel cruising. In the days before TV remote control, channel cruising meant standing at the television and turning the rotary dial on the set. Rotating the dial through all three channels, he happened upon

34

a WWII movie about aircraft carriers.

Hearing the roar of aircraft engines from the TV, the Master Chief looked up from his papers just in time to see a SBD dive bomber take-off.

"Hey kid, you wanted to know how I got my pilot's wings? I flew those in WWII as a First Class Petty Officer." With that bombshell, Mike probed further. Williams continued, "What a lot of civilians did not know at the time of WWII, the United States Navy was short of officer pilots. I was lucky to be picked for the enlisted pilot program. Funny thing, now I'm in a squadron whose only function is to ferry aircraft and my wife did the same job during WWII. Small world, isn't it?"

After breakfast, it was back to the airfield. Next stop would be VRF-31's major rendezvous spot in El Paso, Texas. For this hop, Mike was content to observe Williams and Chance. Touching down at the El Paso Airport and parking the aircraft, he was excited to check into the El Paso Inn. He heard many stories about the place from Chance on their flight from NAS Pensacola. He guessed the stories would make a good cheap romance novel. He was soon to learn about Chapter One - Nights at the El Paso Inn.

The Inn, it seemed, was a mandatory stop for VRF-31 flight crews. While the trio checked in, a terrific amount of noise and laughter was heard from the adjoining bar. Investigating the source, Mike entered and understood the story of the El Paso Inn. Looking around the bar and pool tables, he saw no less than six VRF-31 flight crews in attendance - all in flight suits. Yes, this was the official VRF-31 hangout and he was an official member of the club.

Deciding to grab a brew, he headed for the bar. As the blonde bartender, wearing a low cut shirt that left nothing to the imagination, approached to take his order, he also noticed she was wearing a VRF-31 ball cap with several nice looking metal souvenir type pins attached to it. Mike was curious and asked her, "Excuse me but what do the pins signify?" "I collect them from crew members who strike my fancy and reward them with some exciting after hour's entertainment." Mike figured this was a polite way to say a nice pin could get you laid.

"By the way, you have one I'm missing and my shift is up." Well, even though he was just a small Indiana farm boy, he hadn't just fallen off the proverbial turnip truck, so off to his room they went. Using a variation on Paul Harvey's signature sign-off message of, "And now you don't know the rest of the story", Mike figured in this case, it was anyone's best guess as to the rest of the story.

The next morning one blurry eyed crewman and no, it wasn't Chance or Williams dragged himself into the airplane. Mike immediately requested to be an observer on the hop to Tucson. Williams, having been in the same boat on more than one occasion, agreed. The only observing Blackstone ended up doing was to check his eyelids for light leaks or better known as taking a nap.

The approach to the Bone Yard at Davis-Monthan Airbase was not to be missed by our erstwhile first time crewman and Williams had Chance wake him up. Nothing like being awakened from a sound sleep and not know where you were; unless you count being in a very loud wind tunnel with huge amounts of noise

36

that came from parts unknown. As Mike stood up and looked over Williams and Chance's shoulders he could not believe the sight he was beholding. The Bone Yard was massive.

While Davis-Monthan was and still is an active Air Force base, for members of VRF-31, it was known simply as a place to drop off tired military airplanes whose ultimate fate was to be either stored for further use or dismantled. The facility was created after WWII to handle the thousands of surplus aircraft being returned to the states. At any one time there were hundreds of planes being stored on the four square mile complex.

Little did Mike know that in the next two years he would be flying many planes to this yard and on a few occasions taking some out. On one occasion the U.S. government sold some surplus S-2's to the South Americans. Removing an aircraft from storage was usually a scary proposition. They almost always were missing quite a bit of equipment that was pretty darn important. It was a known practice that when a plane was being sent to the Bone Yard, squadron mechanics would take off some equipment to be used as spares on other airplanes.

With the mission complete it was time to make arrangements to return to the squadron. Instead of returning home commercially, the crew would be taking a Marine Corps CH-34 gas piston driven helicopter out of storage and returning it to Norfolk to be reworked and brought back in to active service.

The CH-34 was built by Sikorsky Aviation in Connecticut from 1954 to 1968. When production ceased over 1,500 had been built. Mike hoped his crew got one of the later models.

Checking over the aircraft, Mike was somewhat alarmed, to say the least, to find some important navigational equipment missing. "Master Chief, what do we do about the missing equipment?" "Son, get used to it. This is about what we expect when taking an aircraft out of here. We have a compass and a radio so we'll just head east and hope for the best. In fact, if we get lost, we can always fly a couple hundred feet off the deck and follow the highway signs." *Great!* Mike muttered under his breath, *fine time to mention that a set of AAA road maps might be needed.*

With time to kill and dressed in their flight suits, Mike and the MCPO headed to the base PX. They needed to pick up some last minute items. Mike wasn't sure if he should be looking for some road maps so he settled on picking up a couple sports magazines. While Blackstone was looking at the magazines, a full U.S. Navy Captain (four stripper) naval aviator walked up to the Master Chief. Blackstone thought nothing of it until the Captain spoke to Williams.

"Excuse me Chief, I noticed you were wearing your aircrew wings inappropriately on your khaki cover." With a slight smile on his face, Williams advised the Captain they weren't aircrew wings but naval pilot wings. He explained they did belong on his cover opposite his enlisted insignia for a Master Chief Petty Officer. "I received my aviator's wings as an enlisted pilot in WWII."

With a sheepish look, the Captain apologized and slinked away like a child being sent to his room. For Mike, a junior enlisted, there was nothing like watching a senior officer being brought down a peg or two.

38

Back at the airfield the CH-34 was ready for flight. For those not familiar, the helicopter was a brute with its massive Pratt and Whitney engine located behind clam shell doors in the front of the aircraft. The crew sat in an elevated cockpit with a fine view of the scenery. There was a major down side to this platform - the engine was made of magnesium. If an onboard fire started, a highway distress flare would seem like a firework's sparkler compared to the engine fire. In fact, while Mike was flying for VRF-31, another crew in a CH-34 crashed in a farmer's field nose first and burned for 10 hours and it was not a pretty sight.

When Blackstone was in Millington at mechanic's school, students were given a demonstration of what would happen if water was used as an extinguishing agent on a magnesium fire. When the instructor sprayed water on the material in a galvanized bucket, the metal exploded with one hell of a bang.

Mike boarded the aircraft and made a mental note to remember that if the CH-34 caught on fire to jump out, run like hell and for heaven's sake, don't grab a garden hose!

This would be Mike's first ride in a helicopter and he was most excited until MCPO Williams told him to get in the left seat. *Oh my God,* Mike thought, *this crazy old fool wants me to pilot the aircraft.* The MCPO could see the terror in Mike's eyes and reassured him, "Mike, take it easy. You are only the co-pilot. On a helicopter the pilot sits in the right seat instead of the left. I will be piloting this baby."

With ADCM Williams piloting and ADR3 Blackstone acting as co-pilot, it was time to head back to Norfolk with the same stops along the way. There would be one slight detour on the trip. Following his chart of their flight, he noticed that the aircraft was heading a little south of Columbus, New Mexico.

Over Mike's headset, "Blackstone to pilot, over." Williams responded, "What's up?" "Master Chief, I'm following our track and it seems we're too far south of our check point at Columbus, New Mexico. Is there a problem?" "Mike, when we head west we always do a little shopping." *OK, so here we are in the middle of nowhere and we're going shopping.* Good thing Mike had released the talk button on his headset when he muttered this latest bit of frustration.

With Mike still confused he watched the Master Chief lower the collective stick in his left hand while pushing the cyclic stick forward in his right and the aircraft started to descend. As the CH-34 got close to the ground, Williams pulled back on the cyclic and he made a soft landing in an empty field. "Mike, watch the aircraft and we'll be right back." Off the two trotted in the direction of the border crossing to Columbus, Mexico. With the engine idling, he had nothing to do except sit back and wait. Blackstone was after all the new guy and what did he know?

Shortly, Mike's two seniors came trotting back toward the helo but it appeared they were walking a little funny and their flight suit pockets were making a clinking sound. They climbed aboard with a jocular, "We're back."

Before resuming their positions, the two emptied their flight suits of Tequila bottles and jars of Jalapeño peppers. The MCPO beat Mike to the punch "Whenever we get near Columbus, we always stop and do a little shopping at Tilley's." Mike figured this was Chapter 2 – Shopping with VRF-31.

Back at the squadron, Mike completed all requirements for duty as Special Duty Aircrewman. The CO pinned his new shinny gold (actual brass) aircrew wings on him. He was now authorized to add the NEC 8258 to his official record.

His assignment with VRF-31 was nearly up and having qualified in three fixed wing aircraft models plus two helicopters; a career decision needed to be made. He could either ship over, re-enlist in naval terminology, and stay with VRF-31 and keep flying or return to the civilian world. Mike chose the latter.

Not sure what to do now that he was a civilian he tried his hand at attending college, a stint as a superintendent of a juvenile detention facility, worked as a Penn State University police officer and finally got a job as a private detective. None of these provided him with the ever changing excitement of his navy life in VQ-2 and VRF-31.

Realizing he missed the Navy, he re-enlisted in the Photographic Interpreter (PT) rating working in naval intelligence. Various duty stations including ships and shore installations made the years fly by. Mike rose through the enlisted ranks until he was commissioned in the Limited Duty Officer program as an Intelligence Officer and was promoted from First Class Petty Officer to Ensign.

Mike was given several first duty choices as a naval officer but the one that intrigued him the most was an assignment to Naples, Italy as a Naval Investigative Service Special Agent.

Mike considered it quite an honor. With his selection, as a naval officer agent, he would be among less than 10% of the NIS Special Agent community.

Checking out of his last duty station with Fleet Intelligence Center Europe and Atlantic (FICEURLANT), he would be on his way to the Naval Investigative Service (NIS) Academy located at the Office of Naval Intelligence Headquarters in Suitland, Maryland. But first a little shopping was in order since NIS special agents wore plain business type clothes and Mike had none.

What does a NIS Special Agent look like? He had no idea so he watched some police detective TV shows and thought he would pick up some ideas. Could a basic detective looking outfit of coat and tie be that different from what a NIS agent would wear? Mike decided there probably wasn't much difference and bought some new togs.

With his new wardrobe packed in his brand new Triumph TR-7 Convertible, he was ready to head to Maryland. He had purchased it as a reward for being commissioned as a naval officer. So now, another new adventure was just beginning for Mike.

CHAPTER 2
THE NIS ACADEMY

Mike arrived at the NIS Academy and was joined by several Special Agent (S/A) trainees. Most notable were: Bob Arkin, a former Dallas policeman; former Federal Oversight Service (FOS) Agent, Tom Goldbloom and John Russo, North Carolina State Police. It would seem to Mike that these gentlemen had much more experience in police work but it didn't faze him as he was determined to hold his own.

S/A Clyde Lowentom greeted one and all to the Basic Agent's Course with his quick New York accent. Looking around the room, he saw some pretty anxious faces and tried to put the class at ease. Lowentom announced, "People you need to forget everything you learned in your former careers in police work." This did not sit well with the class so he continued. "All aspects of working as a NIS Special Agent will be so different that everyone in the class will be starting at the same level of knowledge - zero."

While this bomb shell was digested by most of the students, Tom, the former FOS agent posed the first question of the day about their soon to be status as federal Special Agents. "Clyde, once we are certified Special Agents and we happen to be in a 7-11 store and a robbery takes place – what do we do?" Since Clyde had already deflated some of the students' high expectations, he did not want to come across as being too negative. He answered this new agent in training with, "Well Tom, just take good notes."

The class in unison shouted, "What?" How could this be?

43

Upon graduation, they assumed they would be just like the FBI and other government federal agents. What had Mike volunteered to do? Since he was in the navy and under orders, he would just make the best of it. He couldn't quit, so with determination, it was 'damn the torpedoes and full speed ahead.'

Clyde, still maintaining a very positive attitude continued with the class orientation. "Friends, you only have jurisdiction to include arresting powers on U.S. Navy and other military installations. When you work off-base local police will have jurisdiction." Wow, what a bummer, now the class thought they might just be a step above a night watchman at a shopping center. (This restriction would change in later years when NIS S/A's would have the same arresting powers as other federal officers.)

After the shock started to wear off, S/A Lowentom reassured the class they would have plenty to do in their new roles as NIS S/A's, both on base as well as off. Moving on with his lecture; it was on to the course outline. Topics taught would be firearms training, unarmed self-defense techniques, military law, interrogation procedures, evidence collection, surveillance techniques and writing up Results of Investigations (ROI's) to name just a few.

Figuring students had just about enough thrown at them for their first day; all were dismissed. Mike and the rest of the class headed to the hotel to check in. At the hotel, each room would have four trainees assigned and would comprise a team for the duration of the class. These teams would be for working on group projects or assignments.

Checking over the bulletin board in the lobby, Mike learned he would be in a room assigned to Team 2. The other members would include Bob Arkin, Tom Goldbloom and John Russo. Mike felt he was lucky in the choice of his roommates and could learn some finer points of police work from them.

The new team members sat in the lobby to get acquainted. It was decided John Russo's G-Car would be used as their vehicle for the duration of the training. With nothing more to do except unpack, the team decided to hit the town for a bite to eat and a beer or two later in the evening.

Washington, DC, not being that far from Suitland was the group's chosen destination. John Russo had been told by his friend at the Pentagon that DC was a great place to meet women and the ratio was three women to every man. Mike thought his group ought to be more worried about graduating from the Academy than making a hit with the ladies.

The first bar they entered proved John's friend correct about the ratio of women and he had not exaggerated. The place was over flowing with lovely ladies and very few men. As the night progressed and sensing the gin mill would only lead to trouble, it was decided the best course of action was to finish their drinks and get back to the hotel.

The second day of class found Team 2 driving to the Academy for their first day of real training. Once again Clyde met them and would be their first instructor of the day. He was a real piece of work and it was hard not to like the guy. He cut his teeth on the old school way of doing police work. His vocabulary was at

45

times colorful and spicy with some Clyde-isms thrown-in as he emphasized a point.

The subject for the day was weapons training. All students were instructed that even though they were familiar with weapons, they would have to qualify with the Ruger .357. The Academy's training version had red handle grips which reminded students as well as other personnel the revolvers did not have a firing capability. Actual black handled Rugers would be used for live firing at the range. Training would encompass both classroom theory and range firing. Agents would have to attain a NIS established minimum score to graduate as well as carry the Ruger in their official duties as S/A's.

At the time of Blackstone's training, the standard weapons issue for all NIS S/A's was the Ruger six-shot .357 Magnum revolver and the 12-gauge shotgun. Extra rounds for it were carried in a brown leather pouch holding six cartridges. For male agents the pouch would be secured to an agent's belt while females would carry it in their purse or on a belt if wearing slacks.

Trainees would be taught the tap-tap method of firing two rounds followed by two more and if need be the final two. This was an attempt to impress on the students to never be caught holding an empty revolver. One could see in the early years, before semi-automatic side arms were authorized for NIS agents, having a revolver as a primary weapon would most assuredly place S/A's at a disadvantage due to their slow and limited reload capability.

Expanding on the use of a revolver as a sidearm, a video was shown to illustrate the proper procedure in reloading from the pouch. It was stressed to never look down while reloading; in some instances, law enforcement officers had been shot in the head while reloading. Much like the baseball saying; keep your eye on the ball.

This was one caution he would lock into his memory bank of things to remember. Mike figured it was highly probable he would use this lesson when he reported to Naval Investigative Service Resident Agency Naples. With what he had read about crime in Italy, the bad guys seemed to have no problem obtaining high capacity weapons. Instructors who had spent time in Naples, told Mike the lessons learned at the Academy would come in handy when he was assigned to any protective service details for high ranking military officers and Department of Defense (DOD) officials.

On the first few range days it was apparent most trainees were familiar with weapons. The only exceptions were two females and one male in the class. Karla, Tim and Louise had never held a handgun much less fired one. As days at the gun range continued, it was soon obvious that they could not hit the broad side of a barn with a bass fiddle. Mike thought it was great fun shooting holes in the silhouette targets. Ready or not it was time to qualify. All students received qualifying scores except Karla, Tim and Louise.

These trainees would need a little extra help. Every night for a week they practiced with a BB pistol shooting at a paper target on the wall in their hotel rooms. To their credit they did qualify after only one more attempt. Shotgun qualifications followed the same number of practice days and on qualification day - all students qualified.

Now that student agents were weapons qualified, it was time for self-defense techniques. Mike thought NIS must be on a tight budget for these training classes. Mike along with the others showed up pretty much wearing a mixed bag of work out gear. As a result, on self-defense day, the gym was a lively color palette of blues, grays, green and pink and yes some of the women wore pink sweat suits.

This area of instruction, taught by S/A Whitmore was more like physical conditioning; only four or five good self-defense moves were taught. Mike especially liked the one where he could bend a bad guy's fingers back and drop him to the floor. Everyone had a good time tossing each other around. Even Sue, a petite five foot nothing got into the spirit and tossed some of the larger men.

Evidence collection, instructed by S/A Thosman, was a subject to be taken very seriously by the students. The class was reminded that even with a solid case, sloppy evidence collection, hit-or-miss documentation and faulty chain of custody procedures could discredit the case if it went to trial.

One aspect of evidence collection most interesting to Mike was the art of finger print collection. Using their issued crime scene kits, everyone would have opportunities to practice lifting prints from guns, autos, bottles, etc. The most challenging task was to find out what objects would allow finger print removal.

Popular TV crime programs had led the public to believe that even rocks could reveal latent prints, however, the students would find that was only a myth. During the course of evidence collection, students were given scenarios to work on from initial collection to proper logging of evidence into the Academy's evidence locker.

Mike and the rest of Team 2 had been anxiously waiting for the class on surveillance techniques to include terrorist type scenarios. This course of instruction would comprise both classroom theory and field activity.

The classroom work was boring and at the same time interesting and necessary. Field surveillance went part and parcel with being a NIS Special Agent.

The object of the first practical assignment was to set up surveillance on a suspicious vehicle at a nearby naval installation. Students were given a brief outline of the situation including a vague description of the subject's vehicle and map of the base.

All students were issued their red handled side arms and their student credentials or CREDS for short. The only extra equipment carried would be regulation bullhorns for communications. Departing the Academy, students drove to the surveillance location at a nearby naval installation.

Arriving at the base, student cars split up to cover as much ground as possible. All cars had radio communication. Without having much success, John Russo thought maybe it was only a wild goose chase and maybe there was no suspicious vehicle.

Team 2's radio crackled with, "All cars, this is Team 1, we have the vehicle and all units converge on the gym parking lot." Once all had arrived and took up positions to block any escape, students bolted out of their vehicles with CREDS out and red handled weapons drawn.

Team 1's Jess Brown challenged the occupants using his bullhorn. He announced, "NIS Special Agents, come out of the vehicle with your hands up." He looked pretty official with his credentials in one hand and the bullhorn in the other. The rest of the student agent trainees held up their credentials and pointed their training Rugers at the vehicle. Doors to the van remained shut and no response from the occupants. Brown again shouted, "You in the van, come out with your hands up!"

What was wrong with this picture? Mike thought, *let's see, CREDS held high and handguns being brandished; what did these alleged bad guys not understand?* Feeling pretty silly standing around looking at each other with their CREDS and sidearms at the ready, it was hardly noticed that sirens were approaching and soon the students were surrounded by base police cars.

Base policemen exited their vehicles with guns drawn; yep, no red handled ones here. All students were ordered to drop their weapons. Boy talk about base police not understanding that NIS Special Agents, in training of course, were on a case. They certainly did not need any interference from mere police officers. SAC Brown from Team 1 informed the police in a loud voice that they were NIS Special Agents while still holding his CREDS high over his head. "We don't care who you are – drop those weapons." Sheepishly all students complied.

Suddenly the doors to the van opened and three men exited all wearing naval officer uniforms holding their lunch bags from the Golden Arches.

The students learned a valuable lesson. When operating on

50

a military installation it was sometimes prudent to notify base police a case was being worked and would assistance be needed.

The next day another practical was on tap to determine if a terrorist or hostage situation was in progress at a warehouse and place it under surveillance and resolve it.

Students in their G-Cars were to respond to a warehouse located on a naval installation where an incident was reported to be in progress. Each team would be given a chance to practice ascertaining the situation and to resolve it. Base police had been notified of the exercise by instructors.

All team members entered their respective vehicles and departed for the warehouse. After reaching the base and locating the warehouse all students parked their vehicles and sat on a grassy knoll to observe. Mike's team would be first up at bat.

Driving ever so slowly, Mike found a spot next to an empty semi-tractor trailer and parked the car. His choice would provide good coverage of the building plus the trailer shielded his team from observation. Bob Arkin, the former Dallas cop was elected to man the car and take charge of the negotiations via the car's radio loud speaker system.

Mike, John and Tom would fan out and look for good surveillance positions to cover the building. John made a quick check and found that there was no back door to the warehouse and found his spot behind a large oak tree. Goldbloom was satisfied crouching behind a trash can.

Meanwhile Mike surveyed the area looking for a likely spot to cover the warehouse. He located his target; a large blue U.S.

postal mailbox. This, he figured, would be a good vantage point and it gave him an unobstructed view of the front entrance. It also would provide a pretty good shield since it was constructed of heavy gauge steel. Taking his place, he was all set. Let the games begin.

Now, as Blackstone tried to blend in with the mailbox it became apparent he would be the butt of many jokes. Even though the students were cautioned to take the exercise seriously, they could not help but snicker as they witnessed a 6' 3" guy pop his head up from time to time over the top of the mailbox; much like a child's Jack in the Box toy.

It was quite a challenge for Mike, while he was peeking, to keep his legs aligned with the legs of the mailbox and at the same time hold his red student revolver over the top. He hoped that from a distance he was invisible to any occupants in the warehouse. A funnier sight was not to be seen the rest of the day and the instructors continued to try and keep the students' laughter down.

In a short time, one shady looking male with long stringy hair and a full beard came out of the warehouse holding a snub nose revolver. He took a quick look around and seeing nothing suspicious re-entered the building. Bob, now outside the car, decided this was at a minimum some type of criminal activity or he could be facing well-armed terrorists.

Arkin following classroom instructions to the letter for standard negotiating techniques, ordered all occupants, using the car's loud speaker, to exit the building with their hands up. The long haired male previously seen was observed near a broken window and yelled, "Back off! We have hostages in here and we're prepared to shoot them."

Since none of Team 2 had hand-held radios and shouting at the team's leader was probably not a very professional move, Bob was on his own. Stumped for an idea he grabbed his student notebook looking for any inspiration. Nope, no magic answer was found. He did figure charging the building with guns blazing would not be a wise move. Hoping for the best, he waited a few more minutes and once more made the demand to come out and to send the hostages out first.

More likely than anything Arkin had said or done, the alleged terrorists, following the instructor's lesson plan surrendered. With that, the presumed leader shouted, "Alright, we're sending them out." The door to the warehouse slowly opened and three men and two women exited with their hands raised. Student Agents Russo and Goldbloom escorted them to a safe area. While all this was taking place, Mike continued to hug his mailbox and kept his revolver on the building.

The terrorists were a different kettle of fish. More negotiations were necessary until they decided their position was hopeless. All exited with Mr. Long Hair holding the snub nose.

Arkin was feeling his oats and got a little cocky. Shouting into his hand held mike, "You pieces of crap get down on the ground and you with the gun – drop it!" All suspects reluctantly complied except for the gunman who held on to it while he was spread eagle on the ground.

Since the alleged terrorist would not give up his weapon, Team 2 members were reluctant to approach. While lying on the ground, this subject continued to hold on to the gun and from time to time made threatening gestures with it.

Patience was said to be a virtue but evidently not with Bob, the Dallas cop and he lost it and shouted to the gunman, "Hold what you got scum bag! Don't and you are going to end up on a slab!" A hush fell over the students. This forceful command was exactly what was needed for him to get religion and comply. Looking at three armed men with guns pointing at him; he dropped the gun. All suspects were restrained and the exercise was over for Team 2. The other teams were given their turn and the exercise was over.

All students gathered around the instructors and were given an after action debriefing. Mike's team was the last to be debriefed. As with the other teams only minor comments were made until it came to the release of the hostages.

Mike's team, as did the other teams, had assumed the men and women escorted from the warehouse were all hostages and made no attempt to restrain them. S/A Lowentom pointed out their mistaken assumption, "Students never assume anything in this business – it could get you killed. One or more of your hostages could have been part of the terrorist group and if that was so, all it would take is for one of those clowns to have a weapon and start shooting. The moral of this story is don't ass-u-me anything in police work. We all know what happens when we assume."

Before Team 2 was excused to return to the Academy, the head instructor for the exercise called Arkin aside. "Bob, in the future you might choose to use more professional and less provocative language." Arkin answered, "Well, it sure got the job done, didn't it?" They both had a good laugh.

Back at the Academy, it was more classroom subjects to wade through. With weeks passing and all students receiving satisfactory grades, it was soon time for the last obstacle to hurdle – the final practical.

In order to graduate, students in their respective teams were given a problem involving targeting and surveillance of a known suspect. Each team would follow a separate individual.

All teams would be supplied basic background information covering the scenario including area of operation and a distorted photo of the subject. They would be required to follow the target commencing at the Academy. Successful completion would be to observe the suspect's activity, collect evidence, track the target and finally write up the ROI. Of prime importance was not being burned or spotted by the subject of their surveillance.

Planning would commence the night before the exercise in the students' rooms. Mike was elected Team 2's SAC and set their room up as the command post.

Once assembled back at the hotel, the first item on the agenda was to study the background notes and the photo of the subject. All teams had been cautioned it would be a bad plan to follow the wrong guy. The team members studied the information individually and then as a group. Mike instructed them to jot down any information thought to be relevant.

Second and third topics to be discussed were the equipment needed and what type of clothes to wear. On the subject of equipment, they would of course, carry their NIS Academy S/A student credentials and small notepads for recording events. Hand held radios and cameras would be included in the team's tool bag. John suggested binoculars and all agreed.

Tom piped up and suggested an ingenious idea of concealing the radios. "Why don't we put them in brown paper lunch bags?" The others concurred with his idea. All thought it would look a little strange to see men walking around congested areas talking into hand held radios. Strangers have a habit of being noisy and inquisitive. Bob speculated, "Probably wouldn't be too cool to have our target in sight and have someone ask us what we are doing." There would be no red handled revolvers used on this exercise. This gave the team a clue the surveillance would not take place on a military installation.

Next on the agenda was clothing requirements. It was decided Mike and Bob should wear casual and business attire to blend in with office workers. John would play the part of a tourist with his Kodak instamatic camera dangling around his neck. Goldbloom volunteered to wear clothes typical of a homeless drunk and would conceal his bottle/radio in the lunch bag.

The final topic of the night was the operation area. The instructors had mentioned Crystal City too many times in the briefing leading Team 2 to put it at the top of the list. They would have maps to be ready for any change in a mode of transportation. It was very important to note all possibilities of transportation; such as autos, buses, the metro or taxi cabs.

As midnight approached and hours had been spent covering detailed information on major streets, alleys, shopping areas and a host of other possibilities; it was time to hit the sack. The final plan was to leave any other variables to on scene actions or best guesses on the day of the exercise. The next day would be long and arduous and all agreed to get some rest. Mike couldn't sleep so he went over the plan one more time.

With only limited sleep and a quick breakfast, it was off to the Academy. All teams gathered for the final instructor briefing on the exercise. With student G-Cars waiting, it was time to saddle up. The Final Problem would begin with Team 1. All other student teams would follow in 10 minute increments.

Once in their G-Car with all four about as nervous as expectant fathers at the birth of their first child, it was tough for our agents in training to remain calm. John spotted a lone male who matched their Target's description exiting the main building. Was it him? All members checked the photo and agreed it was a close match. With Tom starting the car; they were ready to rock and roll but wait, he turned around and went back into the building.

The adrenaline was really pumping for the team but since it was going to be a long day, they had to settle down and collect their thoughts. All they could do was sit and wait for something to happen. John likened it to watching a pot of water beginning to boil.

Just when they thought the instructors had forgotten about them, not one but two males exited and both matched the description in their notes and the photo. The chase was about to begin. The team had a big problem; which one should they follow?

Mike instructed the other members of the team to check

57

their notes and the photo more closely. It was decided to keep track of the taller of the two and disregard the other. "Mike, the tall guy is walking towards a four-door sedan" shouted Tom. "Quiet Tom! I can see him." It looked like they were in for a car chase. Unfortunately, while Mike and the others were fixating on this male, the other one had walked by their car and said, "Hey guys what ya'll looking at?" Laughing hysterically, he walked back to the building.

It would seem that our four-some would have an up close personal look at one of their Targets. It was obvious that the other male was a good six inches shorter than their target. Seeing three disheartened faces, Mike tried to keep their spirits up and explained: "Listen, we matched most of the descriptive details; we just got the height a little wrong." They had been close but no cigar and much like the old saying; "Close only counts in horseshoes and hand grenades."

What a bummer, the exercise was less than 20 minutes old and they had already been burned.

OK, so now they would be on the alert to make sure there would be no more slip ups in identification. Just when their confidence was improving sure enough the building door opened and two different males walked down the steps. John got a shot of the two with his Kodak. These were definitely not the two previously seen. They split up and headed toward separate cars. It was still difficult to be sure which one to follow. While sitting and thinking over their problem, one of the two drove his car a distance away and honked his horn and yelled in a mocking tone

"Tallyho!"

Game on! He exited the parking lot with Team 2 in loose pursuit and headed toward the interstate. They were right on his tail. The team thought it was mighty nice of the instructors to have the target driving a government vehicle with official plates. Mike gave himself and the others a Bravo Zulu. Mike thought, *what was so hard about this surveillance stuff? Just keep him in sight, follow the guy, take good notes and make your report - nothing to it, right?*

In unison, the boys sang, "Graduation day here we come" to the tune of the Broadway 1921 musical, 'California here we come.' While Team 2 symbolically patted each other on their backs, Tom screamed, "Mike, he's headed for the Crystal City exit." "Holy Crap, Tom follow him and for heaven's sake don't lose him!"

The target's car careened off the interstate and made the exit with Team 2 in hot pursuit. All they had to do was keep their eyes on the ball or target in this case.

Commuter traffic had started to get congested with cars weaving in and out; still not too bad. Tom was able to keep the target's car in sight with only three cars ahead. Immediately, team members speculated on his destination.

Chaos reigned supreme inside the car with much shouting back and forth. Control was about to be lost for Team 2. No matter what ideas were put forth, no two guesses were the same. All of a sudden, the answer magically appeared right in front of them. Their man made a sudden and quick left turn into a parking lot. They missed the turn and had to take the next entrance into the parking lot.

59

What to do now? He had disappeared, no, he hadn't. John Russo spotted his car only two rows from their position. Luck was really with them. All they had to do was get a little closer and place him under surveillance. Once again, Mike was feeling pretty smug and so were the others. This was until they got a closer look at the car and discovered it was empty. They had lost him; their morale had bottomed out.

What was their next plan? Bob suggested they had one hope and it all hinged on him entering the Crystal City Underground. Since this was all they could come up with, they decided to head for the Underground entrance. Based on the team's background notes, the Underground was a subterranean city with offices, shops and food venues. Mike remembered some facts about the Crystal City Underground from their notes.

The name Crystal City was derived from Crystal House, the first building constructed around 1963. Subsequent buildings were so named Crystal but general usage referred to the complex as Crystal City. The 70's saw the opening of the Crystal City Underground which must have been some undertaking. Cobble-stone streets made the interior look like a turn of the century shopping village. When it opened, it had 30 specialty stores.

Bob was left to watch the team's G-Car and keep a weather eye on the target's car. The rest headed toward the entrance to the Underground loaded down with all their equipment including the cleverly disguised radios in the brown paper bags.

Once inside and hoping he was hungry; nothing else came to mind, the remaining members of Team 2 headed in the direction

60

of the Food Court. They were absolutely counting on finding him at that location. If he wasn't, it would be nearly impossible to locate him in the Underground. With any luck, he would be found munching away on a bagel or some other tasty treat.

When the team arrived at the food pavilion they were met by hundreds of people having a mid-morning snack. Mike had heard much about this Underground. He was amazed at the variety of food choices and the aroma made it hard for him to keep his mind on the task at hand. There were kiosks for hot dogs, pretzels, French pastries, New York style bagels and so much more. Disappointedly, there definitely was no time for a nosh.

Continuing to search for the target it was becoming clear just how challenging this surveillance was turning out. It was time to split up to increase the odds of picking up the Target's trail. Tom would stay in visual contact with Mike and John would go solo. Mike cautioned both to stay within paper bag contact. This was going to be looking for that proverbial needle in a haystack.

Mike was getting frustrated but then again no one at the Academy said the exercise was going to be easy. He sure hoped in the real world, surveillance would not be this tough.

Paper bag situation reports were coming in steadily from Tom, John and Bob but all reported negative results. However, just when it looked like all was lost, a very excited John reported, "I've got him! - I've got him!" Mike tried to calm him down, "John calm down and what is your 10-20?" With the Target located, Mike and Tom would join John. Once together, a three-man surveillance would be set up.

Now in place, activities of the target were noted with John taking touristy photos of shops making sure to keep him in the view finder. Mike noted the subject was calmly sitting on a bench and munching on some type of pastry from a white paper bag.

Tom Goldbloom took up a position approximately 40 feet from the bench to cut off the target's exit. Mike did the same in the opposite direction. Every time a pedestrian would pass by the bench the students would get overly excited. No one seemed to pay much attention to one guy sitting on a bench snacking away. This was beginning to look like an easy surveillance after all. It was a little boring but at the same time nerve racking for our hopeful special agents. The fear of being burned again was ever present. It continued to be 99% nothing to report with the hopes of 1% action.

With our enterprising trio on high alert for any sudden movement by their man, a new wrinkle was thrown into the mix. Walking up and sitting down was the same male they had previously seen back at the Academy. He sat down next to Team 2's target and started reading a newspaper he had with him. It was odd the men never spoke to each other and Mike noted it in his notes.

What was going on? Mike mulled the thought over. After a short while, this newcomer stood up and bid his fellow 'bench sitter' goodbye and departed. Not a minute later, their target got up and picked up the newspaper from the bench. He started to head in the opposite direction from the other male.

A new problem had now surfaced: should they stay with the new person, now referred to as Target 2 or follow Target 1. The decision was made to split up with Mike and John staying with Target 1 and Tom would follow Target 2.

With this new plan in place it was time to proceed. Mike thought it was strange that Target 1 upon leaving the bench walked right by a trash can without discarding his trash from the pastry. He casually put it in his pocket. What made it so strange, the trash can was less than five feet from where he had been sitting.

What was this all about? Who was in the habit of keeping trash? No time to think about it and it was time to continue with the surveillance. Events were starting to happen with Mike's radio crackling, "Mike from Tom, Target 2 is moving in your direction." He was advised to keep Target 2 in sight and report any more updates.

As Target 1 was walking, he would stop from time to time and look in shop windows checking for a tail. The glass would act as a mirror reflecting images. Continuing, he seemed to be heading for the Underground Metro Station. Still nothing for Mike and John to report, except he was really fond of the white pastry paper trash bag.

Wait just a minute! As Mike and John reached the train platform area Target 1 was seen darting quick glances and reached in his pocket and discarded the white bag into a nearby trash receptacle. Figuring this might be some sort of a drop and of some importance, Blackstone decided to grab it.

A loud horn announced the arrival of the train with the PA system confirming it, Mike was forced to abandon retrieving the bag. He was too far away to grab it and board the train. Target 1 quickly entered one of the cars with Blackstone hurrying into an adjacent one.

John, who now was left standing on the train platform had to decide to stay put or go after the trash. Figuring Mike had the situation well in hand, it was time to get the bag out of the trash can. Good idea but before he could retrieve the trash, the train doors slammed shut which startled him.

Just before the doors shut, Target 1 had jumped off and John was now left alone with him. As the train departed, John observed Target 1 smile and wave to Mike as the train left the station. John had just enough time to grab the bag and take up solo surveillance of Target 1. Even to this almost S/A, there had to be something really important in that white paper bag.

Mike, major league irritated for being left on the train, radioed John to keep track of their Target. At the same time, he radioed Tom and cautioned him not to lose his man - something was definitely up. The good news for Blackstone was the train would make many stops along the Metro route. He was able to hop off at the very next station - still in the Underground.

To recap the surveillance scenario to date, we have: Tom Goldbloom following Target 2; John Russo following Target 1; Mike Blackstone trying to catch up and Bob Arkin still with the cars.

John, tailing his man, made a command decision that Target 1 was heading for the exit. He alerted Mike and Tom. In the meantime, Tom advised Target 2 seemed to be heading for a Metro stop.

Excitedly, Goldbloom radioed that Target 2, now at the train stop, stopped at a trash receptacle and appeared to be frantically searching for something. From his vantage point it looked like he came up empty handed.

John Russo reported to all team members including Bob, who had been monitoring all radio communications, that Target 1 did not seem to be in any hurry to exit the building. "John and Tom, this is Mike - what is your 10-20?" Receiving location information, Mike felt that they had a good handle on the situation and headed for Team 2's G-Car to join Bob.

As Target 1 exited the facility, John radioed Bob at the cars, "Bob, Target 1 is out and headed your way." Mike overhearing the alert, started running for the exit. He reached it just as Goldbloom with Target 2 in sight exited the Underground. Target 2 seemed to be headed in the direction of Target 1's car so Tom broke off surveillance and returned to the team G-Car.

Surprise – Surprise! Target 2 was in fact headed straight for Bob's location. Mike radioed John to head for the team's car. Mike now had a visual on both Targets. John acknowledged and also said he was holding the white bag of Target 1's trash but did not have a chance to look inside it.

Bob radioed Mike that Tom and John were with him and both targets had reached the original Target's car. Mike confirmed both had entered the vehicle and casually returned to the G-Car. The hard part was about to begin – the waiting for any new development. Still too engrossed in watching Target's 1 and 2; inspection of that important trash bag would have to wait. All four soon to be S/A's were convinced it held some unknown piece of treasured information.

Quick as a flash, Target 1 started his car and drove out of their parking space. Team 2 was ready for the chase. Much to their surprise and shock the Target did not depart but pulled up next to Team 2. Looks like our intrepid agents were burned again.

Rolling down his window, our boys were advised the exercise was over and for them to head back to the Academy. They were instructed to properly enter into evidence any information collected. Mike felt pretty righteous that Team 2 had recovered valuable and possibly classified information contained in the pastry bag. Mike was quick to announce: "I think all-in-all we did an excellent job for this exercise."

He was asked to give a short synopsis of their surveillance highlighting major points of interest. He responded that they were pretty sure all the important aspects of the exercise were covered including retrieving one piece of important information.

"So what was that important piece of information?" Target 1 wanted to know. Mike was really sure of himself, "Why it's right here in this paper bag you threw in the trash can by the train platform."

"Go ahead and open it, Mike." He now had a sinking feeling something was amiss. Mike proceeded as ordered to slowly open the bag. Inside he felt only a very tiny piece of scrap paper. "It's only a scrap of paper" he exclaimed. Blackstone was instructed to go ahead and read it. "It says, what about the newspaper?"

Target 1 now opened up his newspaper, the same one he had picked up from the bench inside the Underground. Inside was a tiny piece of microfilm which he showed to Mike. "You guys had such a bad case of tunnel vision over the white bag you missed the newspaper and discounted it as trivial and felt no need to report it."

Mike Blackstone, Tom Goldbloom, John Russo and Bob Arkin felt they were ready to join the ranks of NIS Special Agents. The rest of the day was spent writing up the ROI for the exercise. The following day was a wrap-up with critiques covering all subjects taught at the Academy including the Final Problem. To everyone's relief all had passed the Basic Agent's Course.

Graduation day and Mike was on Cloud Nine when he received his diploma. Next item on the agenda was duty assignments but since most if not all had previously been assigned, it would be no surprise. This included Mike who knew he was on his way to Naples, Italy. In addition to diplomas, official NIS Special Agent credentials were presented to the new Special Agents.

One important item was left for our new S/A's – head to the Virginia gun store recommended by some instructors to replace the Ruger. John was happy with the standard issued Ruger .357 so he stayed behind to finish packing. Mike and Tom on the other hand could not wait to replace it. They would have to pay for their new side arms out of their own pockets. No problem for Mike as the Ruger reminded him too much of a Black & Decker drill he once owned.

As Tom and Mike walked into the gun store, they were amazed at the selection of hand guns. Mike's choice would be a

Smith & Wesson (Model 19) .357 Magnum revolver with a 4"
barrel. Tom would choose a Smith & Wesson .44 Magnum with a
6" barrel. You know the gun made famous by Clint Eastwood of
'Dirty Harry' fame. One wondered what elephant Tom planned to
bring down. When Mike made his purchase he thought it
interesting that no purchase permit was required.

Back in their hotel room and putting the finishing touches
on packing, curiosity finally got the better of Mike and the rest of
Team 2. Goldbloom was asked why he had quit the FOS to become
an NIS S/A? He was quick to answer, "FOS agents don't carry
guns." Blackstone watched Tom admiring his new cannon. He
thought, under his breath; *look out world, here comes Tom with his
.44 Magnum!*

Later that day back at the Academy, it was time to finish
packing and check out. It was tough for Mike to say goodbye to all
his former classmates, especially good old Team 2. He had grown
very fond of Tom, Bob and John. All that was left to do was stop
by the mail room and ship his S & W and Ruger handguns along
with his trusty leather ammo pouch to Naples.

Packing his TR-7, Naval Investigative Service Special
Agent Mike Blackstone was off to Norfolk. So much to do and so
little time. Back home, he spent his time packing his household
goods for shipment and also getting his Triumph sports car shipped
to Naples, Italy. It was a tiresome effort to remember all the things
he would have to do such as sub-lease his home and pay all his bills.
In two days he would be off to the air terminal to catch his chartered
flight to Italy.

Those last two days we spent before the flight to have his household goods picked up by the shippers. He next had to have his Triumph at the vehicle transportation depot for shipment. S/A Blackstone was advised to have his catalytic converter removed because Italy did not have unleaded gas. He followed the shipper's advice, paid the $50.00 fee and had it removed.

Arrivederci a Norfolk – Ciao a Napoli

CHAPTER 3

ASSIGNMENT: NAPLES, ITALY

With all of his pre-departure items checked off his list, it was time to check in at the Norfolk Naval Air Station terminal to catch the Air Tiger Line's charter flight which would carry Mike to his new home and duty station in Bella Napoli. Waiting in the terminal, Mike pulled out his welcome aboard package from the Naples' NIS office.

The public address system announcement startled Mike as he was engrossed in all the information contained in his package. "Attention passengers, we will board the aircraft in 10 minutes."

Military Airlift Command charter flights were contracted by the U.S. government to routinely carry military and civilian Department of Defense personnel to and from Italy and other European locations. The aircraft in service for these missions at the time of Blackstone's travel was the Boeing Douglas DC-8. These planes first saw service in 1959 and had 14 modifications throughout its history. Thankfully, Mike would be flying on one of the latest versions.

Accommodations on the aircraft were not too bad but definitely not commercial air. Mike thought the airline put a premium on the number of passengers it crammed aboard the plane. He had about 10" of leg room before the person in front would be in his lap should the seat be reclined.

Once all aboard and the door secured, the aircraft taxied to the run up apron. With the pilot satisfied all systems were a 'Go' it

70

started its roll down the runway and Mike reminisced about his days as an enlisted aircrewman. The planes he had flown with the VRF-31 STORKLINERS always left a little bit to be desired but they had one saving grace – a parachute. Flying commercial air, Mike always felt a little uneasy by not having one and not sitting in the cockpit to see where the plane was heading.

Once the aircraft reached its assigned altitude, Mike passed the time on the eight plus hour flight by reading his recently purchased travel book on Italy. Perusing the book, he found the history of Naples most enlightening. It was a little disappointing to learn the not too flattering introductory information on present day Naples presented by the author. Most prominent was a description where the city was referred to as a huge, filthy and crime ridden with a taste for mischief.

Reading further, he was alerted to the preconceived notion by first time travelers that Naples would be found just like the book described. In fact, he was soon to find the author had been rather kind to the city in his comments. Skipping over more depressing facts and figures, he located a chapter on the beauty of Naples.

Naples from a historical and cultural standpoint was pointed out to have some charming features. Exploring the city, tourists would find numerous grand squares or piazzas and world class museums, such as the Museo Archeologico Nazionale. Mike hoped he would be able to visit it someday. The book highlighted numerous restaurants and of course Neapolitan pizza. His first order of business was to try a Pizza Margherita.

The author went to great pains to describe it being made

71

with fresh tomato, basil, fresh mozzarella cheese made from buffalo milk, olive oil drizzled on it and baked in a stone fire fueled oven. Just reading the description of the pizza made Mike's mouth water.

Trying valiantly to keep a positive attitude while reading the book, he found an even more interesting chapter on the history of Naples. Naples was a Greek settlement founded in 750 BC and was given the name Neapoli or 'new town.' Prospering during both Greek and Roman periods, it remained an independent city until the Barbarians showed up around 1139. They pretty much kept it to themselves and passed it from one generation to the next until Alfonso I of Aragon arrived and claimed it for Spain. This period lasted for the next 300 odd years.

Mike thought he had reached a saturation point until he turned to the last chapter. It contained useful phrases in Italian; he started a crash course in the language. His only previous experience with a foreign language was back in high school when he studied Spanish.

After the eight-hour journey, his charter flight touched down at Capodichino Airport on the outskirts of Naples. The airport was located a short distance from Naval Support Activity (NSA) Naples. The NSA compound was not large by most military standards but would have most of the comforts of a stateside military base. It had the usual military administrative offices, a commissary, Navy Exchange retail store, steak house, movie theater, liquor store and a few more shops to tempt Mike into spending his money.

Newly minted S/A Mike Blackstone was met by S/A Tony

72

Cantanzo, a hard charging Mexican-American- from Newark, New Jersey. Picking up his baggage, Mike and Tony headed for the office G-Car. After spending time at the NIS Academy in S/A John Russo's new G-Car, he was disappointed to say the least when he was shown the office G-Car.

Approaching, he found a rather tired and forlorn well used tan Renault 4-door sedan complete with dents and rust. With Cantanzo sensing Mike's disappointment, he reassured him the Renault wasn't really in bad shape – it was probably the best of their carpool fleet. "Mike, if you think this is bad wait until you see the Dodge – she's a real beauty." Agent Cantanzo went on to explain, "We are at the end of the food chain and most equipment, including cars, are hand me downs from stateside offices or purchased locally; second hand of course."

Departing the airport, the two drove to Mike's new office. Driving in Italy was more like driving the 24 hours at Le-Mans, with little regard for any civilized rules of the road. Mike was immediately introduced to the most important accessories on the car; the gas pedal, the brakes and last but not least the horn. When traveling at maximum warp speed, it wasn't long before they reached the base.

Driving through the security gate and after several nice office buildings were passed, Mike started to get a little nervous. It appeared they were heading for the back lot where some sort of storage building was located. It turned out to be used by the Navy Exchange. Yep, you guessed it; another disappointment was staring Mike square in the face. Parking the car, they walked toward a

73

non-descript looking small office building with one main entrance. Tony, ever ready with a quick quip, "Well, what did you expect, The Ritz?"

Alright, so the car was not so great and well, not a great office building either but hey, he was a certified federal Special Agent and was ready to go out and do battle with the Italian and military bad guys.

Entering the office, he was in luck as an agent training session was in progress. He was introduced to the full complement of S/A's plus the office staff.

Tom Thompson, Senior Agent in Charge (SAC) introduced Mike to: Dave Albright, Assistant Agent in Charge (ASAC), S/A's Jack Lewis, Tim Tosgood, Bill Jones, Ned Hommes and Bob Trailor. The only Italian introduced was college educated Rudalfo Tia. He preferred to be addressed as Dotore or Doctor. In Italy, when one has a college degree, he or she could use the formal title of Dotore.

Mike would be sharing an office with S/A Bill Jones and was shown his desk and began to settle in. What caught Mike's attention was the number of case files on his desk. It seemed there would be no holiday period. He was to be thrown into the briar patch of routine cases. Ok by Mike, he was raring to go!

Jones would be a big help and gave him a brief rundown on some of the types of cases he would be working. NISRA Naples' agents were responsible for major crimes committed by primarily U.S. Navy personnel, Marine Corps personnel and government persons working in Italy. On a case by case basis or requested

74

tasking, NIS S/A's would travel to other areas falling under their jurisdiction.

Continuing with his explanation, their case load would include crimes against property, fraud, counter-intelligence, drug interdiction and homicides. He would cover more types of cases later.

Since it was almost lunch time, Bill along with Dave Albright took Mike to a local place outside the base. The Two Palms Restaurant was a favorite with locals as well as the military. Its garden setting was most impressive and certainly enhanced the scenery of the area.

Looking over the menu Mike was quick to make his selection - a Pizza Margarita. He watched as it was prepared and slid into the stone oven. In less than five minutes it was placed before him. Oh my God, Mike was mesmerized by the beauty of it, reminding him of the Italian flag – red (tomatoes), green (basil) and white (mozzarella cheese). The crust was crispy and blackened from the fire. Diving into the pizza it was an attack on his olfactory senses. "Dave, this pizza is unbelievable; it is the best." "Mike, you wouldn't be the first to have that sentiment. Oh by the way, you might wipe that olive oil dripping down the side of your mouth."

Back at the office, Special Agent Jones pressed on with his briefing, "Mike, all S/A's in the office will be working on background investigations for security clearances in addition to regular case work. While these will not be too exciting, they are important and necessary.

Stateside, this is the function of the Defense Investigative Service or DIS. This duty would fall as a collateral assignment to us. It is one extra duty we all have to do."

He was also informed that he would have a collateral duty of briefing commands on NIS's Command Counter-Intelligence Program. He felt this would be a chance to use his background in naval intelligence and the program was of prime importance. Jones explained that while Naples was a hot bed for crime it did pose a threat from foreign agents. Mike would partner with S/A Jack Lewis in presenting these briefings. The one and only tool supplied by NIS was the video, 'The Collectors' to show to each and every command. Mike would add his own observations.

Mike was given his package containing his firearms shipped from the Academy. He was informed he would have to qualify with his personal weapon, the S&W .357 revolver. As luck would have it, the office was due to re-qualify with their side arms and shotguns the next day. Mike had previously qualified with his government issued Ruger .357 at the Academy. He held up the S&W and the Ruger side by side and told Bill, "You know holding the Ruger still reminds me of a Black & Decker drill but my Smith .357; now that's a weapon."

"Mike, this is a good time to explain carrying your weapon. There is a major change from stateside agent rules for carrying a government side arm. Here in Naples we are allowed to carry 24/7. You will be issued an Italian Porto d' Armi permit by the Italian police. The permit authorizes you to go armed, both on and off base, anywhere in Italy."

With office orientation complete, the next stop would be to drop his luggage off and check into his temporary lodging at a nearby hotel. Bill explained that due to a shortage of local housing, all arriving agents would be authorized time to secure an apartment. The Hotel Termi was selected for Mike as it was close to the base. Dropping off his baggage, it was back to the base to continue his check in.

With Special Agent Jones in tow, his first stop would be the administrative office to pick up his official check in sheet. He needed to visit the housing office, household goods office and other necessary commands including the base hospital and dental clinic. They both were co-located off the NSA compound at the top of the hill.

Bill explained Mike would need to get the all-important ration card for purchasing liquor, cigarettes and electronic items. Ration cards were necessary for all assigned personnel, as a thriving black market existed in Naples.

"Bill, you say I'll need a ration card to buy a TV or VCR at the base exchange?" "Yes, it is a government requirement." Mike was informed that a TV and VCR were not luxuries but necessities in Naples. The down side to living off-base was no English language TV programs on Italian TV. The only programs broadcast were on Italian stations RA1 and RA2. If Mike wanted to catch an American show he would have watch it at the steak house on base. It had access to Armed Forces Radio and Television or AFRTS programming.

"Bill, if I can't get English speaking TV, why do I need a

TV and VCR?" "Mike as you begin to pick up some Italian you might find Italian TV interesting."

"Ok, that explains the TV but what am I supposed to do with the VCR – tape racy Italian commercials?" "You will soon find one of the most popular business establishments here in Naples is the video exchange store. It's just a small little place outside the base where VHS and BETA format movies can be checked out. Believe me you will spend a lot of time in line to get some films for evening entertainment. It will most likely be your last stop after work each day. I, on the other hand, have my wife pick up ours."

Bill returned to his briefing on black marketing. He explained he has found two scenarios for involvement in the trade. The first was many sailors thought it was a way to make a quick buck. The second was when a sailor was married to an Italian national. He would be pressured from the family to buy these items. They in turn would sell the articles on the black market.

Mike as well as the rest of the S/A's at the office would initiate many cases involving sailors caught up in the black market.

In addition to the ration card, Mike was advised to get a base enlisted club card for the EM Club. The card allowed him unimpeded access to the club to facilitate any upcoming operations. Bill thought it a good idea to get one for the Flamingo Club located on the AFSOUTH base. He would also need to get a NATO Allied Command ID Card. It seemed to Mike there was a ton of admin stuff to get out of the way before he could actually start work as a NIS S/A.

A quick check-in at the base hospital and dental clinic and it was back to the NSA compound. Mike needed to stop at the bank to exchange U.S. dollars for some Italian lira. Dollars were accepted on base but most large purchases off base would require a ready supply of lira notes. "Bill, how much money do you think I need to exchange?"

"Mike, let me introduce you to fine art of playing the Lira Exchange Game; an activity you will find most interesting. In the office, we watch currency fluctuations between the lira and good old U.S. greenbacks. When the lira rate is up, we buy more and when it is down, we wait. For example, a few months ago my villa rent was 700,000 lira or $700.00 U.S. Now the rate is up so I bought more. I just paid my rent, it was only $600.00. Most of us keep around $1,000.00 in U.S. currency on hand for lira purchases."

Another most important stop on Mike's list was to check on the status of his household goods and car. To his relief, both had arrived and were ready for pick up. He informed the civilian clerk he would arrange delivery of his household goods once he secured an apartment. His car, well, that was another matter, he would return later to take delivery.

Before leaving the office, Mike was made aware of a very important item he needed to purchase; his gas ration coupon book. The book contained coupons he could use at AGIP gas stations to purchase discounted fuel. At the time he was assigned, Italian civilians were paying over $3.00 U.S. per liter. Mike would have to get used to Europeans buying gas by the liter instead of the gallon. In the early 80's $3.00 per liter was pretty expensive gas. U.S. price per gallon was around $1.35. By using his coupon book, Mike would pay close to the stateside price per gallon.

Having completed these stops, Bill dropped Mike off at the housing office and returned to work. Since all agents lived off base, this was a most important stop. The office was the repository of listings for houses, apartments or villas for rent. Mike would concentrate on finding an apartment and hopefully a roommate to share the cost.

Mike was directed to a board listing Roommates Wanted. Using a map Jones had loaned him he searched the listings. He found a nice sounding villa in Parco Azurro in the Pozzuoli area but the rent was a little steep for Mike; $600.00 per month. On the other end of the spectrum was the Pinetamare Towers. Apartments were more reasonable but Mike did not think he would like to live in a 12 story building not to mention there were eight buildings in the complex. It did have some perks though with a small exchange and food store. He had to be more frugal than the other civilian agents. Civilian S/A's Cost of Living Allowance was twice Mike's allowance for a naval officer agent.

Scanning all the listings he found one that looked promising. As luck would have it while he was writing down the information, the present tenant came in. Lt. Bob Richards introduced himself and advised he had only posted the advertisement for his need of a roommate the day before. They say 'timing is everything in life.' This was especially true with meeting Bob and possibly finding an apartment so quickly.

The lieutenant explained some of the finer points of the apartment. He also revealed that he was a Judge Advocate General

(JAG) officer. He was a defense counsel and as Mike would soon learn, they would have ample opportunities to be on opposite sides of the table. Mike would arrest alleged military wrong doers and Bob would defend them. Since Lt. Richards had the day off, he volunteered to drive Mike out to the apartment.

The apartment was on the outskirts of Naples in a beautiful tree lined neighborhood near an Italian food market owned by Bob's landlord. It was also located next to a train stop. As Bob was driving he narrated a running travel log of the architectural features they passed.

Mike was most interested in an old Roman ruin called Arco Felice. The road they were on went right through it. The only drawback was it was so narrow no two cars could transit at the same time. Arriving and parking the car in the underground garage; a converted cellar, they headed up the marble steps. In Italy, marble was a readily accessible and inexpensive building material.

Reaching the top of the stairs Bob unlocked the two key locks and one dead bolt. As they entered through a very ornate front door, Mike asked Bob, "Why the need for so many locks on the door?"

"Mike, theft and break-ins are a fact of life here in Naples and if you value anything precious or sentimental, I recommend you ship it back to the states." Seeing a certain degree of alarm on Mike's face Bob tried to relieve his consternation. "You know I don't really think we will have much to worry about once word gets out that an armed U.S. federal agent is living in the apartment."

Going from room to room, Mike noticed there didn't seem

81

to be any vents for either heat or air conditioning. Bob explained there was no central heating system or air conditioning in the apartment. Stepping into the living room, he was shown the rudimentary heating system. Occupying a space in the corner of the room was a portable rectangular metal object on wheels with a grate on the front. Mike examined the contraption more closely and spotted a flimsy ordinary red rubber hose connected to a propane bottle: "What the hell is this?"

Bob, walking over and pointing to it: "The heating system." He went on to explain the theory of its operation. "When you are cold and feel the need for a little warmth, it's pretty simple." Reaching down to the gas bottle he turned the knob (no regulator) and struck a match to the grate and waited for the Whoosh!

"Jesus, Bob, isn't that just a little bit dangerous?" "Not really, but last week one did blow up in an apartment down the street. Oh, and by the way, some call this little beauty a bombala which loosely translates to bomb." *Oh Crap!* Mike thought. "By the way, this one's mine; if you want some heat of your own, they sell them at the local negozio di ferramenta; that's a hardware store."

Paralyzed in place, Mike continued to contemplate the Italian heating system, he had a moment to reflect back to the movie, The Wizard of Oz. He felt much like Dorothy when she made that famous statement: "Toto, I've a feeling we're not in Kansas anymore."

It seemed to Mike, he would have to make allowances for almost everything compared to living in the states. Bob casually strolled over to the nearest window and opened it. "Oh, about the air conditioning, if you're hot – this is the air conditioning."

Moving on to the bathroom, Mike was advised the apartment only had hot water at certain times of the day and the water supply could be off for hours but usually would come back on or not. Mike thought, *here comes that Kansas thing again.*

Mike had only been in the country less than a day and he would learn the most important word used in Italy and especially in Naples. The word or words were Domani or even Dopo Domani which when translated meant tomorrow or day after tomorrow. He would soon learn Italians living and working in Naples never seemed to be in a hurry to accomplish projects, such as water and power shortages. Muttering under his breath; *can this get any worse?* Yep, it could and it would.

Next on the tour was the kitchen, he was happy to see American style appliances including a full size refrigerator. Wait just a minute! In the corner Mike spotted the same flimsy red rubber connected to the stove. Upon closer examination, he could see the hose ran through a hole in the wall leading to the same type of gas tank he had seen in the living room. "Good news Bob, if the damn thing blows up at least it would only take out the balcony." Bob saved the best for last and it was off to the spare bedroom.

Walking into the room Mike was pleasantly surprised to see it was large and roomy. It had to measure at least 15' by 15' with the marble floors and two large windows for his air conditioned comfort. Mike figured he would probably have to buy a large rug for the floor so his 'tootsies' would not get cold first time out of bed. Upon closer inspection of the room, he thought something was missing – got it – no closet.

Lt. Richards leaning against the bedroom door guessed what Mike was thinking. Richards was sure Blackstone thought more bad news was coming his way. "Mike, you'll have to buy a wardrobe for your clothes; most apartments don't have closets."

Sensing Mike could use some good news, "Look on the bright side; at least you won't have to buy a converter for your electronics; the apartment is hardwired to take care of converting U.S. voltage to Italian."

Mike was engrossed in his own thoughts and did not hear a word Bob was saying. The distraction was a little voice whispering in his ear: "We're not in Kansas anymore – we're not in Kansas anymore!" Before he knew it, he was shouting, "I know we're not in Kansas and who the hell ships a closet?" Bob, not sure what this Kansas thing was all about, figured Mike had enough culture shock for one day.

Back in Bob's car, the duo headed back to the base. Mike was pretty satisfied with the apartment and told Bob he would like to be his roommate. With this good news, Lt. Richards was a little reluctant to spoil it by passing on one more tidbit of information. "You know I have one minuscule bit of news for you – we don't have a phone so you'll have to work that out at the housing office." It seemed to Mike the little voice about Kansas was going to be a permanent fixture while he was assigned to Naples.

Arriving back at the housing office, Mike attempted to find out the procedure for getting a phone. He was directed to the Italian phone representative. This would be his first introduction to Italian policy for phones. He was pretty sure it would not be the last on other utility questions. He was informed Naples suffered from a shortage of telephone capacity. It would be a long time before cell phones would make their appearance. Mike was told he would be placed on a waiting list numbering over two hundred and fifty applicants.

It was obvious he would not be getting a phone while assigned to Naples. One interesting side note to this story was that even if Mike got a phone, he would be responsible for any charges the previous person had not paid. This insured the phone company would never lose any revenue. It sounded outrageous and he told the clerk in no uncertain terms. "No problem Agenti, if and when your name comes up and you don't want to pay any outstanding phone charges, well then, no phone for you!" Mike could see that being angry was a no win proposition so he tried a new approach.

Even though his patience by this time was wearing thin, he tried to remain calm. "Without a phone, how do I make a telephone call?" The clerk advised him it was not a problem in Italy; just have a Gettone handy.

Gettone – Gettone, hmm, he tried to recall the word in his travel book but came up empty. Trying to be helpful the phone agent reached in his pocket and flipped Mike a copper looking coin. Examining it, he could see it was about the size of a U.S. quarter. Most interesting it had a groove running down the center. He was all set and with his Gettone gift he said a hearty Ciao and departed for his office.

As he walked back he got to thinking about the coin - *at least I can make one phone call provided I know how to use an Italian pay phone. So much to learn.*

Completing his check-in, he decided to drive over to join the AFSOUTH Officer's Club. While driving from NSA to AFSOUTH, Mike noticed a strange site beside the roadway. Some type of demonstration was obviously in progress with burning auto tires and thick black smoke billowing into the sky. Slowing down and looking closer, he observed it was a group of scantily clad females standing around the tires and the road. Some were wearing only panties and bras!

SCREECH! While he was looking at the females, he hadn't noticed a car had stopped in front of him. One of the 'ladies' was leaning into the driver's window with her butt hiked up – which left nothing to the imagination. Slamming on his brakes and swerving around to miss the car, Mike could not believe the man's stupidity. He continued his drive to the base still thinking about the purpose of the gathering.

The club, as well as other NATO offices and commands at AFSOUTH, was located approximately four miles from Mike's office at NSA Naples. Entering the club, he decided to grab a quick sandwich at the bar.

It was in a secluded part of the club with the usual long bar plus a few tables thrown in for good measure. The room was richly decorated with paneling and the walls were covered with military plaques and other military memorabilia

To Mike's surprise, at the bar sat a female Ensign he

had previously dated in Norfolk. This was before he graduated from the NIS Academy. In Norfolk, one evening while at dinner, the officer told him she would be transferring from Bermuda to the Navy Communications Center (NCC) in Naples, Italy.

On their first date in Norfolk she blew him away with: "You know Mike; I'm excited about the transfer but I will miss Bermuda's marijuana." Mike was surprised she would volunteer information that she was a user of illicit drugs. She wasn't satisfied with that confession; she continued to explain that the 'Mary Jane' in Bermuda was primo stuff. She was sadly disappointed that the only 'smoke' available in Naples would be the local crappy hashish.

Walking up to her, they renewed their friendship. She proceeded to introduce him to her friends who were also assigned to NCC. Surprised to see Mike in civilian clothes and not in uniform, she asked what he was doing in Naples. "Why Louisa Ann, I'm a NIS Special Agent here in Naples."

Silence – Silence and more Silence! With members of her party staring at each other; the silence was much like standing in a funeral parlor and not knowing what to say. It was so quiet Mike thought he could have heard a pin drop!

With smoke clearing from Blackstone's bombshell, she and her companions made a pretty lame excuse about having to get back to work and beat a hasty retreat toward the exit.

Mike made a mental note to keep an eye on this officer and her friends when he began working drug operations. While any military member engaging in any prohibited drug activity would get Mike's attention; it was doubly important to watch these people.

They had access to highly classified information. Enjoying his lunch, he thought to himself; *suppose a future date with her was now out of the question? Yea, probably was.*

Returning to the office, Mike decided to ask Bill for an explanation on the roadside activity he had observed on his trip to AFSOUTH. "Bill, I saw some women practically naked standing by the road – any idea who they were?" "Mike those ladies are hookers. The tires are used sometimes for warmth but primarily as a signal they are open for business. They are known as Campfire Girls but as you can see by their dress code there is no connection to the stateside legitimate group of young girls."

Bill thought it interesting his new office mate had not mentioned one old and very fat woman with stringy bleached blonde hair wearing a miniskirt and sitting on a wall. She would have been in company with the other ladies of the night. Bill asked him if he had seen an old woman near the Campfire Girls. Mike did seem to recall an old fat woman wearing a miniskirt sitting on a wall. "That's Humpty Dumpty – a local landmark," said Jones. They both broke out laughing. Campfire Girls and Humpty Dumpty sitting on a wall – what a hoot! What would be next?

Since it was still early Bill decided to take S/A Blackstone on a tour of the Naples area including a stop at the local Anti-Drug Squad Headquarters. Departing the office in one of their primo G-cars, that tan mean machine, it was off for the ride of Mike's life. As they sped toward downtown, it was obvious most traffic laws were on an 'only if you want to basis.' Speed laws were casually observed, traffic lights obeyed (only if you felt like it) and sidewalks could be used as an extra roadway if traffic was stalled on the main thoroughfare.

Thinking it over as they proceeded, he thought; *on one hand it seemed like driver chaos but with everyone having the same idea, it seemed to work.* As they worked their way downtown Mike heard in the distance a driver repeatedly honking his horn. Just when he was about to ask Bill if he heard it, the car came tearing by them with some guy sticking his head out the passenger window and waving a white handkerchief. He was actually more on the sidewalk than the road.

Bill shouted out as he swerved to get out of the way, "Don't worry about that; it's only an emergency ambulance." He explained at the time there was a shortage of regular ambulances in Naples. People in an emergency used their private vehicles and waved a white handkerchief and laid on their horns. Mike thought maybe he should start a journal. The first chapter could be titled – Surviving in Naples.

Just when Mike thought it couldn't get any crazier driving in Naples; they entered the main traffic/railway tunnel leading to downtown Naples. The tunnel layout had lanes leading to and from Naples separated by railroad tracks running down the middle. All was going well with the standard Naples' traffic flow of stop – go - blow your horn! and stop – go - blow your horn! This symphony of movement suddenly came to a screeching halt.

Honk! Honk! The ubiquitous sound of Naples had greeted Mike: horns, horns and more horns! It seemed every driver except Bill was laying on his horn. The sounds bouncing off the walls of the tunnel were deafening. Mike compared it to a rock and roll concert but the comparison would not come close to describing the volume.

Observing that patience obviously was not a high priority with some drivers in Bella Napoli; the Alpha Romeo directly next to them apparently had enough waiting. Suddenly, the driver pulled off to the left, gunned his engine and jumped onto the railroad tracks. While Mike sat stupefied, the crazy Neapolitan proceeded straight down the tracks heading for downtown Naples. "Bill, what the hell's going on? Does that guy have a death wish?" Not waiting for an answer from Jones and wanting a better view he leapt out of the car. Mike figured it was OK seeing how they weren't going anywhere soon.

Mike could see a train's lights approaching and hear the engineer blasting away on his horn but to no avail. Our daredevil paid no attention and kept speeding down the tracks towards the train. Just when Mike thought a terrific accident was imminent; the driver swerved off the tracks and cleared the tunnel. He thought he had just witnessed a scene from of a Keystone Cops 1930's B grade chase movie.

Mike stood next to their car as the train passed and the engineer gave him a cheery look with the famous Neapolitan gesture of a shoulder shrug; he seemed to be saying – no problem! Mike silently thought; *just another routine episode in the daily life of citizens of Naples and more importantly – is this Kansas thing ever going to end?*

Re-entering the car and seeing Bill was not the least bit

concerned, Mike slowly sank back into his seat. "Mike, get used to it. If you want to get anywhere around here, you have to have some pretty big cojones." "Thanks, I'll try to remember that little tidbit of wisdom in the future." Contrary to what Blackstone was expecting and led to believe, Naples, while crowded and a little run down and dirty, did have somewhat of a surreal beauty to it. He would of course have to overlook the piles of trash and garbage in plastic bags littering some streets and alley ways.

As they continued to the port, Bill pointed out some of the areas Mike would become familiar with working in downtown Naples: the Castle area, the Gut, Shoe Alley, Thieves' Alley and the Park Area. Along with the potential operational areas, he also was shown the location of some of Jones' favorite restaurants and pizzerias. Mike was ready for a repeat meal of Napoli's famous Pizza Margarita. He was pleasantly surprised at the number of galleries and museums.

S/A Jones stopped the car outside the port area and pointed out the navy's boat landing dock where U.S. Navy sailors on liberty would come in from their ships. Knowing Mike would be interested he also showed him the area where ferries and hydrofoils departed for the island of Capri and other destinations.

Once inside the secure port area and making the required stop at the port police check point, Mike and Bill showed the guard their credentials and identified themselves as Agente Federale di Stati Uniti and were promptly waved in.

Slowly proceeding and with Mike taking in all the new sights it wasn't long before the car stopped at a small plain building. Agent Jones advised Blackstone they had arrived at the headquarters of the CARB Anti-Drug Squad.

Entering the building and with no security checkpoint, the two agents were met by Sergio di Grasso. This fellow dressed in shabby dungarees and a food splattered shirt was huge. Mike figured he must have topped the scales at 300 pounds. A startling fact since he probably wasn't over 5'3". This Neapolitan giant immediately ushered Bill and Mike into the commanding officer's office.

Entering the room, a most impressive gentleman was introduced to Mike: Major Alphonso Tanta. In a baritone voice and with a handshake like a pair of vice gripes he welcomed Blackstone to Naples. Gazing around the office, Mike noticed it was opulently furnished with rich paneling and a magnificent chandelier above the Major's desk. On a wall behind his 18th century desk hung numerous Italian and foreign awards. What made this room all the more impressive was its stark contrast to the outer offices.

The office décor wasn't the only thing that marked the difference between the regular CARBS and Major Tanta   While Sergio and his fellow agents were to put it kindly, slovenly dressed, Tanta was attired in an immaculate three-piece suit that had come from a custom tailor shop. He also spoke perfect English with a soft dialect.

This would be a short meeting as in the hierarchy of police and military work, Tanta was on a management level with Mike and Bill's SAC while the U. S. agents were more on labor's level with the regular Anti-Drug CARBS.

When the meeting was over, the Major summoned Sergio to escort Mike and Bill to the outer office and lounge area. Sitting around a large table were the rest of the CARBS. Depending on who was asked, these gentlemen would either be remarked as famous for their courage or infamous for their tactics. This shady group of characters were mostly smoking cigarettes and cleaning their 9 mm Berettas. Winstons were the cigarettes of choice and the ashtrays were over flowing. Italians loved to smoke.

Taking the lead, Bill introduced Mike to the group. The cast of characters included, besides Sergio: Joccomo, a smallish fellow who could not have weighed more than 95 pounds soaking wet; Luigi, a handsome transplant from Rome; Paolo, who spoke perfect English and Monti, a 21-year-old oddity from San Diego, California. Blackstone thought it odd that he spoke English without any trace of an accent.

Grabbing a couple of chairs, Bill engaged the CARBS in a spirited conversation with Mike trying to follow along. He could not understand much due to his limited Italian language skills. He did catch a few words but one in particular caught his attention.

Turning to Monti, "What does Ba-Boo mean?" "Oh, it's the Neapolitan way of saying OK or alright. The actual correct pronunciation is Va Bene. I've become used to their unique way of expressing themselves in the Italian language." Mike was very impressed with his command of the English language but still could not get over the fact that he had no accent and he was from California.

Curiosity got the best of him and he couldn't help asking,

93

"So, how come you live in Naples and more importantly why did you join the CARBS?"

"I was born in Italy and my parents moved to San Diego when I was 10 years old. My younger brother, Rudy was born in California. My parents became homesick for the mother country and we moved back. To my surprise, all Italian born males must do some type of military service. Since I was born here they sort of drafted me. I had a choice of joining the regular army totting a rifle or volunteer to serve with the Anti-Drug Squad here in Naples and that's the story."

In Italy, one does not get directly down to business; one must socialize first. The NIS agents wanted to talk about an upcoming joint operation but the CARBS insisted they all go to the coffee bar next door.

The bar was pretty typical with shelves stacked with spirits and aperitifs as well as the obligatory espresso machine. Since it was located in a working class area, Mike thought the owner had made no attempt to spruce it up. It was obvious to Mike, once they entered, this was a regular event. The owner welcomed Bill like an old friend. To his surprise not only would they have a coffee but more correctly Café Correcto.

Bill, leaning over to Mike explained this was coffee with a splash of liquor. The liquor of choice with these CARBS was anise-flavored Sambuca. This was something Blackstone would have to get used to; drinking, with the exception of a small glass of wine with a meal, while on duty. It had been stressed at the Academy – no consumption of alcohol on duty. Since they weren't technically on duty, both agents followed the Italians' lead.

At the end of about 30 minutes, Bill and Mike bid a hearty Ciao and departed for their office. On the way back, Mike asked Bill to drop him off to pick up his car. While driving Mike related his conversation with Monti about the word Ba-Boo and was the one given the correct definition?

Bill, with a snort, agreed that Neapolitans have a unique way with the Italian language including their pronunciation for the word for OK or alright. "You'll find the Italian you learned from your travel book might be of some use in other places in Italy but not so much in Naples." Mike's mental filing cabinet was beginning to over flow with new and ever changing information on dealing with life in Naples.

After picking up his car and his gas ration book, Mike returned to the office. He was surprised to see three agent wives in the conference room. He was immediately introduced and found them very charming and welcoming. The ASAC's wife inquired, "Do you know much about Sorrento art?" Not sure if this was some trick question played on the new guy, he decided to play along. "No" was his quick response. "We are on our way to Sorrento to buy a quantity of Sorrento gaming tables and would you like us to include you?" Mike had seen examples of small pictures made of Italian inlaid wood but had no idea about a gaming table.

Describing the table, Bill Jones' wife explained, "The table is all handmade using Italian woods with intricate designs inlaid into the table. It contains a roulette wheel, backgammon, checker and chess boards. There is even a green felt insert for playing cards.

The price per table is $125.00." Mike had seen those small 10" x 10" pictures priced at around $10.00. The price of $125.00 for a table seemed like a bargain. Deciding to be a team player he was onboard for buying his first piece of fine Italian furniture. The ladies left to start their shopping trip.

With the end of a very busy and hectic day, he would take up his roommate's offer of a drink at the apartment. On his way with his TR-7 racing through the gears he was surprised to see a traffic police officer standing by the side of the road next to his squad car. Slowing down to pass the officer, a round white paddle with a red circle in the center suddenly was pointed in Mike's direction. He decided it would be a good idea to pull over and see if there was a problem.

You bet there was a problem! As the officer approached, Mike could see he was carrying some sort of notepad. Blackstone made an educated guess he must have been speeding. Apparently this was the time speed laws were being enforced by local authorities. Assuming he would be granted the standard police courtesy and let off with a warning, he quickly had his NIS credentials out for inspection.

"Buon Giorno, come problema?" Mike was quick to greet him in his best Italian. "Buon Giorno, velocitae multa; 15,000 lira," responded the officer in his slow halting Italian. Mike was correct, he'd been caught speeding and the fine was apparently 15,000 lira. With the officer's palm facing up and stuck under Mike's face, it was to be paid immediately.

Mike figured it was time to bring out the big guns. Pointing to his credentials, "Signore, io sono (Italian for I am) un Agente Federale di Stati Uniti." "Si an-da 15,000 lira." It was obvious to Mike no police courtesy was forth coming as the officer still had his palm outstretched. Evidently, Mike identifying himself as a U.S. NIS Special Agent didn't carry much weight in Italy. Reaching into his wallet, he produced the 15,000 lira and gave it to the officer.

Deciding his hotel would be a safer option, Mike headed in that direction thinking; *did I actually pay a fine for speeding or buy the guy's lunch?* Thus ended Special Agent Mike Blackstone's first day.

CHAPTER 4
ROUTINE CASE LOAD OF NIS S/A

Arriving on his first official day at the office, Mike was anxious to start his new assignment. His office mate, Bill Jones explained in detail NIS Naples' case load which would include: black marketing in cigarettes, liquor and electronic items; drug interdiction operations covering Italy and other countries where U.S. Navy ships made port calls; fraudulent compensation claims filed against the U.S. government; criminal activity investigations; afloat case work where no S/A was assigned to a host ship; counter intelligence work; DIS background checks and other miscellaneous cases under the jurisdiction of NIS Naples.

In order to set the stage for S/A Blackstone's cases; a little background information would be useful on life in Naples.

Naples, Italy had the reputation for being the home of black marketeering. In fact, it might be best described as a way of life for many residents. With the U.S. Navy present, opportunities were abundant for this illicit activity. The base exchange retail stores at both NSA and AFSOUTH contained a wealth of goods much desired by locals. Stereos, cigarettes and liquor were always high on the criminal's list of prized items. While most of these goods could be obtained at local shops, they would be more expensive than purchased on base. Prices were kept low in order for servicemen to purchase them plus no duty fees were levied on the items.

The U.S. government's answer to controlling black

marketing was a ration card issued to all service members and dependents over the age of 18. These cards were required for the purchase of high value items such as cigarettes, liquor and electronic equipment.

Cigarettes were always in high demand by Italians and Winstons were at the top of the list. During Mike's tour, a carton could be purchased on base for less than $3.00 while the black market price would range from $1.00 to $2.00 a pack: turning a nice profit.

The biggest disadvantage for Blackstone and his fellow agents in combating this illegal activity was the amount of cigarettes authorized patrons could purchase each month. Each service member and members of his immediate family were allowed a ration of six cartons a month. Simple math shows a family of four could buy a combined 24 cartons each and every month. This equaled a lot of 'cigs' even in the 1980's!

A known fact was Americans were switching to light and menthol brands and away from more full body ones. The funny thing was the Navy Exchange would stock two to three cases of full bodied for each one of light or menthol ones. You might have thought someone would have figured out if the ratio of Winstons to lights or menthols was reversed, Special Agent cases might have decreased. It was a known fact that full strength cigarettes were most desired by Italians. Many cases would be initiated by NIS agents against sailors who thought black marketing in cigarettes would be an easy way to make a fast buck.

A classic example of Italians believing in skirting Italian as well as U.S. laws was Blackstone's landlord, Signore Carlo. On the very first month Mike's rent came due he made a proposition. "You know Michele; your rent could be reduced if I had a few cartons of Winstons." Even with his landlord knowing he was a NIS Special Agent; it didn't seem to matter or slow him down when requesting this favor.

Liquor especially whiskey was another rationed item in great demand by locals. This activity would be similar to the story of Winston cigarettes. Service members and all dependent members 18 and over were allowed to purchase one gallon per month per person. The brand Tennessee Walker (TW) was the top selling hard liquor. A bit curious to Mike was this brand was considered inferior by most American consumers in Naples. However, just like Winstons, for every non-TW case stocked, such as Jim Beam, there would be three to four cases of TW.

Even though S/A Blackstone was the 'new guy on the block,' it seemed there was something wrong with this picture. What to do about it? Just like cigarettes, if the Navy Exchange reversed the ratio of TW whiskey to other brands, black marketing might slow down a bit.

One particular case stands out from the rest concerning liquor. It involved a junior sailor married to an Italian national. He had also adopted her 19-year-old son. Mike researched the sailor's purchase records for a six-month period and they showed a disturbing trend. Either the sailor had a powerful thirst or he sold much of his allotment. This young man's family had purchased their entire ration allotment of hard liquor for the six-month period and it was all the brand TW. That 18 gallons was a lot of booze!

Mike felt he had enough evidence to bring the sailor in for questioning. During the interview, he maintained his innocence and stated he had no knowledge of any illicit activity. Trying to lighten up the situation, he tried a new comical approach.

Our wayward sailor was advised if he and his family continued consuming this amount of hard liquor, as the sailor alleged, then their livers were probably in the first stage of being pickled. Our sailor finally realized there would be no escape since Mike had his purchase records. They clearly showed an excessive amount of liquor being purchased. He admitted to giving some of the excess to friends and relatives who were selling it and splitting the profits with him. Case closed.

Rivaling cigarettes and liquor during Mike's tour in Naples was the trafficking of electronics. A ration card to purchase high value items such as TV's, VCR's and stereos was required. Any TV or VCR with the name Sony was much in demand. Just like Sony, Pioneer was a name sailors admired and so did Italians. Pioneer components including reel to reel recorders, receivers, amplifiers, turntables and of course, those four-foot-tall speakers were much in demand by those involved in black marketing. Most of Mike's cases would involve those two brands. An example of the potential profit was the price of a Sony Betamax VCR. At the base exchange, Mike purchased a Betamax for close to $600.00. On the local economy that same unit might cost as much as $1000.

To attempt to control this illicit activity, Naples' S/A's would open Initiative Operation Cases (IOC's) targeting U.S.

101

service members. While all black market activity was to be discouraged, some empathy was felt towards service members who were married to Italian nationals.

For those not familiar with family traditions in Italy, it must be remembered that our sailor married to an Italian national not only wedded his wife but her entire family. Most black market cases involving married service members who had Italian spouses would be the result of pressure being applied to get Uncle Luigi his cigarettes or that nice stereo.

While proving cases involving black market activity wasn't easy; success was always possible.

While all cases Mike worked during his tour with NIS were important; mainstream work for NIS agents was combating drug use among U.S. personnel. As with the general population in the United States in the 1980's, drugs were a major problem with military men and women assigned to Italy, as well as those being stationed on ships. It was a never ending battle to try and combat drug use by American sailors and marines.

Besides the obvious tactic of raiding known drug activity areas with the assistance of the CARB Anti-Drug Squad, Mike would develop sources to be used in his drug ops. No one liked to be a snitch to a NIS agent, however, when one was busted for an illegal activity, he or she usually would do anything to help their case.

An opportunity of turning an illegal drug player into a source would present itself when a subject was arrested. He or she would sometimes be given the chance to help themselves by helping NIS with their drug interdiction operations. For this cooperation, on a case by case basis, his or her charges might be lowered. No promises were ever made by Naples' agents for their cooperation.

Sources were used to purchase illegal drugs from identified service members thought to be trafficking in drugs both on and off base. Mike would be credited with over 12 cases solved.

One important case worth mentioning involved the growing of marijuana off-base by two sailors. A tip was received at the office from an Italian who thought she saw 'strange plants' being grown in her neighbor's backyard.

Based on this tip, Blackstone and Agent Tony Cantanzo with assistance from two members of the CARBS put the residence under surveillance. This was accomplished by using the informant's backyard and peering over the fence and standing by for some development. Mike thought, *Oh, yeah, let the good times roll!*

Sure enough, it wasn't long before two men exited the residence and began working their 'garden.' With the CARB drug agents deciding the plants were marijuana, the drug team raided the residence and the CARBS arrested the two. Mike and Tony bagged around 12 fully matured pot plants while the CARBS attended to the two evil doers; which were identified as U.S. sailors.

Handcuffed and screaming and asserting their ill-informed idea of the U.S. Constitution and Bill of Rights, they began to swear at the Italian drug agents as well as the NIS agents about their rights. Such foul language you would not believe. With M-F's this and SOB's that, it didn't take the CARBS long to aggressively put a stop to it. The two sailors calmed down and were taken to the prison in downtown Naples.

On the way back to the office, Tony explained about the infamous Naples' prison.

"The Naples' prison is unlike any U.S. prison you or any other American citizen could imagine. It looks like it must have been built around the time of Columbus but actually constructed in the early 20th century. Besides the bleak exterior and interior, the daily routine of the prisoners is one that can turn the most hardened criminal into a choirboy. Each cell holds up to 30 men with cots and one toilet which was visible to the guards. The sole entertainment is a black and white TV mounted outside the cell and is tuned to one Italian channel.

Our boys probably will have the company of some pretty tough hombres. The prison houses some notorious Camorra members.

Meals. This will be an adjustment for our two wrongdoers. One meal a day is served and if more is wanted; the family will have to bring it. In the case of our two miscreants – they would have to buy it. Exercise is another matter. Of the prisoner's 24-hour day - 23 are spent in the cell. Each cell is given 30-45 minutes to walk around the outside courtyard inside the heavily guarded prison walls. There will be no college or ceramics classes according to the staff. A prisoner is in for punishment – period!"

Back at the office, Tony brought up an old case which had some loose ends. It involved the theft a few months back of a government .45 Cal. handgun.

"Mike, you remember we thought that the .45 pistol theft was at a dead end?" "Yeah, Tony I remember. Do you suppose these two desperados might have some information?" Mike suggested that they let the two guys sit and cool their heels for a bit. Prison life might make them more receptive.

Waiting about a week, Blackstone and Cantanzo drove to the prison to meet with the two. This would be the first time Mike would see the prison from the inside. Escorted to the interrogation room, Mike and Tony were met by the two sailors. Since it was only a short time ago these two had called the agents every vulgar name in the book - they weren't expecting much cooperation.

What a surprise when they entered the interrogation room. Both men jumped to their feet and addressed Mike and Tony as Mr. Blackstone and Mr. Cantanzo. They both looked like a couple of innocent choir boys albeit 'more the worse for wear.'

Getting down to the business at hand Tony asked them if they had any knowledge of a government .45 pistol that was stolen on base a few months ago. In unison, they blurted out, "If we could shit that .45 to get out of here, we would!" The two went on to describe the conditions of life in an Italian prison. They verified in graphic detail what agent Cantanzo had told Mike earlier about the prison. A pretty sad payday for growing some 'weed.' Since the two had no useful information it was time for Mike and Tony to leave and let them wallow in their own self-pity.

Another interesting drug case involved a USMC corporal who Mike had arrested for trafficking in hashish. Making sure he understood the charges and waiving his rights to remain silent and

105

have an attorney present - Mike began the interrogation. Initially getting nothing but denials from the subject, Mike decided to try a different tack. Blackstone had developed a technique in the past which produced good results. He reached into his sport coat pocket and pulled out a #2 pencil.

"Marine, you're in a lot of trouble but maybe you can help yourself. See this pencil eraser – we know people make mistakes and you've made a big one. If you cooperate with us and fess up to the charges, it might go easier for you and this eraser might help." Mike made him no promises.

Mike got his confession in written form from the marine. It seemed he had bought some hashish from a local dealer and gave small amounts to about five friends on three separate occasions. Mike figured he was not a major player and had him on only three counts of distributing. The young man had no prior arrests.

The Uniform Code of Military Justice made no distinction between selling and distributing or in this case giving some freebies to his friends. Since it was his first offense, Mike felt if the marine kept clean then this would only be a minor blip on his record. Oh contraire! Mike could not believe his assumption was going to be proved so wrong.

The next day his roommate, JAG officer Lt. Bob Richards, stormed into Mike's office. He was really pissed! Mike thought he could see steam coming out of his ears. Richards had been assigned as defense counsel for the corporal Mike had arrested the day before.

Blackstone could not understand why he was so upset. The

marine would probably only be charged with one count of distribution. Mike had worked many similar cases that resulted in a single charge.

"Special Agent Blackstone, do you have any idea how much trouble my client is in because of the confession you got out of him? That written confession is really causing me some trouble. He should have exercised his right to remain silent and have an attorney present during any questioning." Mike tried to diffuse the explosive atmosphere in his office, "Bob take it easy. Your man will probably be charged with one count of distribution."

"One count – did you say one count? I'll have you know my client is being charged with 15 counts of distributing hashish." Oops! Mike felt a slight bit of remorse for the corporal. Simple arithmetic definitely was working against our marine as: 5 people times 3 occasions equaled 15 counts of distribution.

Lt. Richards finally calmed down and expressed his opinion on dealing with servicemen who get caught in illegal activities. "You know Mike; it never ceases to amaze me that it's a given that service members have the same rights as civilians. Time after time, I handle a case where a client should have remained silent or exercised his right to an attorney during questioning by NIS but they just don't! It doesn't cost them a damn dime."

"Well Bob, it has been my experience that most sailors or marines believe if they exercise those rights - it might be construed they had something to hide. It definitely gives us the edge in interrogating suspects."

Fraud cases would be one of the most demanding and would

run a close second to drug cases on the number Mike investigated. They would fall into three broad categories: jewelry, electronics and household goods.

All naval and civilian DOD personnel transferred into the Naples area were allowed so many pounds of household goods to be shipped. The government provided insurance against loss at no cost to the individual. Most personnel were honest but there were a few dishonest ones that Mike would open a case on. The opportunities for those few to take advantage of the system were many.

Most of Mike's cases involved theft or alleged theft committed by locals targeting service or civilian member's household goods. Upon arrival of his shipment, the individual would make arrangements with the base transportation office for delivery to their residence. Using local Italian moving companies, individual employees would have a pretty good idea what was valuable. The moving company's contract required the unloading and unpacking of the entire shipment. Just like honest service members who submitted a legitimate claim for loss; the majority of Italians employed by the moving company were honest.

Military as well as civilians would have their residences broken into and high value items stolen. While this could just be a coincidence, Mike thought it strange it usually happened shortly after movers finished unloading and delivering the goods. This would result in the victim applying for compensation from the government. There were times when Naples' agents were called in to review suspicious claims reported by base officials or tips from informers. This pattern of thefts would also happen when the military or civilian member transferred out of Naples.

From time to time when things at the office were slow, Mike would review suspicious claims and follow up by interviewing the victims.

One such case involved a sailor who claimed his Sony color 27" TV was stolen from his residence. Checking the claim and his inventory of household goods he shipped to Naples; Mike discovered a glaring error. Magically, the alleged victim's 27" black and white TV had turned into a Sony color 27" TV.

Making an appointment with the individual at his residence and pretty sure this individual was involved in filing a false loss claim, Mike read him his rights. As in previous interrogations, Yeoman Second Class Thompson denied any wrong doing and willingly waived his rights. At this point, S/A Blackstone pulled some papers out of his brief case.

Showing him his signed official claim and a written statement from the base official, Mike asked the sailor to explain how his 27" B&W TV shipped in with his household goods magically turned into a Sony color 27" TV when it was stolen. Oops, got you Mr. Sailorman!

With a few lame excuses such as: "Oh, I sold the B&W and bought the Sony from the base exchange electronics shop." Mike was quick to respond; "Nice try but your electronics' ration card shows no such purchase. Oh, by the way, isn't that a 27" B&W TV sitting in that corner?" With this, he admitted some of his buddies told him it was easy to make a quick buck and the government had plenty of money. Mike arrested him and turned the case over to the

JAG office. Driving back to his office he thought that these young people sure did some stupid things. The more Mike worked these types of cases, the more he became convinced the perpetrators were simple minded and not hardened criminals.

Another but rather clumsy attempt to defraud the government was made by a civilian employee. He was subject to the same rules applying to servicemen and other employees. This was a rather disappointing case since the individual was employed at the base Pass and ID office. He like others thought he could make a quick buck at the expense of the U.S. government.

The facts were that he filed a claim for a very expensive portable stereo allegedly stolen from his residence. Value claimed was over $500.00. Again, it was not the big things but the little things that ended one's dreams of quick riches. In this case, it would be a tip from a friend of his who had seen him listening to it at work. He felt it was the same one he claimed was stolen.

Following up on the tip, Mike and Tim paid a visit to the man's place of employment. This would turn out to be one of their easiest cases to solve. Believe it or not, the stereo was sitting in plain view on his desk. Case closed and on to the next one.

Mike believed he was due for a rest; it was not to be, he had a new assignment.

While traveling to exotic countries was a rewarding experience for S/A Blackstone, the upcoming case would be a rather depressing one. While most afloat cases involved illicit drug activity, this assignment to travel to Egypt with S/A Ned Hommes was much different – a homicide. Difficult traveling was an

110

issue but it was the nature of the case that troubled Mike: a murder aboard a U.S. Navy frigate. The ship would be making a port call in Alexandria; their ultimate destination.

On a rather gloomy day in Naples, Mike and Hommes were called in to the SAC's office. As they entered, the look on his face told the duo something important was up. It would be a case involving the death of a sailor in Egypt. The only information the SAC had was the name of the victim, one Machine Repairman Second Class (MR2) Robert Lewis. Anything else, the agents would have to develop on board the ship including the name of the assailant.

The SAC continued with his briefing and explained the main difficulty from the outset was to get to the ship currently at sea. They would fly a navy C-1A aircraft from Naples to NAS Sigonella, located in the eastern part of Sicily. From Sigonella the agents would catch another C-1A for a flight to a 5th fleet aircraft carrier operating in the area.

Mike saw the adventure in this mode of travel while Hommes didn't seem so sure. The exciting part of this flight, at least for Mike, was the A/C, better known as a COD, which stood for 'carry onboard delivery' airplane, would make a 'trap' on the carrier. A 'trap' in naval terms meant the plane would grab a wire on the deck with its tail hook to stop its forward movement. He thought he would keep that tidbit to himself for a while.

Mike, trying to pay attention, was absorbed in his thoughts concerning the travel to reach the ship. As far as he was concerned it would be pretty tame since he did have numerous hours of flight time in aircraft similar to the COD.

Oops, not so fast big guy, his attention was suddenly brought back to the SAC's briefing when he heard the mention of a helicopter. The final leg of the trip would be by helicopter and landing on a moving ship. This revelation to Mike would be an accident waiting to happen. Just like Ned, he would be a 'nugget' which in naval aviation terminology meant a first timer.

Up bright and early the next day, it was time to report to the airport to catch their plane to NAS Sigonella. As Mike was an old hand at flying, he quietly read a paper back novel to pass the time. Ned on the other hand was all eyes and ears. His only experience with flying was on large commercial aircraft. Mike assured him there was nothing to worry about. The flight was a short one and before Hommes had time to worry; they were back on terra firma.

Our duo only had time to grab a quick bite to eat before they were called to board the aircraft for the next leg of the trip. Mike's partner was now an old pro at flying naval aviation, he was more relaxed until Mike gave him the bad news; landing would require catching a wire on the carrier.

"Ned, a little item I thought I would mention about landing on the carrier. The SAC in the briefing didn't mention how we would land. When this plane hits the flight deck, a small hook at the rear of the plane will catch a wire and that's how we will stop."

Hommes seemed to be OK and sat back in his seat. Moments later when the aircraft began to circle the ship, he started getting just a tad nervous. With his face pressed against one of the windows, he spotted what looked like a football field floating in the ocean. With a terrified look, Ned screamed, "We're not going to land on that!" Mike gave him a slight nod and advised him to tighten his seat belt and hang on!

The plane began its decent with our intrepid aviators hanging on for dear life. With the plane violently shaking and with a cross wind causing it to veer from port to starboard, the tires hit the deck. With a loud scrapping sound and with the pilot pushing the twin engines to full power, the agents came to a stop with one final violent jerk.

Mike and Ned remained onboard until permission to exit the aircraft. While waiting Hommes asked why the engines were roaring as the hit the deck? He thought they should have had less power instead of more. "Ned, the pilot needs to have max power when landing on a carrier in case he misses the wire. This will permit enough speed to continue down the deck and lift off for another try."

Exiting, the two were advised that a H-2 helicopter was ready to take them to the frigate. Walking up to the diminutive helo, Ned thought to himself, *how much worse can it get?* He soon would discover that it indeed could and would.

In less than 45 minutes of flight time, the agents were hovering over the ship patrolling in the local operations' area. As it continued to hover, Mike noticed the enlisted plane captain readying a cable suspended from a metal arm outside the door. Speaking into his microphone attached to this flight helmet, "Shipmate, what's up and why aren't we landing?" He was advised the pilot was not qualified to land on the deck so the agents would have to drop down using the cable.

Oh Crap! Mike thought. How was he going to explain this to S/A Hommes? No easy answer came to mind, "Ned, we can't land; we'll have to hook on to that cable and be lowered to the deck." As he was hooked to the cable, he screamed to anyone who would hear him; "Oh God, I'm going to die!" Out the door and slowing descending he kept screaming – "I'm going to die! Oh Lord I'm going to die!" No, he didn't die and landed safely on the ship's flight deck. Mike followed and they were both ready to go to work.

The Commanding Officer of the ship met the two and escorted them to his stateroom for a confidential briefing. He was very cordial and provided refreshments. This would be Mike's first experience of having a senior naval officer paying deference to him. As previously mentioned, he was a newly minted Ensign which placed him at the bottom of the officer barrel: a good three paygrades below the CO. The CO was unaware that Mike was a junior naval officer serving with NIS and not a civilian. He naturally assumed Blackstone was just another civilian Special Agent.

S/A Blackstone and S/A Hommes were advised the ship would be returning to Alexandria the next day; it was decided to wait until the ship was back in port to begin their investigation. Collecting preliminary notes and photos, the agents were shown to their staterooms.

Once settled in, it was just as well they delayed the start. Later that day the seas began to kick up and the ship started to roll 30 degrees from port to starboard and back again. To make matters worse it also was hobby horsing - rocking up and down. It didn't take long for the violent motion of the sea to take hold and add to Ned's woes; sea sickness or Mal de Mer.

Confined to his stateroom, he spent the rest of the day and night in a most pitiful state; it was no cakewalk for Mike either. Even though he had spent many days at sea in the past, it was only on large combatants and not on a floating cork bobbing in the ocean. While he never gave up his lunch, he nevertheless was not a happy camper.

The next morning, with the ship tied up in port, both agents had recovered enough to begin the investigation. The first item on the agenda was to inspect the murder scene. With the assistance of the ship's Master-At-Arms (MAA), agents Hommes and Blackstone were escorted to the Machine Repair Shop. This was a work space where repairs to ship's equipment were performed.

Removing the bright yellow Do Not Enter tape, the MAA unlocked the door. As soon as it was opened it was apparent to both agents that the space had not been touched since the incident. When Mike and Ned entered they were almost overcome by the coppery smell of dried blood – not very pleasant. The sheer volume of blood splatters was hard to imagine. Hommes volunteered his assessment, "I've been with NIS for over 12 years and I have seen my fair share of pretty bad crime scenes. This 10 x 10 space looks like someone has shaken up a soda can and spewed it all over the walls and ceiling." Even the tools had dried blood caked on them. It was so grisly they both thought the space could have been used in some horror flick.

While Mike shot photos of the bloody machine shop, Ned looked for evidence related to the crime. They both searched and examined tools in the shop for any evidence of being used in the attack. Except for the blood, the agents came up empty handed for any clues or usable evidence.

Exiting the shop and glad to be out, Blackstone and Hommes returned to their staterooms to assemble the information collected and correlate it with the material provided by the CO and ship's MAA. The plan for their investigation was to schedule interviews with any witnesses plus anyone else thought to have pertinent facts.

The agents were hearing various opinions on the homicide. The story circulating around the ship was the trouble started at a ship's party ashore with the usual amount of drinking and hell raising. Nothing of significance was developed from the activities at the party; sailors only partied and drifted back to the ship. So far, pretty tame evening at the party but back at the ship events would turn deadly.

The facts of the case developed by Ned and Mike were that a Petty Officer Second Class was found dead in the MR shop. His body was not discovered until the following morning. No witnesses to the crime and no weapon were developed by the ship's investigation. The most important clue was missing - the body.

The agents were informed the MR2's body had been removed and taken to the base morgue prior to getting underway for ship's operations. The NIS team was advised only limited refrigeration was available ashore.

A quick autopsy was performed and the body was shipped home for burial. The agents did receive a copy of the autopsy including a photo to review and would place it in their evidence collection folder.

In Mike's stateroom, the task was to collate all the material collected and form a game plan for the next day. Picking up the autopsy and photo from his stack, Mike was astounded at the brutality of the attack. The autopsy surmised the victim died of massive bleeding from deep puncture wounds to the head and throat area. The puncture to the head was so deep it had penetrated the skull. He never thought he had a weak stomach but the report was getting to him.

The only photo of the autopsy was the sailor laying on a slab in the morgue. The image was pretty awful. He was pictured with a large crudely made stitch running from his throat area down to his lower abdomen. It was obvious not too much attention was paid to sewing him up. Staring at the photo, Mike handed it to Ned, "You know, that's a hell of a way to end up – laid out on some cold slab and stitched up like some old burlap sack of potatoes."

Over the next two days, Agents Blackstone and Hommes conducted over 12 interviews with some startling results. It appeared the victim, MR2 Lewis was known as a bully around the ship. He stood 6'4" and weighed close to 250 pounds. The word on the ship was 'it wasn't healthy to get on the wrong side of him.' Hommes concurred with this appraisal – Lewis was a big guy.

Information gleaned from several sources revealed that he would routinely pick on a couple of individuals but to no great

117

degree - mostly verbal assaults. However, there was one sailor he would single out and took great delight in causing him misery. The sailor was identified as Seaman Alcott. He was small in stature, not standing 5'1" and weighed less than 100 pounds. Obviously, Alcott would be no match for Lewis. He never thought Lewis' behavior was worth mentioning to the attention of ship's XO or CO.

After all interviews were completed, it was decided to recall one particular individual who had given some startling opinions including factual information. Our nervous sailor was brought back in for a second interview and was reassured he was not a suspect. Seaman Apprentice Hatcher, the young sailor, told his story to the agents:

"Most of our berthing mates went to the party together and had a good time; except for my friend Richard. As usual Bob, the MR2, would pick on him. Nothing serious, just the same old tired name calling and a little pushing and shoving. Getting no reaction from Richard, Bob said he was bored and was going back to the ship. He planned to go to the MR shop and listen to some tunes. A short time later, Richard and I decided to return to the ship. On the way back, Richard seemed to be more upset than usual. Once back onboard, I turned in for some sleep and assumed Richard did the same.

This however was not to be the case. Hearing Richard talking to himself, his rack was next to mine, I sat up to see what was bothering him. I saw him sitting on his bed, still wearing his liberty clothes. I was shocked to see him holding his buck knife in his right hand. It was open and he was banging the knife on his leg.

Richard was ranting and raving about he had had enough of Bob and wasn't going to take it anymore. I heard him say he was going to do something about it. I told him to forget it and go to sleep.

I woke the next morning and saw him sleeping in his rack and thought all was well, until I heard that Bob Lewis was found dead in his shop. I could not believe my friend was involved so I kept quiet and went about my duties."

Blackstone and Hommes thanked him for his honesty and cooperation. They requested and received a written statement from Hatcher and dismissed him with the caution not to speak to anyone about his interview.

Taking a break and grabbing some lunch, the two agents reviewed their progress and decided they had enough probable cause to call in Seaman Alcott for interrogation. The MAA was requested to bring him to the agents.

Entering the room, Mike and Ned were surprised to see just how diminutive their man was in person. He definitely did not fit the profile of a killer. The agents identified themselves as NIS Special Agents and told him to sit down. Alcott was so nervous Mike thought he heard his teeth chattering. Agent Hommes advised him of his rights since he was now the subject of their investigation. Surprisingly, he had no problem executing a sworn signed waiver of his rights.

It was determined Mike would be the lead interrogator with Ned assisting. Blackstone decided a straight forward approach would be the best course. With a few minutes of silence in the room, Mike looked at the suspect. He put forth the question - no he made the statement: "You did it - didn't you." Looking down at the table, Alcott responded, "Yes Sir, I did. I stabbed MR2 Lewis with my knife."

Even though Mike wasn't the most experienced agent with NIS, he was pretty sure this was probably the shortest murder confession on record. S/A Hommes asked him if he would mind telling his story in his own words. He agreed and would tell the agents what transpired that fateful night:

"It all started long before that night when I was the object of continued periods of harassment by MR2 Lewis. Nothing big but mostly verbal as well as poking me and making fun of my small size. The night of the party my friends and I were having a good time and as usual Bob, that's MR2 Lewis, would come over and give me a hard time. We both had been drinking. After a couple of hours my friends and I had enough of the party and Bob so we returned to the ship.

Once back on the ship I went to my berthing compartment along with my shipmates. Sitting on my rack I got to thinking about the treatment I had been receiving at the hands of Lewis. I don't know but for some reason I pulled out my buck knife and started pounding it on my knee. I know I was saying, no, I was mumbling some words but I can't remember them.

I remember I stood up after a time, I decided to confront the Machine Repairman and asked the fellows in my compartment if they had seen him. Someone spoke up, I don't remember who, and said he thought he saw him heading to the MR shop. I left my compartment and walked to his shop.

I opened the door and walked in. Lewis was sitting slouched over one of the workbenches with his back to me. Hearing the door open, he turned and saw me. He started yelling at me and once again started making fun of me. I just wanted to tell him I was tired of being picked on and wanted him to stop.

I think that made him mad and he stood up and took a few steps towards me. I thought maybe this time he was really going to hurt me; he was not only drunk, but getting madder. I pulled my buck knife from its pouch, opened it and pointed it at him.

'What are you going to do with that – stick me?' he shouted and started towards me again. He was so mad, he had spittle coming out of his mouth! I was really scared and he just kept coming and coming. My hand was shaking and I yelled at him to stay away from me!

He just wouldn't listen and lunged at me and I guess I stabbed him. Lord knows how many times - I just kept flaying away with my knife and he fell to the floor. Oh my God, there was blood everywhere – on him and all over the shop. I closed my knife and put it back in its pouch. I closed the shop door and went back to my berthing space. I took a shower, changed my clothes and went on deck and threw them overboard and went to bed. I didn't mean to hurt him. I just wanted him to stop picking on me – I'm sorry."

Ned pointed to the knife on the sailor's belt. "Is that the same knife you used to stab the MR?" Alcott answered, "Yes" and agent Hommes took custody of the knife. Examining it he could see reddish/orange residue on the blade and was pretty sure it looked like dried blood. Seaman Alcott was asked if he had used the knife or cleaned it since the night of the stabbing and he responded "No."

The subject was asked to complete a signed sworn written statement. With his confession in hand, he was released to the custody of the Master-at Arms and confined to the ship's brig.

Months later Mike found out that the sailor was returned to the states to stand trial. He was found guilty and sentenced to 15 years in prison. As he digested the information on the trial, Mike thought; *what a waste – two young men ruined – one dead and one to spend many years of his young life in prison.*

With their investigation completed and with reluctant satisfaction, Mike and Ned departed the ship for the return trip to Naples. This time, however, it would be by commercial air transportation and the flight would take them through Cairo, Egypt. They would have to remain overnight and chose The Ramada Inn for their lodgings.

Up the next day, Mike's plan was to visit some of the sights since their connecting flight would not be until that afternoon. He wanted to visit the Museum of Cairo where relics from King Tut's tomb were housed. Ned decided to hang out at the hotel. Hommes would meet Mike at the airport with their luggage. Arriving and with the admission line stretching around the building, he decided to visit the Souk. The Souk was a marketplace where all kinds of merchandise could be found at ridiculously low prices. The sky's the limit and the goods ranged from gold jewelry to furniture.

Navigating the maze of shops, he had his eye on only one item – an authentic camel saddle. He found just the right one; it was beautiful with a green leather seat. Bargaining with the shop owner

122

and reaching a fair price, he made his purchase. Time was running short so Mike and his camel saddle headed for the Cairo International Airport.

At the entrance Mike found S/A Hommes standing guard over their luggage. "Ned, where do we go to check-in and also check our luggage to Naples? "You know Mike I have been watching this place and don't have a clue."

Confusion would be a polite way to describe the airport. No organized line or permanent ticket counters; just temporary tables with flight numbers. What a mess! With perseverance, the agents found where to check-in for their flight and made it onboard. For the agents it was time to catch some 'winks' before arriving home. Mike and Ned would have only one connecting flight and then hello Naples.

Mike had just returned and checked into the office and was advised not to not unpack his bags. Mike along with Tony Cantanzo were assigned to two operations for visiting ships. The first would be in Greece and then onto Morocco. They would fly to Souda Bay, Crete in a navy aircraft and switch to a commercial flight to Athens.

The operation in Greece would be pretty straight forward; much like the ones worked in Naples. The interdiction operation in Morocco would be a revelation to Mike. One interesting note was highlighted by the SAC regarding the Moroccan legal system. It was during Mike's tour in Naples that Moroccan laws concerning drugs were in place. He was advised that unlike U.S. law, as well as other countries, it was not against the law to sell drugs -

only to buy them.

Tony who had worked with Moroccan Anti-Drug Agents in the past told him, "Mike, don't be surprised when we work with the Moroccans; the sellers will be the police." OK, so this was getting really confusing to Mike. Apparently, it was OK for Moroccan cops to approach a sailor and offer drugs and this was not entrapment – go figure? This would be another major learning curve for Mike mastering other countries drug laws. So many differences to get used to and so much to learn and so little time.

It was time to get to the airport to catch their plane to Souda Bay. Mike would spend the flight quizzing Tony on what to see in Crete. Mike hoped he could do a little sightseeing.

Arriving in Souda Bay and with no time for sightseeing before the next flight, Mike and Tony decided to hit the base retail store. Strolling the aisles, looking for any neat item to bring back, Mike spotted his prize – an authentic brown Flakoti rug. These rugs were hand made from the wool of special long hair sheep. Such a deal to be had considering the value of the U.S. dollar overseas. It made it too hard to pass up. The rug only cost $25.00 and back in the states closer to $150.00!

Departing Crete and flying Olympic Airways and landing in Athens, the agents rented a car to use for the OP. Checking into their lodgings, a message was waiting from the home office. Bad news – due to a change in the port call for the ship, the operation had been cancelled. Mike and Tony were advised to proceed to Morocco. Since they could not get a flight until the next day there was time for a little sightseeing.

Museum hunting would be the plan for the afternoon. Tony thought there would be only enough time to explore the National Archaeological Museum.

The Museum, considered one of the greatest in the world, contained the richest collections of artifacts. The construction of the building began in the 19th century. During WWII it was closed and the relics were sealed in special protective boxes and buried, in order to avoid their destruction and looting.

Arriving at the building Mike was anxious to get inside to see what treasures it held. Time to pay their admission and travel back in time. The museum was divided into eight collections. With only enough time to check out one, they decided on the Egyptian Art Collection.

This collection dated back thousands of years and housed more than 6000 artifacts. Obviously, there would not be time to see all 6000, so Mike and Tony concentrated on ancient tools, mummies and a 3000-year old loaf of bread with a bite-sized chunk missing. All too soon the museum was closed for the day, so Blackstone and Cantanzo headed back to their hotel.

The next morning, checking in at the Olympic Airways terminal, it was time to board and head for Morocco. Once in Morocco and working with the Moroccan police; it was a real eye opener for Mike. Just when he was getting used to the antics of the CARBS back in Naples; the Moroccans would go one better.

On the first night working the OP, their partner, a Moroccan sergeant, walked up to a couple sailors and asked if they would like to buy some good 'smoke.' Never missing a golden opportunity to get high, the two made the purchase and were promptly arrested. This scenario would repeat itself over the next two nights. Lucky for the wrong doing sailors; the Moroccan authorities turned them over to the commanding officer of the ship for punishment.

Returning from working in Morocco and with his normal case load up to date and no new ops on tap, he finally would take a few days off. He decided to do some sightseeing around Naples. Having discovered a new found interest in historic sites, he would visit the Museo Archeologico in downtown Naples. This museum was the repository for ancient art recovered from Pompeii and other finds from around Mount Vesuvius. With traffic at its usual hectic 'every man for himself' pace, he decided to leave his car at the office and take the commuter train.

Finding the museum and paying his admission, he entered with his trusty guidebook in hand: where would he start? Like most museums around the world, the rooms were filled with so many treasures it was hard to absorb it all. His guide book listed the top ten; he would visit only those rooms. While all exhibits were impressive, he was most captivated by rooms that contained weapons and jewelry. After spending a few hours, Mike was reaching overload and decided there would be other opportunities to revisit during his NIS tour.

Before catching his train back to the base, he visited the Galleria Umberto. Once inside a visitor might describe it as a shopping mall but that would be a major understatement. It was more like a picture from an art magazine.

The Gallery was designed by Senore Rocco and built in

126

1891; named for Umberto I, the King of Naples at that time. It was planned and still in use as a public retail center with shops and cafes. The real showstopper was the huge stained glass ceiling covering the entire facility. Looking up at the ceiling with its hues of blue, green, red, and yellow Mike compared it to a multi-colored Tiffany lampshade because of the iridescent colors. He hated to leave but it was time to catch his train.

Standing on the train platform, Mike remembered vividly the advice given about riding the commuter trains during rush hour. "Don't!" As his train pulled up to the platform, it was a sight to see. It was so overcrowded that some passengers had their noses pressed up against the windows. Luckily a number exited but not nearly enough.

Entering the train and looking for a seat; forget it – standing room only. Did we say standing room; it was more like arm pit to arm pit. Straps hanging from the ceiling were designed for safety. Mike decided to count them but as he counted he discovered there were only enough for about half the current occupants.

As the train lurched forward jostling the passengers: what was that smell? In Naples and many other cities in Italy, washing clothes was done by hand and hung on balcony clothes lines. Hand washing never seemed to get the clothes 'odor-free.' Since he was an old navy salt, the colorful clothes drying reminded him of multi-colored ceremonial naval flags hanging from a ship's rigging. Because of this manual washing of clothes and showers were not a daily occurrence, the body odor was overwhelming to put it mildly.

Mike would be eternally grateful for the short ride and made a quick exit for some well needed fresh air at his stop. Walking to his car, he decided to check in at the office. No problem for Mike as he was on vacation - bad plan! He was greeted by at least a half dozen fellow agents as he entered the building.

Upon entering the conference room, a briefing on an operation was about to be discussed. The office had received a request from the CO of a navy ship anchored in the Bay of Naples for NIS assistance. With only limited information to go on concerning possible drug activity; it was time to saddle up and head to the port.

Arriving at the port the team boarded a launch sent from the ship. All aboard and they were on their way. It was a quick ride to the anchored ship. Their boat pulled up next to the boarding ladder of the navy submarine tender. As the boat slammed into the side of the ship with each passing wave, each member of the six-man team cautiously made the leap to the boarding ladder. It was no easy task as the ladder precariously hung from the side and it was a long climb up to reach the entrance way.

Captain Mike Reynolds, the CO, was a handsome man in his mid-30's and quite young to be the commanding officer of a major warship. He radiated an air of supreme confidence and leadership. He would stand for no nonsense on his ship.

The CO lead them to his stateroom and once inside he briefed the agents on the problem. The ship's MAA had discovered some sort of drug activity on board. The Captain was not sure of the extent, therefore, he decided to request NIS assistance. It was thought best to have MA1 Thomas, who initiated the ship's investigation, brief the agents.

MA1 Thomas entered the room and began the briefing. He related that based on information from an informal source, he had apprehended one of the crew in possession of a small amount of hashish. Thomas discovered this was not an isolated incident but was more widespread. The sailor stated that as many as 10-12 more sailors and one officer were involved. After briefing the XO, it was determined professional investigators were needed and NIS was contacted.

After the MAA departed, the CO advised three separate staterooms were available to be used as office/interrogation rooms. The agents moved to one of the staterooms to go over a game plan. It was decided to split into two man teams in separate rooms for interviews/interrogations. The ASAC decided S/A's Trailor and Blackstone would be the lead agents on this investigation. They would collate all information submitted to them by the other members of the team.

With a game plan in place, the sailor that the MAA had popped was brought in for interrogation.

Bob instructed the sailor, Seaman Apprentice Thomas Littleton to be seated. Since it had been determined he had been caught with an illicit drug and thus was in violation of the UCMJ, Trailor advised him of his rights. After being read his rights, upper most being the right to remain silent and have an attorney present, he agreed to talk to the agents. After Littleton signed the waiver, it was time to begin.

Mike was ready to start and ready to put his plan into action. "Tom, can I call you Tom and is that OK?" It was OK with Tom. While not promising him anything, the sailor was told that if he cooperated, Mike's well-worn #2 pencil eraser might be used to modify the charge against him or a least lessen it. The key was to learn from the mistake and move forward. Agent Bob Trailor took over the interrogation.

"Tom, you probably know we have information of others involved in this drug operation and we will be talking to them. When we talk to them, if we hear your name and involvement mentioned; that's what we call corroborating evidence and sailor you are in bigger trouble."

Littleton started to mist up and sob. Mike reassured him it would be in his best interest to cooperate in their investigation.

Trailor continued, "Let me explain some facts to you, when people get caught in a jam, they will drop a dime on anyone with the hope of mitigating charges against them. They would even give up their own grandmother if they thought it would help. Tom, help us to help you." Trembling, he agreed and began to tell his story to the agents:

"It all began when I was running short of money. SN Masters from the deck division had heard about my problem and offered to help me. He said there was an easy way to earn some extra money. He told me that all I had to do was have YN3 Sampson verbally give me the location of my first pick-up of hashish. Seeing that I was afraid, Sampson said the group had been doing it for some time with no problems. He even heard from another sailor in the group that the head man of the organization was an officer. Reluctantly I agreed to do it just the one time to pay some debts.

The procedure was for me to pick up a small amount of hashish hidden in several possible places on the ship. The hiding places could be in overhead piping or electrical boxes – pretty much anywhere. After making a sale, I was to place the money, less my commission, in a secret location on the ship. The location was specified on a note with the hashish I picked up to sell. At the drop I would find further instructions to locate the next package of hashish to sell.

All communications were verbal to locate the initial pick-up of hashish for a new employee of the group. An example would have Masters in an innocent conversation quietly say; 'Go to the main fire hose station on deck 2 and look behind it for the package to sell.' I never got any other instructions except from SN Master."

He was thanked for his cooperation and was asked to provide any useful names of sailors on the ship. Tom identified a SA Tim Johnson, HT3 Higgins and a YN2 Jason Jones. At the conclusion of the session, Tom signed a written confession of his involvement. He was advised not to discuss this meeting or the contents with anyone. As Tom rose to leave, he stopped and said, "You know, I knew it was only a matter of time before I got caught and now I'm glad it's over. Thank you."

As the day came to a close with all agents concluding their respective investigations and with additional buyers and sellers identified, it was time to wrap it up and debrief the CO.

Reassembling in his stateroom, the ASAC went over the results of his agents' efforts.

It was discovered that a total of five sellers were identified selling hashish to nine plus buyers. The hashish was procured by a Seaman Masters while he was on liberty in Naples. Despite their best efforts, the name of the officer involved was not obtained. All sellers in the ring told basically the same story of the operation. Instructions for pickup of monies and drops of hashish were handled solely by written notes secreted in various parts of the ship.

One consistent name the agents kept hearing was SN Masters. When brought in for questioning, he was the only suspect to exercise his right to remain silent and seek guidance from an attorney. It was evident to the interrogating agent that Masters knew the officer involved but was not going to give him up.

The CO asked Albright if there was anything else that could be done about SN Masters to get him to talk? Before he could answer, Mike jumped in with, "CO, he had every right to remain silent and seek attorney assistance." Before continuing the ASAC gave Mike a disapproving look and proceeded to finish briefing the CO. "Captain, when Masters heads toward court-martial, he just might get some religion and drop that important dime on the officer in question." All NIS S/A's were thanked for their hard work.

The ASAC on the ride back to the port, reminded Mike that NIS agents don't try any cases or pass judgment but merely gather the facts. He was also sternly reminded to, "Never side with a suspect and never lecture a commanding officer." Mike would have to remember that he was not a naval officer looking

132

out for his troops but a NIS S/A solely charged with investigating crimes.

Assembling back in the office, a round table discussion was held and ROI's were written up by each individual agent participating in the investigation.

Mike thought now he could surely get back to his sightseeing. Once again he was proved wrong. The SAC apologized, "We need to reduce the backlog on those DIS cases."

Mike reluctantly grabbed his stack and began to set up appointments. He knew these interviews were important for individuals requesting a clearance or an upgrade.

As previously mentioned, in the continental U.S. and territories, DIS agents conducted these investigations for access to Secret and Top Secret material. However, this function for clearing naval and DOD personnel overseas would fall to NIS agents. Once every couple of months all outstanding background cases would be divided up among Naples' agents to process.

Looking at his stack of files, Mike picked the top one and began the paper drill. Working these cases were very time consuming and pretty boring and usually nothing ever developed.

When a military or DOD civilian's job required access to sensitive information, he or she would fill out paperwork listing residences, employment and references; much like any application requiring the same types of information. Only references that could be verified from personnel stationed in Naples would require action on the part of Naples' agents. While most people, when talking to an agent were truthful, they would be wary of saying anything negative about a co-worker. One interview was most interesting to Mike as it actually revealed some startling information.

This case dealt with a request to verify a reference listed by a Communication Technician Specialist Third Class (CT3) stationed in Norfolk, Virginia who was seeking a Top Secret security clearance. The CT designation identifies personnel by the nature of their work and would be privy to most sensitive information.

The sailor's listed reference was working at the Naval Communications Group, Naples, Italy. This was the same unit Blackstone's Bermuda Drug Lady was assigned. Time to drive over to their building to interview the reference. For brevity, Mike met the individual and took his statement. Unlike other personnel he had interviewed in the past, this individual was very talkative and open about his opinion for the CT's access to higher classified material. He stated the following:

"I have known CT3 Flowers for about four years and was stationed with him prior to coming to Naples. He was a nice guy but in my opinion suffered from a bad case of low self-esteem. He would continually embellish stories about himself to look important especially about his job working in naval communications intelligence.

I recall one time when we were out drinking, he was busy chatting up a nice looking woman at a local bar. I did not pay too much attention to the conversation until I heard him discussing a secret project we were working. He wasn't necessarily divulging classified information; it was the mere fact that he was telling her where he worked and he had access to secret stuff that bothered me.

In my opinion, he should not be given a higher security clearance and maybe a closer look at his current security status is needed. It is not that he is necessarily untrustworthy, it is only when he has been drinking and trying to impress; he gets into trouble."

Thanking the individual, Mike returned to his office to write up his report. Once again this case reminded him that he was only responsible to report his findings and not to form an opinion.

The next day started out much like every other day with Mike driving to his office at the NSA compound. His daily morning routine was to walk to the base espresso bar and get a jolt of good Italian coffee and a sweet roll or cornetto; the local version of a croissant. Back in his office, he munched on his sweet roll, drank his coffee and read the latest Stars and Stripes newspaper. He was now ready for the day ahead.

On this particular day, Mike was stuck in the office as duty agent along with S/A Tim Tosgood. A good day to catch up on paperwork which was a never ending chore. Like any other vocation, a NIS agent's world seemed to revolve around mountains of paper.

As Blackstone was settling in, the office secretary advised him there was a phone call from the Executive Officer from the base hospital. Picking up the phone, the XO requested NIS assistance on a troubling event that occurred the previous evening. Alerting Tim to the situation, they drove up the hill to the hospital to interview the commander.

While Mike drove, Tim looked over the preliminary information they had received. At the front desk, the receptionist telephoned the XO and the agents were sent to his office.

The agents were ushered into his office to be briefed on the problem. Commander James reported that on the previous night, a staff nurse was concerned about the circumstances of a father who brought his 11-year old daughter in for treatment. The injury according to the father was due to the little girl grabbing a hot frying pan from the stove and burning her finger tips. After receiving treatment, they returned to their off-base residence.

The nurse sensing something was not quite right decided to check the little girl's medical records. She thought the father's story was a little fishy and she remembered previous treatments for the same type of injury. The records showed that in the last month, the girl had been treated twice for the same injury to her fingers. With this information she alerted Commander James.

Both agents concurred there was enough information, including descriptions of the father and the girl, to pay a visit to the father's off-base residence. Special Agent Tosgood agreed with the nurse on the father's story.

"Mike, since the residence is off-base, we better alert the local Italian police." In case of trouble, Tim and Mike would need assistance from the Italians. The local police station told the agents a regular police unit would meet them at the residence.

Arriving at the residence, S/A's Blackstone and Tosgood parked their G-Car and exited the vehicle. A tall man was seen on the porch with a young girl. Approaching the porch, the agents could see she was being held against her will.

Both agents froze! Tim cautioned Mike that he could see the man holding a knife to the girl's throat. "Stop right there and don't come any closer or she gets cut." This was not looking good so both backed away toward the Italian police cruiser where both police officers had remained in their car.

A short conference was held with the police who showed no interest in getting involved. They felt it was solely a U.S. military matter. The police stated, "We are only here as observers." Blackstone and Tosgood both agreed the police could not be counted on for any help. After checking their notes on the descriptions of the father and little girl, Tim came up with a plan.

"Mike, I'm going back to the residence and try to talk him out of this, remember, I have a wife and two kids. If he makes a move towards me with the knife or tries to hurt the little girl, what are you prepared to do?" "I wouldn't like it, but if he does, I'll take him out." With that assurance, Tosgood slowly headed back toward the residence. Opening his coat to show that he was unarmed, Mike's partner began to talk to the father of the girl. He continued his approach while he was talking and got about 15 feet from the porch. Before Tim could go any further, the man shouted "Stop!"

With his partner diverting the man's attention, Mike cautiously took up a position behind a low cinder block wall directly in front of the porch. Using the ledge on the wall as a prop, he drew his .357 S&W from his shoulder holster and took up a shooting position. The distance was only about 30 feet and as a qualified expert with the revolver, there was no doubt that if it came to it, the man was going down.

Mike had never been nervous while qualifying on the firing range back at the Academy but this was the real thing and with sweat beading up on his forehead and his pulse racing; it was a different story. Mike said a silent prayer; *please Lord just let the guy put the knife down and we can all go home safe.* Even with some trepidation, Mike was prepared to shoot to save Tim and the little girl.

Tensions were at a high level but whatever S/A Tosgood was telling the man seemed to calm him down. With Mike continuing to draw a bead on the man, he dropped the blade and released the little girl who ran crying back into the house. Handcuffing the man and placing him in their car, it was time to head to the office.

Once back at the office and while the subject was escorted to the interrogation room, Mike debriefed the SAC on the events. Joining Tim, the interrogation of the subject began with the standard speech about the man's rights. The subject was Petty Officer Second Class Tompsen who elected to waive his rights and executed the standard form. Surprisingly he was ready to talk to the agents.

With practiced professionalism, both agents set the man at ease and asked him to just tell what happened with the little girl. After rambling on and on with his eyes darting back and forth he stated, "I would from time to time burn her fingers with a cigarette to teach her a lesson." With that damning admission, the agents concluded the interrogation and the subject signed a written statement. The case was turned over to the JAG office and Mike hoped his roommate would not be assigned to the case.

Sitting alone in the interrogation room, both agents had time to reflect. "You know Mike, that was some scary shit and to tell you the truth, I wasn't sure how it was all going to end." "I didn't either but you can rest easy because if you or the girl were in danger I would have taken the shot." "Thanks Mike."

Now alone, Mike ran the events over and over in his head. Unlike TV and the movies, shooting someone in real life was not to be taken lightly. The director can say "Cut" and it's a 'do over.' Mike and his fellow agents would not be granted that luxury. Thinking back to the Academy when he sat in the weapon's class on shooting situations, he never imagined that one day he would have to face the real thing.

One collateral duty for Mike was providing NIS Foreign Counterintelligence Program briefings to area commands. He didn't mind this tasking; he felt as a permanent naval intelligence officer as well as a S/A, guarding the country's secrets was of prime importance. Routinely on a requested basis, Blackstone and Jack Lewis would provide security of classified material briefings along with showing the video: The Collectors. The video showed various scenarios for the collection of information by foreign agents.

Mike thought he had 'hit the deck running pretty hard' and deserved a rest but once again duty called. It would be a trip to Bahrain. It would be a drug interdiction OP with ASAC Dave Albright. At least there was some good news – they would travel commercial all the way. Their flight would originate in

Naples and fly to Rome. The connecting flight would take them to Saudi Arabia and then catch a flight to Bahrain.

Flying from Naples to Rome was a no brainer and they made their connecting flight with no difficulty. After a long flight to the kingdom of Saudi Arabia both agents were anxious to reach their destination.

Exiting the aircraft, the two collected their luggage and headed for customs. Since they had nothing to declare they by passed it and went straight to passport control.

"Welcome to the Kingdom of Saudi Arabia and passports and visas, please." Mike looked at Albright for an explanation about visas. He had none and no one at the office had thought to request them. It was assumed all that was needed was either their tourist or official passports. After all, they weren't staying in the kingdom - only passing through. Oops, there goes that Assume Guy rearing his ugly head.

In short order, airport police showed up and our duo were taken into custody. Dave explained the situation and the visa problem was solved. They were forcefully told to take seats at the boarding area for Bahrain and not to move without permission. Mike thought it was like being back in grade school. Blackstone remembered he would have to raise his hand to ask for permission to use the bathroom. Only this was no grade school, he would have to ask the cop who was his guard in case nature called.

Not soon enough, their flight was called and it was onto Bahrain. Well at least there was some humor in this last flight. It would be a short one.

"Welcome aboard Bahrain Airways Flight A and please fasten your seat belts." Mike was ready for a leisurely flight but Dave knew differently. The aircraft roared down the runway and lifted off. Just as Mike felt the plane level off at its cruising altitude; it began its descent. "Dave what's up? Is there a problem?" "There's no problem Mike, we will be in the air only about 20 minutes."

Back on terra firma the agents headed off to rent a car. There would be no problem since both had international driving licenses. One thing they would have to keep in mind was foreigners would be considered at fault in any traffic problem. It seemed the logic for this approach was in the belief that had you, the foreign driver not been in their country – no accident could have taken place. Traveling in foreign countries sure had its surprises – go figure this one out!

With the car rented and driving so very carefully Mike and Dave reached their 5-star hotel. Checking in Dave had no problem with the price of the hotel room since his civilian per diem would completely cover this high cost area. Mike who was on the navy plan would be a whole different story. His per diem would only cover 85% of the bill. He would have to argue with the Navy Dispersing Officer over the difference once he returned to Naples.

Walking through the lobby Mike was in awe of the opulence of the place. Leather chairs and sofas, fountains flowing and he thought he saw gold leaf throughout the lobby. Since it was late afternoon and Mike was thirsty – really thirsty, they decided to hit the bar. The bar was as impressive as the lobby. Crystal glassware, gold filigree chandeliers and very expensive looking tile were in abundance. Mike wondered what a beer was going to cost him in the bar?

Locating an empty table, the two were ready to decompress. After ordering two beers (at $8.00 apiece) it was interesting to watch the different array of patrons. The bar was filled with men in western attire, Middle Eastern dress and casual touristy clothing. Also Dave noticed there seemed to be a number of flight crews milling around. Mike noticed a few of the crew were pretty fine looking women. He always was a sucker for a woman in uniform.

Mike and Dave were about to order another round when two stewardesses walked up to their table. They both were tall statuesque blondes with smiles that would melt butter. "Hello gentlemen, mind if we join you?" Mike was ready to answer when Dave piped up, "Yes we do." This had the obvious effect and they rejoined their compatriots.

"Dave, what the hell's the matter. All they wanted to do was sit and talk and have a few drinks." Dave quietly explained the situation, "Mike first they sit down. Next we all have a few drinks. Later it is suggested to go upstairs for more drinks. Before you know it Mike you have gone past socializing. Need I say more?" Mike took the hint and dropped the subject.

Over the last of their beer, Mike was interested in the number of men drinking in the bar and wearing robes and Keffiyeh head gear. "Dave, who are the gents in the robes sucking down all the booze?" "Oh, they're Saudis who come over to Bahrain to drink, party and anything else they can't do back home." "So if they are over here it's OK but back home in Saudi Arabia it's a big no-no?" "Yep, you got it."

Finishing their drinks, they left the bar and headed to their rooms. Dave was paged by the front desk. Bad news just like in the past for Mike - the 5th Fleet ship's visit had been canceled. Mike was directed to fly home to Naples and Dave would head to Beirut, Lebanon to investigate the bombing of the Marine Barracks. The news had reported a high casualty number.

The only flight they could book was for the following morning. Dave volunteered to show Mike the Souk. Mike had been to one in Egypt but was interested in buying some jewelry. Jumping in their rented car it was off to the Bazaar.

The Bahrain Souk was much like Cairo's except the gold selection was much greater and varied. As the agents walked the street, they were greeted by a number of gold shops. Mike thought that every other shop was selling some type of gold. Store after store had broom handles filled with 22 kt. gold bracelets. Picking one at random, Mike entered. He was looking for a nice pair of earrings for his mom. He selected one pair and asked the price. He was surprise when the clerk dropped them on a scale. In Bahrain gold jewelry was sold by the ounce – no matter how detailed or the work involved to create it.

The next morning Mike was off for home and Dave to Lebanon.

CHAPTER 5

THE FLEETS INPORT NAPLES

Whenever the fleet would pull into Naples harbor, NIS Naples would initiate drug interdiction operations or merely devote extra man hours to monitoring servicemen's activity while their ships were in port. An important aspect of duty in Naples was to keep sailors safe and out of trouble while on liberty. On an informal basis, the CARBS would sometimes be needed to assist Mike and his fellow agents with activities of sailors which would not take place on base.

Naples was known as a city where one could find any kind of diversion – legal or otherwise. The Castle area as well as the Gut were well known areas to off duty sailors. As with most young people, sailors and marines when told not to do something – well, they usually tried.

The Castello Nuovo or new castle (in English) dates back to 13th Century when it was used by Charles I Anjou, the King of Naples. It was situated in the downtown area. Located on a slight rise, it was an impressive site. The castle was first constructed in 1279 and finished in 1282. Pope Boniface VIII was elected and the ceremony took place at the Castle around 1290. In the ensuing years, the site was the scene of more important events as well as numerous military battles culminating with the annexation of the Kingdom of Naples by King Charles VIII of France for Spain.

From an architectural view, the most outstanding feature was the white sided marble arch standing over 100' in height.

144

When one entered through the Bronze Gates into the Piazza del Duomo that history came alive. Visitors would stroll the grounds and imagine those early Italians, who had walked before them centuries ago.

The Castle was used as local administrative offices but after dark it took on a different character. While not strictly off limits during the evening, the grounds surrounding it were sure to find some kind of mischief for the sailors and marines.

Besides drugs, which were readily available throughout Naples as well as the rest of Italy, the main activity centered around a young man's desire for some female companionship hoping it would end in a sexual encounter, better known as getting laid. Unfortunately for Sammy Sailor, this would require the services of a prostitute or 'puttana.' Paying for sex with a prostitute could result in much danger from robbery to contracting a sexual disease. However, the real scare was finding out your lady of the evening was a gay male impersonating a female prostitute or a 'ricchione.'

On one evening while Mike and Sergio were patrolling along the Castle; he received a first class demonstration. Just as they rounded a corner, a couple of beautiful women approached our dynamic duo. Blackstone was taken aback by their beauty and remarked to his CARB partner, "Those sure are some kind of fine looking women." Sergio busted out with a hearty laugh, "Michele, those are Ricchioni; you know, male prostitutes that pass as women." Now that Mike thought about it, the two seemed to be overly tall for Italian women.

Mike still did not trust his eyes and was finally convinced

when the two walked by. He heard both of them chatting in very strong low baritone voices. Boy, Mike had a lot to learn and the learning curve seemed to be getting steeper all the time. It was a quiet night and not much activity around the Castle so the team moved on to the Gut to rendezvous with other NIS agents and CARBS.

In order to reach the rendezvous, they had to cross over many side streets and alleys. Always alert, Mike spotted numerous cars parked on a side street. What got his attention was the cars had their windows covered with newspapers and were fogged up. Asking his partner for an explanation, he was told young people in Naples lacked privacy for intimacy and found it where they could.

The Gut, a seedy and rundown alley, could best be described as the worst slum (whores, booze, guns and drugs) you could ever have imagined. Anything and everything was available.

Arriving at the pre-arranged rendezvous location, Mike was briefed that he would continue with Sergio di Grasso while Tony Cantanzo would be partnered with Joccomo; Albright would work with Paolo; Jack Lewis teamed up with Monti.

The attack plan was pretty simple. Mike and Sergio along with Albright and Paolo would work one side of the alley, moving sailors along towards the exit. On the other side, Tony and Joccomo with Jack and Monti would convince sailors or marines the area was out-of-bounds. Pretty easy tasking for the agents and CARBS. They would enter all establishments and would announce the Gut was off-limits. As Blackstone exited the Gut, he noticed his CARB was lagging behind but did not think much about it. He never was

146

the fleetest of foot. Meanwhile Mike had reached his G-Car and waited for his CARB and the rest of the teams.

Just when he got comfortable leaning on the car and eating a slice of cold pizza; out came a U.S. sailor in a dress blue uniform with the big guy in hot pursuit. Mike heard him scream at the top of his lungs in Italian, "Attento! Alto!" Alerted that he was obviously chasing the sailor, Mike grabbed him. He was placed up against the car with the side of his face kissing the roof. Mike waited for his partner to catch up. As the CARB walked up wheezing and gasping for air, Mike noticed he had his thumb in his mouth and was sucking on it.

Meanwhile the sailor shouted every obscenity he could think of including "Get your M-F hands off me!" Knowing the Italian's disposition and temper Mike waited. Moving closer to him, Mike asked, "Qual e il problema?" Instead of answering, he looked at the sailor and angrily pressed his injured thumb against the sailor's nose.

Evidently Sergio's thumb got our antagonistic sailor going and he was screaming about his rights as a U.S. citizen. While he continued with his verbal assault on our duo, Sergio explained: "I tried to stop the sailor inside the Gut. But instead of complying, he shoved me against the stone side of a shop wall and caused me to bang my thumb against the wall and cut it." As Mike listened our misguided soul mouthed off again and was rewarded with Sergio pressing his massive body against him in a threatening manner.

Ok, it was obvious the sailor wasn't getting the big picture! It was time for Mike to calm Sergio down before he really got pissed at the sailor.

"Shipmate, have you ever watched the movie 'Midnight Express?' No? Too bad because the movie shows exactly what a foreigner can expect from police authorities. You would have a pretty clear picture of what awaits you at the hands of this very large police officer." It seemed to Mike, civilian travelers including U.S. military members, believed they had the rights granted to them by the U.S. Constitution and the Bill of Rights when traveling abroad; they're only good back in the states.

In this particular case, the rights of our misinformed 'swabby' were at the mercy of one Sergio di Grasso. Still not getting his point across, the sailor continued with his diatribe which resulted with Sergio grabbing and shaking the young fool.

Pulling the CARB aside, Mike could see there was only one solution to the problem. He returned to the sailor and very softly advised him he had two choices: (1) to continue with his verbal assault and be arrested and end up in the downtown prison for an assault on a police official or (2) shut up! A light came on for our wayward sailor and he chose the correct option. The petty officer apologized and returned to his ship. Blackstone played Dr. Kildare to Sergio and bandaged his thumb.

The rest of the teams arrived and the ASAC determined all agents as well as the CARBS would call it a night except for Mike, Tony and Monti, the young CARB. Since the evening was still young they were directed to work around Fleet Landing. This docking area at the port was where enlisted and officer liberty boats dropped off ship's personnel or picked others up and returned them

148

to their ships. No civilian boats were allowed to use this dock and it was patrolled by members of the Shore Patrol.

With Fleet Landing close enough to walk, the agents decided to do just that. While they were headed in that direction, a trio of young Italians approached from a side alley. "Hey sailors, hashish?" they asked in halting English. It appeared these youngsters had mistakenly assumed our trio of agents for sailors returning to their ships. Oops, wrong assumption!

Monti, as the local law enforcement representative took the lead. He spoke smooth English to the three, "You guys speak English?" The leader of the three, looked left to right and shook his head in a negative manner. Without a pause, he proceeded to pull out a small tin foil wrapped package for inspection. Monti alerted Mike and Tony the tin foil contained a small amount of hashish. He planned to arrest them. Now, this was where Moe, Curly and Larry from 'The Three Stooges' came into play.

This would be his first solo arrest and he was extremely nervous. In a hushed voice, speaking out of the side of his mouth, queried the NIS agents, "Are you guys ready?" The U.S. agents whispered, "Yeah, we're ready." Without a pause, he said again, "Are you guys ready?" For the second time, Tony responded in a hushed voice, "Yeah, we're ready."

While this laughable exchange was taking place, the trio of young Italians began to sense something was amiss and started to back away from the agents. As the teens slowly moved away, Mike, Tony and Monti casually moved to cut off their exit. The teens weren't sure what was about to happen but it was clear they sensed something was wrong and continued to back away from the agents. The CARB again whispered out of the side of his mouth, "Are you guys ready?"

Agent Cantanzo had just about enough of this nonsense and had reached his limit of patience. Shouting, in his best Jersey accent; "Jesus Christ, we're ready already!" With that declaration, the three desperados were jumped, put into custody and handcuffed. It seemed to Mike, it was a lot of work for 1-2 grams of hashish.

The scene continued with the two NIS agents restraining their two captives. At the same time, Monti violently jerked the leader by the shoulders. He was nose to nose with him. Not doing it once but at least two more times until the frightened teenager snapped to some sort of attentive stance.

Standing aside, the NIS agents continued to hold the other two teens while Monti interrogated the leader. Mike and Tony thought it looked like he was lecturing the kid. By now this wrong doer was scared and in tears. It appeared he had seen the error of his ways - attempting to sell drugs to sailors was a bad idea.

As he walked over to Mike and Tony, the junior CARB instructed Blackstone and Cantanzo to release their captives. Once released, the three terrors of the night disappeared into the back alleys of Naples.

As the trio resumed their walk toward Fleet Landing, Mike made a point of asking why the young leader was roughed up? He was in custody and handcuffed. It was obvious to both NIS agents that the teen had not resisted arrest. Mike had previously observed suspects in CARB custody receiving similar physical intimidation.

"Respect! We must have Respect!" With Blackstone and Cantanzo full attention, he explained. "I have been taught by senior Anti-Drug members that bad guys must have a fear of us and thus respect our authority." With Naples' history of lawlessness, one could see how they felt the need to establish control quickly. It seemed to Mike that David's show of force demonstrated to the teens just who was in charge. He apparently had been taught that lawyers had their laws - the CARBS had their own.

Italian rule of law or the CARBS interpretation was definitely open for discussion. Since he would be working closely in the future with these gents, Blackstone would have to go along and hope things never got out of hand. In the future, Mike would have plenty of opportunities to observe this respect gathering technique by more senior members of the CARB Anti-Drug Squad.

Reaching their destination of Fleet Landing, the Shore Patrol lieutenant in charge advised the weather was worsening and liberty had been cancelled. He would only have one more boat scheduled to arrive to pick up stragglers. Tony decided it was a good time to call it a night. Mike and Tony headed to their car with Monti doing the same. The end of a most enlightening evening was in sight for Mike after experiencing an episode of – When Sammy Sailor met the CARBS of Napoli.

With ships in port, off-limit areas would not be the only places sailors sought out entertainment. There were more and safer options available to visiting sailors and marines as well as those stationed in Naples. The USO located in Naples provided a little piece of home for servicemen out on the town. It was a good place to go for a hamburger, drink a Coke or watch a movie. It had a most prized commodity - telephones. Only a short cab ride from the port was another place for sailors and marines to look for some innocent fun. EDENLANDIA, while it could not be compared to DISNEYLAND, provided all the entertainment associated with an amusement park.

The park was located just outside Naples' city center. It opened in the mid 60's with all standard diversions: roller coaster, Ferris wheel, arcades and food stalls. While most activities were harmless, it also had a darker side: prostitution and drugs. Those Camp Fire girls would sometimes be in attendance outside the entrance as would local drug dealers. From time to time, NIS S/A's would be in attendance to show a presence and cautioned servicemen on the pitfalls of dealing with prostitutes and drug thugs.

The most popular place for the majority of ship's personnel with time on their hands was Carney Park. The recreation area was a place where they could play ball games, have a picnic, go swimming or just relax in the sunshine and enjoy a beer or two.

The park was named for Admiral Robert B. Carney who was a past Chief of Naval Operations (CNO) in the 1950's and 1960's. It was established by the Morale, Welfare and Recreation Command of the U.S. Department of Defense. From its inception, it was designed to provide recreation facilities for military personnel and their families, authorized DOD personnel with their families as well as single sailors, marines and allied military members. It was located in a 93-acre park like setting albeit in the center of an extinct volcano crater. Mike often wondered just how extinct it was on the

152

times he had worked inside the park.

Surrounding the crater area was a forest with tall pines and shrubbery with numerous footpaths leading up from the base. A short list of activities included: a golf course, swimming pool, ball fields, tennis courts, picnic areas and a snack bar. An unusual feature was a short iron railing which bordered the only road and formed a complete circle around the park.

It was normal procedure for a few NIS agents to work Carney Park during visits by ship's personnel. No assistance was needed from Italian local police agencies as Carney Park was considered working on a military base for jurisdiction purposes.

With six U.S. Navy ships visiting, the SAC, Tom Thompson, had decided his agents would be on hand in the park. Three teams of two agents each would be present. Mike would be working with Dave Albright, the ASAC.

Assisting the NIS teams were members of the NSA base military police along with some Shore Patrol who would routinely be tasked with keeping order in the park. Their normal charter called for them to handle minor infractions. With NIS agents present, they would be another set of eyes and ears and report any suspicious activity.

Agents Albright and Blackstone, dressed in casual civilian clothes, would start the OP by milling around much like any off-duty sailors. The two would be on alert to respond to criminal activity falling under NIS jurisdiction.

The day was in the summer and it was steamy hot. It wasn't just hot; it was more like the Sahara Desert kind of hot! Mike and

ASAC Dave Albright decided to keep to the shady side of the park. While taking a break and sitting on one of the picnic tables two sailors, in summer white uniforms, were observed standing by one of the footpaths leading up into the woods. Darting glances back and forth and quick as a flash, the two disappeared into the wooded area.

The ASAC was very familiar with Naples and Carney Park. He asked Mike, "Does that look normal to you?" "Not really Dave, nothing up there except trees and secluded places." They decided to act on this suspicious behavior. A plan of action was developed which called for Mike to follow the two sailors up the path while agent Albright would circle around on an adjacent one. Game on! They headed for the pathways.

Arriving at his footpath and seeing the ASAC disappear on the adjacent one, Mike cautiously moved up the trail. Knowing he did not have visual contact with the subjects, he had to rely on picking up any unusual sounds. As he continued his climb upward, he froze; voices were heard not too far ahead. The two had to be up in a clearing that Mike could barely see.

Silently, he moved up to a position behind a tall pine tree only yards away from the two. Continuing his surveillance, he observed the taller of the two pull something out of his pocket, cup it to his mouth and light it. He passed it to his buddy who cupped it likewise and smoked it. Either they were short of cigarette funds and were sharing a butt or this was some kind of smoking narcotic. With the wind blowing toward Mike, he smelled the unmistakable odor of marijuana. He found it odd as it was hard if not impossible to find in Naples – time to investigate.

Jumping out from behind the tree, Mike announced, "Alright freeze, NIS Special Agent and hold it right there." Holding up his NIS credentials, he approached the pair. "You're both under arrest." He thought, wrongly, that since he was a properly identified federal agent, this would be a no brainer bust and was expecting no trouble.

Standing a few feet from the two, he heard the taller one; a very large muscular seaman, shout, "Oh, Shit!" and lunged at Mike. Before he had time to react, a very large fist was heading in the direction of Mike's face. Good thing he had heard the warning and only received a glancing blow to this jaw. After striking the blow, his 6'4" assailant grabbed him and they both crashed to the ground. Rolling around in the dirt with Mike trying to restrain him, the two began to roll down the footpath. Yelling at the top of his lungs, "Agent Down!" He hoped for some assistance from the ASAC or members of the military police. The fight continued with Mike's assailant beginning to get the better of him.

Fearing the other guy might jump in, Mike while struggling with his man and could see out of the corner of his eye that the second sailor didn't want any part of the fight. The last Mike saw of him; he was running in the direction of the adjacent path.

It was bad enough that a pretty good tussle was going on but then, Mike felt the man trying to get his hands on his shoulder holstered service revolver. *Oh Crap!* Mike thought, *this asshole is going to try and shoot me over one lousy joint.*

With Mike continuing to shout for help, the pair cartwheeled down the path. Mike had his hands full trying to subdue the sailor and at the same time keep his revolver from him. What seemed like at least 30 minutes but more like two, Mike emerged with our sailor at the bottom of the footpath.

To Mike's relief, members of the base military police and Shore Patrol rushed to his aid. Mike had his man face down kissing the dirt while the Shore Patrol cuffed him. With the situation under control he sat down to collect himself.

The humorous part of this whole episode occurred when the sailor's head had somehow ended up under the aforementioned iron railing by the road. Evidently in all the excitement, nobody had noticed the sailor's head was protruding under the railing.

One police officer in an effort to get Mike's subject to his feet resulted in a most comical sight. Mike was not sure the sailor saw much humor in it. It was lift him up – bang his head and back down. Lift the sailor up – bang his head and back down again. This comical scene went on until the Petty Officer in Charge of the Shore Patrol realized what was going. He slid Mike's offender away from the railing and got him in a vertical position.

Patting down our wayward sailor, Mike discovered a small plastic bag containing suspected marijuana and some rolling papers. Retaining this evidence to be entered into the NIS evidence locker, Mike turned the sailor over to base military police who loaded him into their van.

Now, he could really sit down and collect his thoughts on what just occurred. With his heart still pounding and his adrenalin still pumping, he spotted the ASAC approaching with the second sailor in tow. S/A Albright's man was loaded into the van with his partner in crime and away the van sped to deposit the two at military police headquarters.

With the ASAC sitting down, Blackstone continued to massage his bruised and swollen chin. Mike asked, "What happened and where the hell were you?" Albright explained, "I heard you yelling and tried to move laterally through the woods but got stuck a couple of times. Just when I got free, here comes this sailor running and stumbling in my direction, screaming something about fight! – guns! – yelling! I took him into custody and figured we'd sort it out once we were back down out of the woods.

Say Mike, except for damage to your clothes and a few cuts and that nasty bruise on your jaw, I figured you came off lucky." Examining the bruise and scrape on the side of Mike's jaw, he exclaimed, "It looks like if you had been hit square on; we would be taking you to the hospital with a broken jaw." "Yeah, you know how we are always saying, 'Shit Happens!' Well, Oh Shit! in this case, saved my bacon not to mention my face."

Mike had just about all the excitement he could stand for one day. The two left Carney Park and headed for the office. Mike would fill the ASAC in later on the whole story of his apprehension of his assailant. Back at his desk, Mike started the draft of his report. Not able to finish, it was time to go home. Interrogating the two could wait till tomorrow. It was definitely - Miller Time.

Just when Mike and the other office agents thought they might catch a break with the majority of ships in Naples harbor due to leave; new tasking came in from one of the ships. It was reported that a sailor had tried to jump ship by literally going over the side. It was also another possibility that he was pushed or simply had fallen overboard. Unfortunately for him, he forgot or didn't notice a painting barge was tied alongside. Ouch! He fell approximately 30 feet and hit hard.

Bob Trailor was tasked to go up to the base hospital to question the sailor. Meanwhile, the SAC assigned Mike, Tony Cantanzo and Tim Tosgood to conduct an investigation onboard the ship once S/A Trailor returned from the hospital.

Once Bob arrived back at the office, he briefed the three assigned agents on his interview with the injured crewman from the ship. He was not able to get too much information as the individual was still disorientated from his fall. The sailor did dismiss the idea that he was pushed or simply had fallen over board. He had intended to jump ship from the ship but misjudged the distance he needed to clear the barge.

Trailor did not think the story was that simple so he pressed him for more. Reluctantly, the crewman volunteered he was not really trying to go AWOL but was afraid for his safety. Still wanting more from the injured sailor, S/A Trailor pressed him and the sailor told him there was an extortion ring operating on the ship. The sailor owed the group money at 25% interest per month and could not pay it back. He additionally provided the name of the sailor on the ship responsible for collecting payments, as well as a friend of his who also owed the group money.

Time for Mike, Tony and Tim to head out to the ship to verify the injured seaman's story. The ship could not delay its movement so the Naples' agents would ride the ship to its next port of call in Catania, Sicily.

Arriving on board the ship and not wanting to lose any time, they started the investigation by meeting with the XO and ship's MAA. The XO stated he had heard rumors of some crewmen lending money but thought it was just shipmates helping out others short of cash. Agents Blackstone, Tosgood and Cantanzo informed him of the details provided by the sailor who had jumped from the ship. An investigation was opened and the three investigators were ready to proceed.

Usury is defined generally as the making of unethical or immoral monetary loans with abusive interest rates. To Mike that translated into plain old loan sharking. In this case, it appeared the extortion group was known to use violent threats to receive payments. The actions of this group would fall under violations of the UCMJ.

The three agents split up to cover more ground. Mike and Tim sent for the injured sailor's friend, Seaman Apprentice Garcia. Tony Cantanzo was shown to the area of the ship where the injured sailor had fallen and made notes as well as shot some photos. He noticed the painting barge was still secured to the ship. Tony half chuckled to himself; *watch that first step – it's a doozy!*

Entering the interview stateroom, Garcia was reluctant to talk at first but eventually opened up. He provided Blackstone and Tosgood with names of others who were in debt to two crewmen on the ship. He also confirmed the name of the sailor who was the collector of loan payments.

With the ship underway and cutting to the chase, the agents compiled their information and went right for the jugular and called in Petty Officer Second Class Potts and advised him of his rights. This was the fellow identified by both Garcia and the injured sailor as the Money Man. Initially denying any involvement, S/A Tosgood clued him in on the legality of his situation.

"Shipmate, you are in big trouble. We have your name as the head of this extortion ring on the ship. We will corroborate the allegation against you with others naming you. It will be some serious brig time." The subject decided to give up the other members of the extortion group and also surrendered his accounting book. The others were subsequently called in and all confessed and gave details of their 'loan business.'

Synopsis of the case revealed the nuts and bolts of the operation. It was known throughout the ship when you were short of money until payday, the group was there to help; just don't miss any payments. In the 1980's payday aboard ship was every two weeks and paid in cash.

The procedure, in place for collections, would be for one member of the group to be stationed near the pay table. Once a debtor collected his pay, he would report to the collector and pay up. If he skipped paying, he knew what awaited him. This was why the injured sailor decided to jump ship. The Naples' agents closed down the ring and departed the ship once it reached Catania.

The old saying "Never a dull moment", certainly applied to Mike's life as an NIS S/A in Naples. Returning from Catania he tried to squeeze some local sightseeing into his schedule - it was disappointment time again.

The SAC called him into his office with a new impromptu assignment. "I understand you are a music lover and I have something for you I think you'll like. Franco Zagusso and his band are scheduled to give a free concert in the San Paolo Stadium this week. I want you to go and mingle with the crowd and dissuade any service people from getting into trouble; no arrests – just advise them." Well, it wasn't sightseeing but it did get him out of the office.

On the concert date, Mike arrived downtown and parked his G-Car. He proceeded to work the crowd outside and be on the lookout for any servicemen activities that were suspicious. While not an Italian opera fan, it was interesting to hear Zagusso sing two Neapolitan favorites in addition to his regular songs. From inside the stadium he could hear a rousing ovation at the conclusion of O Sole Mio (O My Sun) and Torna a Surriento (Comeback to Sorrento.) After about two hours, Mike had enough of this Initiative Operation and called it a night.

CHAPTER 6
WORKING DEDICATED OPERATIONS WITH THE CARB ANTI-DRUG SQUAD

Mike's tour in Naples required the use of local police assets when working off military installations. With this requirement, most cases involved working with CARB Anti-Drug Squad. As seen previously, Naples S/A's used the affectionate moniker of CARBS when referring to these gents. The squad was unique, wild and an unorthodox group of individuals you could ever imagine who had police identity cards and carried high powered handguns.

In the two years he worked alongside the CARBS, he could not recall them showing any sort of badge verifying their authority. Their preferred badge of identification was the 9 mm Beretta. The CARBS attitude reminded him of the Bandito's famous quote: "Badges? We don't need no badges. We don't got to show you no stinking badges. We got guns!" The quote came from the classic movie 'The Treasure of the Sierra Madre' starring Humphrey Bogart.

The CARBS or loosely translated as carrier of carbines was a military organization which was formed hundreds of years before Italy became an independent country. This force was founded by one powerful man named Victor Emanuel I; the Duke of Savoy and the King of Sardinia. They had the distinction of arresting Giuseppe Garibaldi, one of Italy's founding fathers. In downtown Naples next to the train station was an impressive piazza named in his honor. Visitors would see a statue of him overlooking the piazza.

In Naples, drug trafficking was a common occupation, in which a ready source of customers always existed. While strictly being members of the Italian military, Anti-Drug CARBS would focus primarily on combating illegal drug activities. Mike and his fellow agents would primarily work with them in and around Naples except for an occasional special operation in another city.

Thousands of sailors off navy ships spend liberty in and around Naples throughout the year. NIS Naples was tasked with working with these Italian gentlemen to keep drugs away from USN and USMC personnel. The drug of choice being the readily available hashish or hash for short and brought into the country from various locales throughout the Mediterranean.

On one noteworthy occasion, Mike's office was called to assist in a drug bust at Cappodichino Airport outside Naples. The CARBS had a tip that a 4-door blue Renault with four Italian nationals would be arriving to deliver a quantity of hash which would ultimately be sold to U.S. servicemen. The operation would include two Italian agents and two American agents.

The call came from Major Tanta advising the bust was on and to meet the Italian drug agents at their office at the port. The CARBS would be Sergio di Grasso and Joccomo with S/A's Mike Blackstone and Tony Cantanzo rounding out the team. Meeting at the CARBS office, the operation plan was discussed. With time a serious consideration there would be no coffee because it was time to get to the airport.

At the airport all agents, both American and Italian, concealed themselves along a row of bushes and a chain link

163

fence bordering the road. In short order, a screech was heard and a blue Renault was observed heading for the main gate but instead of entering the airport, the car made a U-turn and headed back in the direction of the agents.

Sergio, crouching alongside Mike, jumped up and pulled his 9 mm Berretta and trotted, running was out of the question, to the front of the car screaming, "Alto!" He stood, seemingly without a care in the world, and pointed his Berretta at the driver. No badges and no ID, just one big gorilla with a gun, shouting and standing smack dab in front of the car. The rest of the agents, with service weapons drawn, surrounded the car. Slowly the big guy moved to the driver's door. He questioned the occupants and in less than a minute, the car was waved on.

Sergio sauntered back to the assembled agents as Mike shouted, "What the hell?" to anyone and everyone. Laughing at some private joke, he explained that they were a bunch of high school students out for a joy ride. Mike and his partner were a little concerned to put it mildly. With all the firepower present it would have not taken much for the situation to explode. The CARBS on the other hand seemed nonplussed over the matter.

Tony jumped into the conversation, "Hey, what if they didn't stop when you ordered them to?" "We shoot them! We are the CARBS!" Blackstone and Cantanzo weren't sure if these two were kidding or not. They weren't in any hurry to find out the answer.

Mike would have so much to learn working with these guys. Resuming their stakeout positions, the game was still on.

164

They did not have to wait long as another blue Renault, matching the vehicle's description, entered the roadway leading to the terminal area. Unlike the previous Renault, this one was moving slowly and obviously looking for something or someone. As it approached the agents' positions, Sergio once again jumped out screaming "Alto! – Polizia!" He had his trusty weapon drawn and the Renault slammed to a halt. The entire team had followed his lead and joined him with their weapons pointing at the car. In an instant all four doors opened and the occupants fled.

No gun play - just the bad guys scattering like cockroaches caught in daylight with the agents in pursuit.

Mike took off sprinting as di Grasso, huffing and puffing trotted after another suspect. Mike soon had his man but alas Sergio's had escaped and he was pissed. As Mike was checking his suspect's jacket pockets for any drug evidence, his Italian partner walked up wheezing and coughing. Sergio's three pack a day cigarette habit appeared to be catching up to him. Mike reported he found no weapons, drugs or drug paraphernalia. The CARB, with a disbelieving look on his face said he would give it a go and grabbed the jacket from Mike.

Mike felt confident he had made a thorough search but was surprised when a small tin foil wrapped package was pulled from his suspect's jacket pocket. "Michele, look what you missed." No, Mike had not missed a thing! It appeared the rules of evidence were slightly different in Italy or at least in Naples. Walking back to the other agents' location, Mike noticed some sort of field interrogation in progress at the chain link fence.

This particular interrogation could not be confused with any sort of interrogation technique Mike had been exposed to at the Academy. Mike's big CARB determined that Joccomo was not having any luck with the suspect. He would take over the interrogation and walked over to the suspect who was handcuffed to the fence.

Leaning into the man's ear he whispered, "Dove il droga?" Mike took that to mean "Where are the drugs?" No response from the man. Again he was politely asked, "Dove il droga?" Mike wasn't sure what else was said to the man but he screamed, "No droga! - Mi Dio, No droga!" For this unacceptable response, Sergio grabbed the man's head and screamed in his ear which caused him to quiver and wet his pants. Mike took what was said to the man as a very menacing threat. This was not a pretty sight for Mike and Tony to watch but this was an Italian or rather a CARB Anti-Drug Squad interrogation not a NIS one.

As much as Mike thought this was unacceptable, it did produce the desired results. The handcuffed suspect gestured to some bushes with his head, it was the only thing he could move. Mike's big Italian casually strolled over and reached down; he came up with a plastic bag. He walked back toward the assembled group and with a big grin on his cherubic face, exclaimed "Guardare – Droga!" Opening the bag which revealed two hashish bricks.

A few weeks later, Mike's office got another call from the Major requesting NIS assistance for a big upcoming event the next week. The Rolling Stones were scheduled to come to Naples. Yes, we're talking, The Rolling Stones – you know Mick Jagger, Keith

Richards and the rest of the boys. Assuming much drug activity would be taking place and sure to draw many sailors and marines; he requested two NIS agents. When the ASAC asked for volunteers, it took Mike less than a second for his hand to shoot up which was quickly followed by agent Jack Lewis. Mike was in, so Jack figured he had to come along. "Jack, it will be great fun - just the right amount of work and rewarded with a free concert – "Yahoo!" "Your enthusiasm for working at night is absolutely nauseating Mike."

The concert date was set for the third week in July at the San Paolo Soccer Stadium in Naples. Since neither Mike or Jack had ever been inside the stadium, a little research was in order. Mike went to his desk and pulled out his travel guide.

San Paola Stadium was built and opened in 1959. At that time, it was among the largest stadium, in Italy seating over 50,000 fans. The local soccer team, Team Napoli, called this stadium home. Mike figured he had enough background material so it was time to prepare for the big event.

This would be the second major event in Italy for the month of July. Less than a week earlier, the Italian's Gli Azzurri (The Blues) soccer team won the world's biggest sporting event – the World Cup. Following on the heels of that event would be the Stone's concert.

The stadium crowd was the largest he had been around in one place. The mass of humanity at the stadium defied mere words. He estimated there were at least 40,000 fans waiting to enter plus more who would remain outside since the concert was sold out. The area outside resembled a small city with tents and bedrolls spread out. The crowd was very orderly since there was a strong presence of uniformed Italian Municipal Police or Polizia Communale. They had been assigned solely for crowd control. Even with the police in heavy numbers, Mike could smell the ever present 'smoke.'

The NIS team located the CARBS. They confirmed the concert was sold out. The CARBS estimated the crowd unable to get tickets numbered close to 2,000. These people would have to be satisfied with listening to the music because the 1980's did not have large outdoor screen TV's. Deciding to split up and circulate among the throng, Mike went with Sergio while Jack moved out with Joccomo. A Shore Patrol van was on hand to transport any arrested military miscreants while the CARBS had a police van available.

Based on haircuts and western style civilian dress, plus a few cowboy hats here and there; the agents were sure numerous military personnel were present. Mike was feeling generous and when he found a couple of sailors trying to score some drugs he let them off with a warning. Sergio was not so generous. Mike helped him apprehend two known dealers.

After about two hours working the outside of the venue, Mike radioed Jack that he and his partner were headed inside and for them to do the same. There was one slight problem for the two teams. They had no admission tickets and as the old saying goes: "No Tickee – No Laundry."

To his disbelief, di Grasso marched right up to the ticket office and notified the employee that he was a CARB and flashed his credentials. As if by magic, he walked away with two tickets for admission. Joccomo was radioed to proceed to the ticket office and obtain their two tickets in the same manner. Satisfied all would be granted admission Mike followed his partner through the entrance gate.

Once inside Mike thought it was funny this episode with the CARB and his credentials. It was the first time he had seen them displayed. Mike would remember in the future never to under estimate the power of the CARBS, especially Sergio.

Now inside the stadium, he was amazed by the sheer size of it and the mass of humanity down on the stadium floor plus an equal number in the stands. It was hot and humid for July so the promoters had installed huge water sprayers in an effort to cool the crowd. As evening approached, it was obvious to Blackstone they would not be able to observe much in the way of illicit activity among servicemen. Mike made a command decision - watch the show!

The lights dimmed and the warm up band came on stage: The J. Geils Band. A pretty cool band but you could tell the crowd was waiting for Mick and the Gang. After their last set, the stage lights went dark and the crowd started a boisterous chant of: Mick – Mick – Mick!

On came the lights and there they were – The Rolling Stones! What a thrill for Mike. He was a big fan of their music but this was the first time he would see them in person. He, of course, was only one of 40,000. The noise was off any recognized decibel meter and it was hard to hear the song with the fans singing along.

Mick and the rest of the Stones were really on. Jagger's voice throughout the performance was strong and forceful. In addition to the sprinklers trying to keep the crowd cool, Mick thought he would help by throwing a bucket of water on the front row seats ala the Harlem Globetrotters. The big difference was Mick actually had thrown a bucket of water while Meadowlark Lemon would only throw a bucket full of confetti.

Jagger, not known for wearing a lot of clothes at his concerts, played true to form; he too must have felt the extreme heat and humidity. Coming back on stage after an instrumental set, he ran across the stage wearing only his Spandex trousers and waving a cape as he sang, 'Jumpin Jack Flash' and what a gas it was.

All too soon the concert was coming to the end but Mick had a special finish to the concert. With the stage lights dimmed, he was transported from the wings riding a type of crane with a platform attached. Jumping on stage with a rousing ovation from the crowd, he belted out 'Satisfaction' and the show was over.

Just when Mike thought the show could not get better; spectacular fireworks erupted, much like ancient Mt. Vesuvius. At the conclusion of that spectacle, the concert was truly over. It was a fitting ending to one over the top performance by the world famous Rolling Stones.

The stadium lights came on illuminating the stadium floor and what a mess. It looked like something from the Woodstock Concert, held in the farmer's field in upstate New York in 1969. Mike watched as thousands of fans sloshed through the mud toward the exits. The amount of trash left behind would fill a small landfill.

Once outside the stadium it was back to work for Mike and Jack. The mess outside was even worse than the one left inside. Blackstone and Lewis were overwhelmed by the number of fans outside who had been content to listen to the music. Numerous bedrolls and tents were rolled up and packed away. A great majority of these Stones fans had followed the band from gig to gig. Their next stop to see or at least hear them would be in Nice, France at the Parc des Sports de L'Ouest.

It was a very good night. No arrests of any marines or sailors were needed and it looked like the CARBS only had the one arrest before the show started. Saying good night to Sergio and Joccomo, the American agents were done. With Jack heading home and Mike to his apartment, it was time for a well-earned nightcap. Before he turned in for the night he checked the TV news to see if the Stones concert was covered.

Turning on his Sony to RA1, the only reception he could get, he was surprised to see the local news replaying the concert. No, Mike did not see himself among the crowd or on any clips but he thought it would be pretty cool to tell his kids someday about the time he saw the Rolling Stones in concert in Naples, Italy.

Joint operations conducted with the CARBS were always exciting but at the same time could be most dangerous. The one Mike was scheduled to assist would involve a raid by Major Tanta and his boys with assistance of NIS agents from the Naples office. The raid was to target a known major drug dealer. He was a major supplier of hashish in Naples which would ultimately find its way to local servicemen or ones visiting from American ships.

Once again meeting downtown at the CARBS office, it was coffee first: details second. It seemed, with very few exceptions, there was always time for a little coffee before a joint OP.

Returning from the coffee bar, it was disclosed the target was living and doing business in an apartment in the Gut. This alley had the well-earned reputation of one nasty place. The smell from previous OP's reminded Mike of a combination of a garbage dump and a backed up toilet. Naples sanitation services were not known to be overly efficient; the piles of uncollected trash and garbage were in every nook and cranny.

As the meeting progressed, team assignments would be divided between S/A's Blackstone, Tony Cantanzo, Bob Trailor and the Italians, Major Tanta, Sergio and Joccomo. The Op Plan called for Mike, Bob and Sergio to rush the front door; at the same time the others would cover the back door. With all details covered, it was time to hit the street.

Leaving the office, it was decided to use two Italian agents' unmarked vehicles and leave NIS Naples' Dodge at the CARBS office. With the Major taking a sad look at the NIS agents G-car, it was thought best. Mike along with Bob jumped in di Grasso's car; a very sleek and mean looking black Alpha Romeo. Tony got in the other car with Tanta and Joccomo. With the black Alpha weaving in and out of traffic and with Joccomo doing the same; a progression of slammed brakes, honking horns and much hand gesturing made the trip one nerve racking experience for Mike.

The teams parked their cars and waited just outside the Gut for the signal to make their approach to the apartment. While

172

waiting a bad ass looking silver BMW slowly passed Sergio's Alpha which made Mike a little nervous. He alerted the CARB and whispered, "Those two guys look suspicious. Shouldn't we stop and question them?" "No – No, Michele! They both are assassins for the Camorra; we never bother them - it is not healthy." *Wow!* Mike mumbled to himself, *those guys didn't look over twenty and this tough CARB was afraid of them!*

After the BMW passed, the agents were out of the cars with guns drawn. Mike, Bob and Sergio took up a position covering the front door. Joccomo radioed they were in position at the back door. All set and it was time to go!

Bang! Bang! Bang! Sergio pounded on the door with his massive left fist and at the same time held his 9 mm in his right while he shouted: "Aperto! – Polizia!" As expected there was no response. As Mike waited he saw the CARB ram the door. It gave way with a loud crack. With guns at the ready and in shooting positions, the Americans were disappointed to see two frightened Italian teenagers standing in the middle of the room with their hands shaking in the air and one had pissed his pants.

With Joccomo handcuffing these two desperados, both teams began a search for any evidence. Not too hard to find as sitting on the kitchen table were scales, bags and two hashish bricks which were in the process of being cut into smaller portions. Interestingly to Mike was another brick on the table which looked a little funny and definitely different from the other two. Beside it was a foul smelling greenish-brown liquid in a pot on the stove.

Mike called Sergio over to explain this odd brick. He

looked at the pot and busted out laughing. "That brick is really pressed camel shit and that messy 'goo' in the pot is hashish and vegetable oil. Our dealer has been known to spread the liquid on cakes of camel shit and pass it off to your servicemen as the real thing." "Well, I guess that's where the phrase – 'This is some good shit' originated." With that Sergio walked away laughing like an over-stuffed teddy bear.

After collecting the drugs, paraphernalia, a stack of lira notes and the two suspects; it was back to the CARB office. While the main dealer was not apprehended, it was still a successful joint operation. Two kilos of hash and one 'camel brick' would never make it to the streets.

Back at the Anti-Drug office, it was time for the required photo session. Every time a bust was made, the Italians were famous for recording it photographically. Mike had noticed a magical thing had taken place; the two pure confiscated hashish bricks had grown to four bricks just in time for the photo!

Wait just a minute. On closer observation, Mike was sure he had seen those two additional bricks before on another bust; the one from the airport. The CARBS obviously believed when dealing with publicity, more was always better. No one could say these guys lacked imagination when it came to public relations.

Standing around the office and with Mike's dogs barking, he whispered to Tony, "I'm tired and I just want to get back to the office, write up a short synopsis for the SAC and go home. What is the holdup?" This was not going to happen anytime soon as the star of the show had not arrived.

What was missing? They had the confiscated drugs, the bad guys and a group of successful drug agents – all that was needed was a main player. Major Tanta entered after taking a quick shower. The rest smelled like a backed up sewer from the Gut.

It was Kodak Time. All agents gathered around the night's haul and with the Major front and center; the photographer snapped the shutter, the flash went off and three tired NIS agents disappeared into the night.

The weeks flew by with Mike continuing to work routine cases including the time consuming but necessary DIS background investigations. New tasking came in and once again it was time to call out the cavalry a.k.a. the CARBS.

A U.S. aircraft carrier was making a port call in Livorno, Italy. The ship's NIS assigned afloat S/A requested the Naples office assist with a planned drug interdiction operation. Mike would be one agent with Tim Tosgood the other along with two representatives borrowed from the Naples' Anti-Drug Squad.

Not trusting any of their G-Cars to make the trip, Tim rented a pretty cool but older FIAT 131. Packing some overnight clothes plus side arms, shotguns and handcuffs, it was time to depart in order to arrive at the port city before the carrier.

Tim would do the driving to Livorno which allowed Mike to settle in the passenger seat for what was supposed to be a leisurely drive on the Autostrada. Tosgood who was the office prankster had other ideas.

Departing the base parking lot and heading out the NSA main gate, Tim jammed his foot on the gas pedal and with tires squealing, they headed for the toll road and Livorno.

Once the NIS agents were on the no speed limit highway, the CARBS followed in one of their sharp Alpha Romeos. Tim increased their speed to 80 mph and put his favorite cassette tape in the player. Not only was the Fiat put to its upper limits, Mike was subjected to the blaring sounds of honky-tonk music. Just to keep Mike awake, Tim from time to time, would slow down and suddenly speed up give Blackstone an unexpected rush. Tosgood seemed to derive a great deal of pleasure watching Mike lurch back and forth because the seat back would not lock in place.

"Just checking to see if your seat belt is still working." Tim thought it was pretty funny – Mike did not see the humor in it. Unbeknownst to Mike, Tim was told about the seat at the agency.

After a stop for lunch and some three hours later, our dynamic duo plus the two assigned Italian agents arrived at the port city of Livorno and met with the afloat agent at a local café bar.

Special Agent Rob Chris was assigned to the aircraft carrier for a routine tour and had been able to cultivate some sources for use in drug buys. Mike was surprised at how young he was – probably not yet twenty-two. Mike felt old at his 35 years of age. With Mike, Tim and the two CARBS introduced to Rob; it was time to get down to business. Adhering to Italian custom, all had the required coffee with the CARBS having their splash of Sambuca.

S/A Chris laid out his ideas for the Op and the Italians advised they had identified a local drug dealer who would make a good target. The final plan was agreed upon and two of Rob's sources would circulate around the port area when liberty call was announced on the ship. It was hoped the drug dealer would make an appearance.

Later that evening with the operation in progress Mike and Tim grabbed a seat on a park bench near the main square. Chris was located a short distance away with the CARBS having a few drinks at a bar. It wasn't long before the target, an ex-U.S. Army civilian approached the two sources from the ship. It was obvious to Mike and Tim that a drug deal was going down.

Tim was first to speak, "Mike, if we take off running across the piazza to catch that scum bag, he'll just run – got any ideas?" With that Mike stood up and grabbed Tim by the hand. "Ok, Tim, let's give them our best impression of two gay caballeros out for a stroll." Swishing away, they sauntered in the direction of the sailors and the drug dealer.

"All right freeze - NIS Special Agents" Mike roared when they got within 10 feet of the group. The sailors froze according to the OP plan, but the drug supplier had other ideas.

Tim remained with the two sailors while Mike took off running after the dealer. He had not noticed the CARBS were in pursuit as well. Too bad he missed that observation as he also forgot the caution he received about working with the Italians when a chase was involved. As he was closing in on his subject he heard very slight noises whizzing past his right ear.

Bing! Bing! Holy Shit! The CARBS had fired at the guy with Mike in between. While it was scary to say the least it did have the desired results. Just as he reached his getaway car, one in which he had driven to the piazza, he gave up and the Italians arrested him. With three handguns pointed his way, the dealer figured it was the right course of action. Oh and just for good measure, Mike found out later the car was seized as part of the bust. Never a dull moment working with the CARB Anti-Drug Squad.

The holidays were always fun to share with the CARBS, especially Christmas time.

On Mike's first Christmas in Naples, the ASAC asked if he would like to accompany him on his annual Santa Claus run to the CARBS. It was time to deliver their presents. Noticing a large box in his office stuffed with goodies, Mike inspected it.

Agent Albright narrated while Mike held up each item: "The Fritos are for Major Tanta; he's mad about them. The NIS pen is for Sergio; I'm not sure why he wants one – but he does. The Mountain Dew, well, that's for Joccomo. That NIS hat is for Monti; I guess it makes him feel part of the team. Paolo is the chow hound and has a crush on the Slim Jims. The last item you have is for Luigi - he gets the T shirt."

Grabbing the box, it was up-up and away to visit the CARBS.

CHAPTER 7
OPERATION RED BLANKET

The day started like any other at Blackstone's office in Naples, Italy. Mike checked in on a cold windy December day and found out the Brigate Rosse or Red Brigades had kidnapped U.S. Army General James Dozier. At the time, he was serving as Deputy Chief of Staff at NATO for the Southern European land forces with his HQ in Verona, Italy. He became the only flag officer to have been captured by a terrorist group.

The facts were that four Red Brigades members, posing as plumbers, kidnapped the General from his apartment in Verona. With the Italian government reluctant to mount a rescue attempt, President Reagan requested assistance from H. Ross Perot. He was not needed; after 42 days in captivity, the Italians rescued Dozier.

Prior to the General's abduction, the Red Brigades claim to infamy was the 1970's kidnapping of Italian former prime minister, Aldo Moro. During that kidnapping, the terrorists killed two Carabiniere body guards in Moro's car and three police officers in a following car. Two months later after 55 days of imprisonment, Aldo Moro was found dead inside the trunk of a car in Rome.

As a result of the Dozier kidnapping, the Naples' NIS office would go on 24-hour Protective Service details for the area admirals and generals.

This new and dangerous operation would be known as Operation Red Blanket. With this new additional assignment, a list of requirements would be needed. High on the list was to take inventory of the weapons S/A's would use against these heavily armed terrorists.

The standard NIS weapon per agent was a six shot Ruger .357 Cal revolver (this was before agents were authorized to carry a semi-automatic side arm) and a 12-gauge shotgun. Agents could if desired purchase and carry a different sidearm.

The history of the Moro kidnapping illustrated that the Red Brigades had access to high velocity automatic weapons and would not hesitate to use them against any agents protecting VIP's. It was determined NIS Naples would need some additional firepower.

The leading candidate was the 9 mm UZI. The Red Brigades was armed with an assortment of weapons including the Beretta 9 mm semi-automatic pistol plus the 9 mm UZI. It was decided to request a shipment of UZIs from the states.

Without the UZI or a similar high capacity weapon, agents would be restricted to a slow reloading from their ammo pouch carried on their belts; two rounds at a time. This cumbersome method would be alleviated later when use of speed loaders was authorized for NIS agents. The speed loader was a round cylinder containing six cartridges.

Waiting for the shipment of UZIs, Mike and his fellow agents would have to make do with the weapons on hand. Weeks past. The UZIs arrived and it was off to the tufa stone firing range. Actually, this was just a rock quarry located on the outskirts of Naples where paper targets were propped up against the walls.

With all admirals and generals safely ensconced in their offices on base, all agents met at the tufa stone quarry. It was time to fire the new weapons but not before some preliminary orientation provided by Bob Trailor, a certified firearms instructor. This instruction would be necessary as the agents had previously been trained and qualified on the Ruger .357, their personal side arms and the pistol grip 12-gauge shotgun. It was easy to see facing off against a Red Brigades terrorist with his 9 mm Beretta was something each agent did not want to contemplate while holding his trusty six shooter.

It was time to see what the UZI could do. Mike was like a kid in a candy store waiting to fire the weapon. When Mike got his turn at bat he was amazed at how quiet it fired and with almost no recoil. Instead of the expected loud multiple bangs his .357 S&W revolver would make; all Mike heard was a quick brrup-brrup each time the trigger was depressed. The sound reminded him of Jiffy Pop popcorn starting to pop. Wow, what a weapon! After all agents qualified, it was back to the office to continue with Operation Red Blanket.

Like the old story goes, bad news travels fast and so it was for Naples' agents. The bad news was waiting back at the office. Unfortunately, the arrival of the UZIs was brought to the attention of the Italian military and police authorities. The SAC was advised weapons with automatic firing capacity would not be permitted by non-Italian military or police personnel.

Sadly, after only one live firing session, they were packed up and sent back to the states – bummer! The agents assigned to protective service details would be short handed in manpower and they would be outgunned by the Red Brigades as well as any other bad guys.

Terrorist organizations and operations in the 1980's were very different and would change as time passed. The Italian Red Brigades was a left-wing paramilitary organization group founded on Marxist-Leninist principles. It operated much like other countries indigenous terrorist organizations, such as the Baader-Minhof (Red Army Faction) in Germany and the French Libertarian (Left Action Directive) in France. These terrorists operated before such international terrorist groups such as Hamas, Al-Qaida and Hezbollah came on the scene and operated across country borders.

Sitting in his office, Mike reflected on this new operation. He thought this was going to be most interesting and possibly a dangerous time in his career with NIS. His office would not be receiving any additional manpower and as a result there would be only enough agents to provide two-man security teams for each general or admiral assigned to the Naples area. This could only be a prescription for disaster as two much less one NIS agent on duty at a time would hardly be called a security team.

Mike was taught there was a minimum number of agents required for a properly manned protective security detail and it sure wasn't going to be one or two special agents! Mike was learning this was the real world: you made do with what you had and sometimes that wasn't much.

Meeting with the SAC, the two man teams were assigned with Mike and S/A Tim Tosgood drawing the two-star admiral for COMFSURFMED and known as the Principal or Admiral and would require 24/7 coverage by the team.

Before Operation Red Blanket had barely started a horrific object lesson taught by the Red Brigades occurred in the downtown area. An Italian judge was murdered in his vehicle while stuck in one of Naples' daily traffic jams. A scooter with two assassins pulled up next to his car and fired numerous rounds from a 12-gauge shotgun into it. Besides the judge, his driver and security guard riding with him were killed. The trailing police in their vehicle were helpless to assist. When finished with their evil deed, the two casually drove off weaving between stalled cars.

Mike thought if they could assassinate an Italian judge in broad daylight they would have no qualms about shooting a U.S. VIP and even less a NIS Special Agent.

The standard routine for the Operation Red Blanket would be for one agent to report to the office and work on his cases. In the event the Principal needed to travel off-base, that agent, would be his escort to provide security.

At the end of the work day, the on-duty agent would escort him to his off-base residence. If lucky, he could catch a few cat naps from time to time during the night. The following morning, the night Special Agent would escort the Principal to his on-base office.

On base and with the Principal safe, the night agent would go home and get some sleep. The night agent's partner, now in the office, would continue routine duties and escort the Principal to his home at the end of the work day. The following morning, the routine would be the same with the night agent taking him from his residence to the office and then head home to sleep.

This security detail duty might sound pretty dull and tame. The drive to and from the residence to work involved only racing through the streets at warp speed. Social functions for the Principal away from the residence was a different story. Much more planning would be involved but it still boiled down to one agent trying to do the work of three. The entire detail for off-residence forays would encompass the properly security cleared driver and the NIS Special Agent in the front seat with the Principal riding in the back with his wife or other dignitary.

On one occasion, Mike was on duty at the residence when the Admiral and his wife announced they would be going to an important cocktail party. No advance notice for this one, Mike would just have to wing it. At the agreed upon time, Marco his civilian driver arrived. Mike would follow Standard Operating Procedures for the movement. He exited the apartment to perform a security check of the area for any suspicious activity or persons. Satisfied there was no apparent threat, the Admiral and his wife would leave the upstairs and would follow Mike down to the unmarked staff car. Mike would ride shotgun and in this case, it was meant literally; he was armed with his shotgun and sidearm.

On the way to the party, Mike was startled by the sound of the Admiral rummaging in his briefcase. "Do you need any assistance?" Mike was shocked when the Admiral responded, "No, just checking to see if my .38 revolver was in the case." Unbeknownst to Mike or anyone else at the NIS office, all Principals had been armed due to the limited number of agents to provide protection.

Thinking to himself: *Oh great! Not only do I have to worry what's in front of me but at the same time what's behind.* He was now sure he was going to get shot either by the Red Brigades or his own VIP playing with his new toy.

Arriving at the residence, Mike was out of the car to make a quick check of the area. Satisfied, he opened the back door and escorted the couple into the villa.

Once inside, Mike maintained a low key presence but at the same time kept a weather-eye on all avenues of ingress and egress to the party. His Principal seemed to be having an enjoyable evening. Soon it was time to depart. The Admiral had an early morning meeting to attend on base. While he and his wife made the rounds saying their goodbyes to the other guests, Mike stepped outside to conduct the standard exit protocol.

Approaching the staff car Marco advised Blackstone that two young men were sitting on a scooter across the street. Marco thought they were acting a little suspicious. Deciding to investigate since scooters were known to be vehicles of opportunity for terrorists' nefarious deeds. Mike discovered after he talked to them they were only a couple of teenagers hanging out. Seeing no apparent problem, he returned to the residence to collect his people. Prior to re-entering the residence, he ordered Marco to have the car running just in case.

Once back inside Mike briefed the Admiral on the situation with the two teenagers and instructed both to move quickly to the car. As Mike opened the door he noticed the two teens were not in sight. He headed straight for the back door of the staff car at a hurried pace. Opening the car door, he shouted, "Let's go now!" The Admiral and his wife ran to the car. While driving, Mike apologized to the Admiral for his gruff language in ordering him to the car. "Mike, you just keep on doing what you need to do to keep my wife and me safe. You'll hear no complaints from me."

Arriving home, Mike deposited his charges safe and sound in their apartment. Mike thought; *a nice easy night's work.* Of course while he was thinking that he had his fingers crossed.

Once inside, the Admiral made the announcement, "Mike, we'll soon have dinner, are you hungry?" Addressing him as Sir, which would be a proper military response, he was surprised when he was told to call him Chuck while in the residence.

Mike would find this informal arrangement a difficult adjustment to make. Habits, engrained in 10 years of naval service would be hard to break. As a newly commissioned officer, he was still trying to adjust to moving in such lofty circles with VIPs. Any navy person would find this lack of formality with such a senior person out of the question; definitely against protocol. Of course, this two star had no idea he was a lowly Ensign, the bottom of the officer barrel. As mentioned previously, almost all NIS Special Agents were civilians; so as far as the Admiral and everyone else in the U.S. Navy were concerned, Mike was a civilian.

While dinner was being prepared, Mike was settled into his room; unpacking his shotgun and spare rounds. Chuck shouted from the kitchen, "Mike, we're having steaks. How do you want yours cooked?" Hesitating, Mike responded, "Well Sir, ah - Admiral, oh, I mean Chuck; medium rare would be fine with me."

Time to eat and what a strange scene it was for Mike. Upon entering the dining room, Chuck and his wife were already seated. With Mike standing and looking a little sheepish, he was instructed to pull up a chair next to the Admiral and dig in. With one and all enjoying the meal, Mike felt more like a family member, certainly not an armed special agent charged with their protection. After dinner, it was announced: "Movie and Popcorn time."

One would have to have been in the apartment to appreciate the picture of the three. The stage was set with his charges on the couch and Mike in a chair behind them. Dressed casually in shirt and slacks, he would look just like an ordinary guest in for a movie. One large difference would be this guest was armed with a S&W handgun secured in a shoulder holster.

Standard procedure, when in the residence, was to be armed with a sidearm at all times. It would be a very bad plan for Mike to be looking for his weapon when trouble materialized.

The rest of the evening Mike spent on his rounds: he checked and re-checked doors and windows and the balcony area. Prior to the couple retiring for the evening, Mike would make a sweep of the outside perimeter for the last time. The night passed uneventfully and it was time to get the Admiral to his office. After he was safe on base, Mike headed to his office to brief Tim on the last night's activity. With turnover complete, he decided he needed some breakfast and then home for some well-earned sleep.

Weekends and holidays were always a difficult proposition. Not the type to sit around in the apartment, Chuck and his wife liked be out and about. There were always dinner parties to attend.

It would be more stressful than during the week when the Admiral would spend a good part of the day on base.

Mike was just settled into his role of guarding his Principal when he was surprised to learn it would change. The Admiral with his wife would be returning to the states for a few days.

With S/A Tosgood tied up in court, Mike was available. He was assigned to assist in the protection of a USMC General visiting the Naples area for an overnight stay. Since he would be staying off-base in a civilian villa, the Marine Detachment's CO requested NIS to assist in the one-night assignment. Mike was volunteered.

Arriving at the residence, Mike introduced himself to the General and went over security details. This VIP would be the only occupant so Mike was sure if any others showed up - they would be the bad guys. Mike was shown the layout of the house including where the Principal would be sleeping. Being an old school marine, he alerted Mike in graphic detail that he had no intention of being a kidnapping victim. "Those damn punk Red Brigades got Gen. Dozier but they sure as hell aren't going to get me."

Entering the bedroom, Mike was shown the layout and a hallway leading to it. Just before leaving the room he noticed a pair of Colt .45 handguns on the nightstand next to the bed.

As they walked to the kitchen, Mike wondered why the display of the Colts? "Sir, why are the two Colts on your nightstand?" "When I go to bed, if anyone comes down the hallway – they're dead meat!" Good info to know as Blackstone had no intention of entering the General's field of fire. The rest of the evening was spent chatting and grabbing a bite to eat.

The General had an early morning flight so he would hit the sack early. Mike decided to make a tour of the outside perimeter. Patrolling the grounds, nothing was out of the ordinary until he noticed a bush close to the General's bedroom window, move ever so slightly. Thinking this might be trouble, Mike drew his weapon and assumed a shooting position. "Freeze! Come out with your hands up!" Before Mike had time to react, a camouflaged marine sergeant emerged. "Hold your fire!" screamed the marine. With his heart beating a mile a minute, Mike holstered his weapon.

The sergeant told Mike the old Marine wanted more than a solo NIS agent for his security. He borrowed the sergeant and two more privates from the NSA Marine Barracks. The CO of the Marine Detachment authorized it. Mike felt pretty confident the outside perimeter was in good hands. It would, however have been nice to have been brought into the loop about the extra manpower.

Back inside the house, he grabbed a seat at the kitchen table and spent the night listening to the snoring coming from down the hall. Daylight soon arrived and it was time for the General to depart for the airport. No problems were encountered by Mike on his drive to the airport. The mission was now completed and it was time to check back with the office and head home for some well-earned sleep.

With the return of Mike and Tim's Principal, it was back to the routine of protecting their VIP two star.

Much like any ordinary individual, the Admiral liked to go out to dinner with his wife. On many outings, Mike would be under a great deal of pressure, protecting the Admiral and his wife against any known or perceived threats. On those nights or afternoons, it was advisable for Mike's Principal not to eat at the same restaurant and to vary his routine.

Terrorists would like nothing better than to operate against a target who adheres to a predictable schedule or routine. Every time they left the residence, Mike would perform a check of the outside, collect the Admiral and his wife and deliver them to a restaurant. While the couple enjoyed their meal, Mike would take up station covering the main and back entrance.

On one occasion, Mike did have a close call delivering the Admiral to AFSOUTH from the NSA compound. He had to attend a NATO (North Atlantic Treaty Organization) conference. Since it was less than five miles to the AFSOUTH base, Mike figured this would be a no problem detail. With Marco driving, they exited the NSA gate and were on their way. Outside the base there was only one narrow road that led to the two lane thoroughfare. This was the same route Mike had used previously to go to the AFSOUTH Officer's Club.

Approaching the intersection, Marco slowed the car down; they had a red light. In the Naples area, traffic light rules can be a little confusing. A green light means GO while a red light means STOP but sometimes it could mean GO. These variations in traffic laws always seem to be left up to the whim of the local driver. Mike had learned to never assume anything while negotiating traffic in Naples.

Seeing the way clear and using the red light means GO

system, Marco gunned the engine and made the right turn and headed toward AFSOUTH. Just when Mike thought things were going a little too smoothly, it happened.

Stopped in their lane of traffic were two cars with their drivers outside in a heated discussion with typical Neapolitan hand gesturing. Mike determined this was either a minor accident or a clumsy attempt to get them to stop. Choosing the latter scenario, he shouted to Marco, "Floor It!" The staff car swerved around the cars, jumped the sidewalk and kept going. With Mike's trusty S&W in his right hand, Marco had the car roaring at a dangerous speed. Slowing down as they approached the main gate to AFSOUTH; they entered to the relief of Mike and he holstered his Smith.

Mike deposited the Admiral in the meeting room. Marco and Mike decided it was time to throttle back and have a coffee. Thus far, that most of Mike's details during Operation Red Blanket were 99% routine and 1% terror. At the conclusion of his meeting, the two star was safely returned to his office at the NSA compound and Mike returned to his regular duties.

Good News! A contingent of NIS agent volunteers from various stateside offices were on their way to Naples. Mike and his fellow agents would soon be relieved of their Red Blanket duties.

Mike had seen, just like the fiasco with the UZIs, good news could and would be followed by bad. The good news was they were going to be relieved. The bad news was Mike and Tim would have one last detail to perform.

A change for this particular assignment would be the Principal. It was to be the Commander in Chief for U.S. Air

Forces Southern Command (CINCUSAIRSOC.)

He would be the highest ranking officer Mike had been assigned to protect: a four-star flag officer. Additionally, S/A's Blackstone and Tosgood would have help from the ASAC. The Admiral's normal team of Hommes and Trailor were unavailable due to a mandatory court appearance. Mike and Tim's two-star was back in the states again on government business.

The detail departed the office and arrived at the villa to collect the Principal and his wife. Villa Nike had been the official residence of the highest-ranking U.S. military officer in southern Italy for the past 62 years. Even though it was showing its age, Mike thought the grandeur of it reminded him of a rich Italian nobleman who may have lived in the residence. The views from the back balcony of the Bay of Naples, Mount Vesuvius and the Isle of Capri were absolutely majestic. As he leaned over the railing for a better view he was accosted by a huge animal; the family's Great Dane. The ASAC saw what had happened to Mike. He got a big laugh at Mike's expense and told Blackstone the dog was just saying hello.

The motorcade was pretty small; just two cars. The ASAC would ride shotgun with the four-star and his wife in a staff car while Tim and Mike followed in their G-Car. Traffic was light and after a short uneventful ride, they arrived at the marina where the Admiral's barge was kept. They would be riding in some kind of style. Mike's only experience was riding in cramped liberty boats for enlisted personnel. A senior naval officer barge, using naval terminology to describe it, would be a boat tricked out with luxuries.

192

The vehicles were parked and the Principal and his wife were escorted onboard.

Casting off the barge headed out into the Bay of Naples; it was nothing but light winds and smooth seas. Thinking the threat would probably be minimal, the agents would try to enjoy the scenery. The holiday atmosphere was broken by a small speed boat heading in the agents' direction. Not wanting to alarm the Admiral or his wife who were down below in the cabin changing clothes, the agents moved to the port side of the vessel and drew their weapons. Great care was exercised to keep them low and out of sight.

Mike and the others thought trouble was coming their way. The ASAC ordered Tim to guard the door leading down below while he and Mike kept on eye on the speed boat. Just when a collision was eminent, it swerved to the right. The last the agents saw of the boat; it was headed in the direction of the port of Naples. The joy riders were seen waving and laughing merrily. Weapons were holstered and it was back to enjoying the scenery.

Coming topside, he asked, "Did I miss anything? "Nothing much, Admiral." The agents were surprised with a tasty breakfast for all to be served by his two stewards. The stewards also were assigned duty as part of the regular boat crew.

Approaching two hours, the harbor of the Isle of Capri loomed into sight. The barge was tied up adjacent to the town wharf area in Marina Grande. It was now time to go on high alert. Exiting the boat, the agents were greeted by a crowd of over 500 tourists. Mike certainly hoped this throng of party goers were innocent tourists. Only one bad guy would turn events ugly.

Mike pulled the ASAC aside and voiced his concern, "Mike, that's why we get the big bucks." "Dave, maybe you get the big ones but I'm just a lowly Ensign."

What a mess! With much pushing and shoving through the crowd, Mike was glad it was only a short walk to the two local police cars with drivers. The ASAC along with the Principal and his wife hopped into one car while Mike and Tim were directed to the other. Jamming the car in first gear and slamming his foot on the accelerator, the Admiral's driver was off with Blackstone and Tosgood's car trying to keep up.

While the lower Capri Town was full of small shops and places for beachgoers, the group's destination was the top of the island or Anacapri. This was where lunch was planned at a famous seafood restaurant. Before the meal the Admiral's wife wanted to do a little shopping in Anacapri's exclusive boutiques.

Travelling up the island at warp speed, Mike felt more like he was in the movie, Grand Prix, starring James Gardner. It appeared these police were nothing but frustrated race car drivers or just wanted to scare the crap out of their Nordamericani passengers.

The one road leading to the summit spiraled round and round. One would think safety and a reasonable speed would be the order of the day. This would not do for intrepid police race car drivers. At mind boggling speeds and sometimes screeching brakes, both cars roared in the direction of the top of the Isle of Capri.

Looking out the car window and down the steep drop, Mike sure hoped these guys knew their business of driving these cars. The only time these crazy drivers would throttle back was on meeting huge tour buses coming down the mountain. When this meeting occurred, our agents were reduced to looking straight down and forced to watch gravel and small rocks plummet down as their car moved over to the edge of the road to let buses pass.

Mike thought all along he might end up getting shot on one of these protective details; instead, there was a high probability he was about to take a very quick one-way ride straight down to the bottom of this beautiful island. An image of a squashed bug came to mind.

Still among the living, Mike and the party reached the top and what a sight it was: right out of a scene from the Garden of Eden. In reality they had reached the Gardens of Augustus. The bright red geraniums and fragrant dahlia flowers reminded Mike of perfume shops back in the states.

While the Admiral and his wife were casually dressed in festive attire, much like other tourists enjoying the day, the security detail was of course dressed in their standard protective service detail uniforms of suits, ties and radio earplugs in their ears.

Their clothes would not have been all that noticeable except it was August and even with the breeze - hot and muggy. Mike thought they stuck out like a sore thumb. It would not have taken a rocket scientist to figure the portly older gentleman surrounded by three official looking gents was of some importance - a good target for the Red Brigades.

While the Admiral accompanied his wife in her search through the various shops, Blackstone advised the ASAC that he would break off and go to the restaurant. The NIS agents were on their own as the police escort had returned to their station.

After a short walk Mike located the restaurant named, IL Tavola di Mar or The Restaurant by the Sea. It was located in a most fashionable area of Anacapri. Entering the eatery, Mike was greeted by the owner who communicated in Italian and broken English all preparations were in order for lunch. A quick check of the restaurant and adjacent areas was made. Mike's only concern was it was located next to a souvenir shop and many shoppers were in the restaurant eating lunch. Mike was reluctantly satisfied and walked back to the others.

With his wife's shopping completed, it was time for lunch. Greeting the Admiral and his wife with the traditional twin cheek kiss, they were led to a table with a spectacular view of the Bay of Naples. The ASAC joined them for lunch since he had known the couple for a number of years. Ordinarily, this familiarity would be unusual for a NIS agent. To an outsider it would look like three old friends having lunch. To be sure, the ASAC would be ready in case trouble broke out. He was armed just like agents Blackstone and Tosgood.

With the Admiral, his wife and the ASAC safely seated; S/A Blackstone took a table covering the front entrance while agent Tosgood positioned himself and watched the back door.

Mike thought if nothing else duty on a security detail meant at least a good meal. He had heard much about the restaurant's signature soup dish – Frutti di Mare and decided to order it. Tim, on the other hand, was not keen on seafood; a Bistecca was just right for him. What a shame - Tim just didn't know what he was missing with the local seafood. Mike tried to enjoy his soup dish; it was difficult. He constantly scanned the room for any suspicious indicators.

At the conclusion of the typical Italian two hour five-course meal, it was time for the Admiral and his wife to be driven back down to the barge. Exiting they were met by the same two original police drivers. Mike had nicknamed them A.J. and P. Jones. Since Mike felt he was lucky to be in one piece after the nerve racking drive up the island; he hoped he would arrive at the bottom in the same condition. A leisurely drive to reach Capri Town was not going to be in the cards.

With all onboard, the two drivers gunned their engines and with screeching tires headed for the roadway. Speeding by slower cars and even buses, it wasn't long before the Polizia automobiles were pulling up to Marina Grande. The police sped off and all the team had to do was get the three-star and his wife to the barge.

They were almost to the barge when all of a sudden a motor scooter raced by the group and a loud bang was heard. Was this an attack or at least a diversion? Mike and Tim scrambled to cover the Admiral and his wife. With hands on their service revolvers, inside their opened coats, all agents scanned the crowd. The ASAC moved in the direction of the Scooter Men as they began to drive off. He determined no threat was coming from the scooter and gave the all clear. It was time to get all onboard the barge. The sports world had a saying: "No harm – no foul." It certainly applied to this episode.

With the engines revved up and boat in gear, the coxswain

headed out of Marina Grande for the return trip. The Admiral and his wife decided to catch a short nap and headed down below. The team found seats and reflected on the day's activities. They theorized on different scenarios for the scooter incident.

The ASAC volunteered, "You know, if those two had been Red Brigades shooters, there was little we could have done to prevent an attack on the Admiral or injuries to the civilians. I figured they would have just sprayed bullets in our direction and if any innocents got hurt – too bad." It only reinforced Mike's feeling without sufficient manpower and firepower, agents assigned to Red Blanket stood a good chance of ending up in a body bag.

The Admiral re-entered the cockpit and showed them the purchase he made on the island. Displaying a very colorful hat, he would add it to his extensive collection. *OK, so he has a hat collection*, Mike tried to think of any significance. The ASAC surmised what Mike was thinking.

"The Admiral's hat collection numbered close to 50 including a dress Carabiniere hat with plume. When he made a formal visit to foreign dignitaries, he would usually receive a hat. It would represent the country he visited." The ASAC, who had been privy to a tour of his hats, related it was most impressive: ranging from a simple peasant hat to a Cardinal's red Galero.

Pulling into the marina, it was time to get back to business. The Principal's staff car was waiting. Agent Albright and the Principal plus his wife entered the car. Mike and Tim followed in their G-Car and all arrived safe and sound at the residence. Special Agents Hommes and Trailor had concluded their business with the

JAG office and resumed security for the Admiral.

The next order of business for the team was to go back to the office and check in. At the office, they received an update on the arrival of the NIS S/A's from the states. The first group had arrived and had started setting up their own Red Blanket operation. It would be a lot different from NIS Naples' operation.

This was to be a first class operation with over 30 volunteer agents representing various NIS stateside offices. They would have the agents for fully manned security details. Their agents would be solely dedicated to security and have no other duties. Mike and his fellow agents were definitely jealous. It was obvious money for expenses would not be a problem. State of the art communications equipment would allow the agents to have a 24/7 command center. Their G-Cars would be rented late model Renaults and Alpha Romeos.

One thing these relief agents had in common with the Naples' folks was the restriction on armament – no semi or automatic weapons allowed. Just like Mike, these agents would be armed with revolvers and shotguns. One stateside agent did get creative as he carried two revolvers.

With the turnover complete and the stateside agents on duty, Mike could finally relax. He thought his worries were over. The Red Brigades was someone else's problem or so he thought.

A week later, Mike and his date were eating at a local pizzeria by the name of Bagnoli Jo. Enjoying his Pizza Margarita, he was shocked to see his former Principal and his wife walk in. He thought nothing of seeing Chuck and his wife. His detail was probably outside. Mike was way off on that assumption and no agents appeared. Blackstone excused himself and went outside to check.

Oops! No G-Car! No Agents! Running back inside, he called the command post using the pizzeria's phone. Reaching the duty agent, Mike alerted him that the Admiral and his wife were off-base with no agent security team. He was assured by the duty agent they were safe eating on base at the Steak House. The agent was told the Principal would notify the command post when he was ready to leave for his residence.

"I guess he changed his mind because he and his wife just walked into the pizzeria where I was trying to enjoy a quiet meal with my date. This place sure isn't the Steak House!" The duty agent was still not convinced, "Are you sure its COMSURFMED?"

"Listen pal, I have spent many days and nights with the Admiral and I sure as hell know what he looks like." Excitedly, the duty agent told Mike to stay put and guard the Admiral until he could get a team to him ASAP.

Just as the agent was about to hang up, Mike questioned him, "Do you think it might be helpful if I told you the location of the pizza place?" Not giving him a chance to answer, Blackstone gave him the name and address.

Mike advised the Admiral that he would be providing his security until the regular agents could get to the restaurant. He was thanked for his diligence.

So much for a leisurely meal and some well-earned time off. He would be back on duty and on high alert. Returning to his table and informing his date of the situation, he patted his left shoulder to reassure himself he was armed. It was a true axiom that a NIS S/A in Naples was never really off-duty and was always armed. In less than 15 minutes, COMSURFMED's detail arrived and Mike finished his meal.

CHAPTER 8
PROTECTIVE SERVICE DETAILS

Protective Service Details were just another duty of NIS agents assigned to Naples, Italy; it just became more challenging with the kidnapping of General Dozier. With the arrival of the specialized contingent of NIS Special Agents from around the U.S. and turnover of protective service details completed, NIS Naples' agents were free to resume their regular duties. This would include the protection of visiting military and civilian VIP's.

When a DOD VIP visited Naples, S/A Blackstone and his fellow agents would be called upon to perform security for those individuals. These details would be more in line with established standard practices. They would be fully manned and following procedures similar to other federal agencies charged with the protection of high ranking dignitaries.

Mike was involved with many VIP visits especially with these three noteworthy dignitaries: Secretary of Defense (SECDEF) and his wife; Assistant Secretary of Defense (ASECDEF) and his wife; Vice Chief of Naval Operations (VCNO) respectively.

Standard operating procedure prior to their arrival would include inspections of travel routes, determining weapons and communication requirements, issuance of identification pins, agenda of visits and meetings, agent assignments, clothing requirements, location and inspection of lodgings. Any and other requirements would be addressed once the Principal arrived.

The pin used by NIS special agents and by other federal

202

agents was a unique identifier for persons involved in protecting high valued targets. Every agency had their own designs which signified who should be close to the Principal and who should not.

S/A Blackstone and all the other Naples' agents assigned to details would be issued a pin in the form of the number 3. Depending on the circumstance and length of the assignment, agents would be directed to rotate the pin clockwise, this would signify a W. In a similar manner, the pin could be used as an E or M. The pin would usually be worn on the upper left lapel of the coat. These pins were used as a resource to deny the opportunity for any bad guys to infiltrate the detail or the activities of the Principal.

The Naples' office was advised that the current SECDEF would be visiting Naples from Greece to see the sights and make official calls on NATO and U.S. military officials. Prior to his arrival, agents executed the standard protocol for such a visit. Mike would be assigned to the detail along with ASAC Albright, Tony Cantanzo and Mike Middleton. Due to a demonstration by over 1,000 left-wing members against his visit, S/A Jack Lewis was added to the team. Intelligence was received of a thwarted assassination attempt while the Secretary was in Greece.

Traveling on his personal government aircraft, the SECDEF arrived at CAPO airport, located north of Naples. NIS Naples' agents were on hand to start the detail. In addition to the Principal, other DOD members and press corps personnel accompanied him. These people were known unofficially as strap hangars. In the early days of official air travel when not enough seats were available, those without seats were assigned numbered floor spaces with straps (seat belts) for security; thus the term 'strap hangers.'

An interesting incident occurred with a well-known member of the news media. He tried to hand his luggage to Mike. In his best professional manner, Mike advised the Press Guy he was a NIS S/A and not a baggage handler. In a huff, Press Guy carried his bags and threw them on the transport.

Motor vehicle movement during normal NIS protective details in Naples would include the VIP's car with a S/A riding shotgun and the remaining agents following in a government chase car. Additionally, sometimes there would be an Italian police lead vehicle for the motorcade. All other official persons would be riding in buses or vans without NIS security.

For this detail, there would be a police cruiser leading the way, followed by the Principal with Mike on board and bringing up the rear were the remaining agents. The mini-van with the others; well, they were on their own. In addition to Mike in the front seat was the security cleared Italian driver. The SECDEF and his wife would ride in the back seat.

The motorcade exited the airport to travel to the Hotel Excelsior in downtown Naples; the only 5-Star hotel. Exiting the Tangenziale highway and with the police leading the way; there was no need to stop and pay the 500 lira toll. Naples streets were notorious for being narrow and congested. The only street leading from the toll road was known as 'squeeze alley' by the locals. It was one narrow street aligned with numerous small shops and businesses. Alleys also intersected the main road.

The motorcade proceeded down the congested street, with

the Italian police car clearing traffic. Mike saw something in the distance which made his heart jump. From a side alley a semi-tractor trailer rig pulled in between the police and the Principal's car. The timing of his move seemed suspicious.

Mike's heart was pumping madly and with the kidnapping of General Dozier still fresh in his mind, a kidnapping or assassination attempt was thought to be in the offing. Mike pulled his weapon from his holster and shouted, "Mr. Secretary get down!" The rig was blocking both sides of the street. A civilian taxi was so close to Mike vehicle, he could have reached out and touched him or asked him for some Grey Poupon. Mike determined the only way to clear the semi would be by using the adjacent sidewalk as an emergency roadway.

With the motorcade at a standstill, Mike leaned out of his window and speaking in Italian promptly told the taxi to move out of the way. Instead of moving, the Italian began to shout and argue!

Mike, taking a page from the CARB's playbook and to get the taxi to move, he pointed his .357 S&W at the driver and shouted: "Stati Uniti! Io Agenti Federali! - Adnare Avanti!" Seeing this rather forceful demonstration by Mike as he stared at one huge gun, the taxi driver decided it was definitely time to andiamo and get the hell moving. The taxi immediately drove up and over the sidewalk with the motorcade in hot pursuit.

Arriving at the hotel, the NIS agents from the chase car jumped out and made a security sweep of the immediate area. With no obvious danger, Mike opened the VIP's door and escorted him and his wife into the lobby. Naples' S/A's would set up a command post in the adjoining room to the Principal's suite.

This was Mike's first detail covering a member of the President's cabinet and was amazed at the huge amount of communications equipment needed by the Secretary. During his visit, Mike and the rest of the detail would accompany him on all his official visits and any sightseeing trips.

The day after his arrival, the Principal was scheduled to hold a military informal meeting in the hotel. Mike was notified that the SECDEF's wife had made a request to visit the ancient city of Pompeii. An Italian driver was detailed and Mike was assigned as her security escort. While it was not a usual practice to safe guard VIP's family members, ASAC Albright thought it best to provide one.

Even though she was thought not to be a high value target, Mike performed his SOP for the exit from the hotel. Satisfied Mike signaled her to come out and get in the back seat of the car. Mike hopped in the front seat and they were off for Pompeii. This city was made famous when it was covered over in ash from the eruption Mount Vesuvius in 79 AD.

A call was made earlier from the hotel to the Director of Antiquities for Pompeii and authorization was made for her to visit some areas of Pompeii off-limits to regular visitors. Once in the city and escorting her, he reminded himself to ignore the sites she was shown. Highlights of her visit were: The House of Golden Cupids; The House of the Faun and even a Brothel.

The House of the Golden Cupids was named after gold-leaf amorini in the bedrooms. The villa was purported to have belonged to the family of Nero's second wife.

In the courtyard of the Faun House stood a three-foot-tall bronze dancing Faun. It was later moved to a museum Naples. The wife was impressed by the colored geometric marble floors and told Mike the family must have had lots of money.

The Lupanarium was one of many brothels located throughout the city. Mike was a little embarrassed by the walls decorated with faded images of erotic acts. The casual visitor would say they pointed to some of the more adventurous acts performed by the prostitutes of the day.

The SECDEF's wife had enough site seeing for the day and requested to return to the hotel. Concurring with her, they headed for the exit and the staff car. Back at the hotel and without any incidents to report, Mike rejoined the other members of the team. They were interested in all the sights Mike was privy to.

The next morning the Principal had to attend a meeting at NATO's Southern Headquarters located on the AFSOUTH base. While the base was secure it would be a maximum security effort to deliver him safely.

The Secretary's staff car, NIS G-Car plus the police cruiser were placed outside the main entrance to the hotel. For this movement all agents would be armed with side arms plus Mike would carry a 12-gauge shotgun. Mike and Tony exited the lobby for the standard security check. With no sign of any demonstrators or other threats it was time to bring out the Principal.

Tony radioed the agents in the lobby that the outside was all clear. The Secretary was ready to move and he was quickly escorted to his car which was surrounded with the rest of the NIS team. The Polizia cruiser turned on his blue lights and with his siren blaring, the motorcade departed with screeching tires and nervous NIS agents on high alert. Even with a police car leading the way traffic was reluctant to move for the motorcade. Some enterprising Neapolitan drivers even tried to sneak in behind the police cruiser.

With the 20-minute hair raising ride almost over, Mike could see the NATO gate only two blocks from their position. As the vehicles entered the base it was not time to relax for the security detail. Italians had easy access to the base and it would only take one to be a threat to the Secretary.

Screeching to a halt at the HQ building all agents exited the vehicles and scanned the area. The Principal's door was opened and he was quickly rushed inside the building. The team including the police 'stood down' and remained with the cars outside the HQ. The meeting with senior military officials was scheduled to last less than an hour. Mike and Jack Lewis volunteered to be espresso runners and brought back coffee.

The ASAC who was stationed inside the complex radioed the team on the status of the meeting. He advised the doors to the conference had opened and it should be only minutes before the Principal was ready to depart. The outside agents prepared to leave the base.

Just like the Indianapolis 500 race with the famous "Gentlemen - start your engines," the detail's engines were started for the 'race' to the hotel.

"ASAC to Cantanzo, we're ready to exit" was heard in Tony's earpiece. Tony informed one and all the Principal was ready to leave the building. All were now on high alert as the Secretary came out with the ASAC and was ushered into his vehicle.

Same preparations as before and the motorcade roared out the gate and headed for the hotel. No incidents were encountered and he was safety deposited back in his suite.

A final function for their VIP was to be a guest at a farewell party at a private residence in Rome, Italy. The SECDEF and his wife wanted to see some of the Italian country side so a decision was made to drive to Rome.

Departing Naples with the two, the motorcade arrived safely at the Grand Hotel. Checking into this previously security cleared hotel, the Secretary and his wife were ensconced in their suite. Leaving agents Cantanzo, Lewis and Middleton at the hotel guarding the Principal, Mike and the ASAC departed to make a security sweep of the residence.

The residence was on the outskirts of the city and the only access to the property was by a dimly lit road. Mike noticed several areas covered with trees and dense brush - a perfect site for an ambush. Entering the residence, a quick check was made of all rooms plus points of ingress and egress.

Returning to the hotel, a short briefing was conducted in the agents' room with Mike assigned to be the agent inside the residence. The rest of the detail would remain outside the party providing perimeter security. S/A Middleton volunteered to remain at the hotel to maintain security.

At the appointed hour for the drive to the party, procedures were kept pretty much the same as previous details. The trip was made without any mishaps and all arrived safely. At the residence, Mike took up his position inside, while agents Dave Albright, Jack Lewis and Tony Cantanzo met with Italian security agents assigned to the party. The plan would be during the party, one NIS S/A and one Italian would sweep the outside area on a rotating basis with the remaining NIS agent and his Italian counterpart. The Italian presence was dictated by the many senior Italian officials attending the function.

The residence was a nice single story villa which made Mike breathe a little easier; he would only be concerned with one floor. The only way in or out was through a front and back door. Since it was a cold night; no activity was planned for outside in the back yard, therefore, Mike had the back door secured.

Mike felt reassured all would be well outside with coverage by NIS and Italian security agents. His only worry would be inside the residence. Still, he could not help but think - *if the bad guys got through the team outside, well then, one guy with a six shooter wasn't going to be much of a deterrent.*

The first guests began to arrive and Mike took up his position at the front door. Checking party invitations, he was satisfied all was going well.

One humorous occurrence struck Mike's funny bone. An Italian gentleman upon entering the front door, handed Mike his party invitation. He proceeded to hand his hat and coat, followed by a request for a cocktail.

Maintaining his best composure, Mike informed him very politely he was not the valet nor the bar tender but a NIS Special Agent assigned to protect the U.S. Secretary of Defense. The residence's valet arrived to take charge of the man's hat and coat and escorted him to the bar.

Remaining at the front door foyer, Mike thought how could that guest have assumed he was the valet? *Let's see we have a man in suit, an ear piece in his ear and a funny pin on his lapel and oh yes, a bulge over his left coat area - yep, he must be the valet.*

The last guest was accounted for and the front entrance was secured. Mike's plan was to circulate around the interior of the residence, trying not to look too conspicuous. Of course he would remain vigilant. He would spend the rest of the evening keeping his eyes and ears open. Not much of a threat inside because the guests were either high ranking Italian military or civilian officials. The odd U.S. embassy type was also thrown into the mix.

Dinner was served and unlike other details there would be no eats for agent Blackstone. As the dinner progressed, he found a comfy chair and checked in with the outside detail by radio. Informing the ASAC dinner had been served, Mike estimated it would be at least a two-hour dinner. Mike felt sorry for the outside NIS agents considering it was a bitter cold night. *That's why they got paid the big bucks,* he mused.

As predicted, the dinner lasted close to two hours and guests started collecting their hats, coats and wraps. It was time for the Principal to depart. Mike advised him he would be the last to leave. As the last guest departed, Mike radioed for the Secretary's car to be brought to the front door. He received the all clear from the ASAC and the Principal and his wife were hustled out and into the car.

Ignoring any speed limit signs, the detail was soon back at the hotel. With the SECDEF safely deposited in his suite, the NIS team gathered to debrief the evening's events. Pretty standard stuff until Mike told the valet story. With all having a good laugh at Mike's expense, a suggestion was made for him to wear a welcome tag for the next party. Hi, my name is Mike and I am a NIS Special Agent.

The next morning it was time for the SECDEF and his party to be driven to the airport. His plane had been flown up from Naples the previous day. He thanked all Naples' agents for their diligence and departed. Mike and his fellow agents loaded up their car and headed back to Naples. Another successful security evolution was in the books.

Months passed while Mike's office continued to work normal cases. It was not long until another VIP, the Assistant Secretary of Defense (ASECDEF) was due to visit. With this visit scheduled it was time to put on their protective detail hats.

At the appointed day and time, the detail team, including Mike, arrived at CAPO to meet the ASECDEF's plane. The purpose of the trip was to attend some low key military meetings. However, he was anxious to visit with his extended Italian family and to see some of Naples. The plane taxied up to where the detail was positioned. The Principal and his wife were placed in the back seat of a staff car with Mike in the shotgun seat. A speedy ride downtown to the Hotel Excelsior and the VIP and his wife were safely checked into their suite. This was the same hotel used by the SECDEF for his visit.

On the following day, the Assistant Secretary requested to visit the downtown waterfront. It was a hot and steamy August day and he and his wife strolled along one of Naples' picturesque waterfront areas. He was dressed much like his fellow tourists in very casual clothes; Bermuda shorts and a flowered short sleeve shirt and his wife wore a very pretty colorful print dress. So far the scene looked pretty normal unless passerby's noticed the couple was surrounded by official looking men wearing suits with ear pieces stuck in their ears. When all this was added up, it would beg the question - what or who were these people? Could they be some important dignitaries?

This detail was more standard in appearance than previous Red Blanket operations as more agents were available. One agent was placed in front of the Principal, one agent was on either side and one agent followed.

Hmmm, do you suppose if there were any bad guys lurking around they might get the idea the casually dressed gentleman might be a target of interest? Mike dismissed this thought. To his and the other agents' relief, no problems materialized. A successful outing was concluded with the couple enjoying a delicious gelato and safely delivered back to their suite.

On the second day of his visit, while the ASECDEF was scheduled for an official meeting at the NSA compound, Mike was informed he had spousal escort duty again. The destination was to Herculaneum. This was another site of the 79 AD eruption of

Mount Vesuvius where much devastation and loss of life took place. Located a short distance from Naples, it was in the direct path of the volcano. It was not as well-known as Pompeii but did have a very interesting history. This detail was made as an exception to the rule much like Mike's last one for the SECDEF's wife.

Mike exited the hotel first for a quick check of the area and was met by Angelo, the security cleared Italian driver. He was instructed to have the car running while Mike went to collect the Secretary's wife. Driving to Herculaneum, Angelo gave a pretty good running monolog on items of interest.

Parking the car, the VIP's wife was met by the site officials who would show her what Herculaneum had to offer. Since this was Mike's first visit, it was hard not to be distracted by all the antiquities.

This detail would provide Mike with a once in a lifetime experience since she would be given a behind the scenes tour of areas. These areas had not been opened to the public. One building led to another and another until Mike's party arrived at one with a locked door. It was opened to reveal a recently uncovered Roman woman's skeleton. She still had gold rings on her boney hands.

The discovery and photo of the woman made the cover of the May 1984 issue of National Geographic. Much of what Mike had seen was pointed out in the article. No one, including Mike, saw their name in print.

Arriving back at the hotel, Mike was advised the couple would be having dinner at a local pizzeria with some of the Principal's relatives. The chosen restaurant would be Antica

214

Pizzeria da Michele located just off Via Cesare Sersale near the train station. He was anxious to try authentic pizza made in a wood-burning oven.

The time set for the dinner would be 8:00 PM which left time for the agents to plan the evolution. The ASAC would ride with the Assistant Secretary and Mike and Tony would be back-up in their G-Car. One agent would remain at the hotel for security. Tony related the pizzeria was located in a quiet neighborhood where mostly local residents liked to eat. There was enough time for a security check of the restaurant.

The couple were collected from their suite and deposited in the back seat of the staff car. Dave Albright assumed his position as shotgun and Mike and Tony were ready to roll. Instead of making like a speeding bullet, the ASAC decided on a normal speed limit drive to the restaurant. He felt it would draw less attention.

Entering the pizzeria, the Principal and his wife were greeted by about, what Mike assumed were relatives, 20 men, women and children. After much chattering and kissing all were seated.

The ASAC had volunteered to remain with the cars while Mike and Tony provided inside security. Finding a table to cover both the front and back doors the duo decided they had to eat. Two pizzas were quickly ordered plus one sent out to the Dave. Even though they were grabbing a fast nosh it did not mean a lessening of attention to the mission.

Mike believed the Principal thoroughly enjoyed meeting his relatives and he heard much laughter and saw extensive hand gesturing. The scene looked like any normal family gathering sharing stories and some pizza. The dinner came to an end and the Assistant Secretary signaled he was ready to depart.

Thankfully for the NIS agents the drive back to the hotel was uneventful and the couple were safe and sound in their suite. On the drive to the hotel, the Principal had informed the ASAC that he and his wife would be flying out the next day.

The next morning at the airport he warmly thanked all agents for their efforts. His wife personally thanked Mike for his security service. Once again it was back to normal duties.

It is said that things come in threes and so it was with protective service details. It wasn't long until another VIP detail loomed on the horizon. This time it would be for the outgoing Vice Chief of Naval Operations (VCNO) who needed the services of the NIS Naples' office. His official visit would include stops in Rome, Paris and concluding with a visit to Germany.

The expected date of the Admiral's arrival in Rome was received at the Naples' office. The ASAC assigned, Jack Lewis, Ned Hommes and Mike to accompany him on the detail. The team was briefed that they would handle his visits to Rome and Paris. Another security detail would meet the VCNO in Germany.

The first item on their to do list was to assemble the equipment and personal items needed. Besides individual suitcases containing personal clothing, each agent made sure to bring both passports; one for tourists with the familiar blue cover, and one for official use with its maroon cover. Mike had been instructed to almost always use his blue tourist passport. The maroon one usually brought unwanted curiosity by the country officials.

Meeting in the ASAC's office, a checklist was developed for the equipment needed for the detail. Their armament, packed in an aluminum suitcase, consisted of four .357 revolvers, pistol griped shotguns, handcuffs, radios and .38 cal. + P hollow point ammunition.

While the equipment suitcase was being loaded, Mike as the new kid on the block, wondered how they would get the suitcase through French customs once they flew to Paris from Rome. He was advised by the ASAC it would not be a problem. "Mike, an official from the U.S. Embassy will meet us and assist with our clearance into France." Sounded OK to Mike but what the hell did he know anyway?

The team departed early from the office for the drive to Capo. Since they would use a domestic flight there would be no worries about passports or customs. It was a short flight and after landing and collecting their luggage, they rented a car for use as a temporary G-Car.

Driving straight to the hotel final arrangements were made for the arrival of the VCNO. Satisfied with the hotel the team headed to the airport. This would only be an overnight visit; the main reason for the Admiral's trip was to attend conferences in France and Germany.

Arriving at the airport, Mike was surprised to see two Italian motorcycle policemen waiting for the arrival of his plane. Right on schedule, the plane landed and was parked on the tarmac. No time was wasted. The Admiral gingerly walked down the aircraft stairs to the embassy provided staff car. It seemed to Mike that he was in a hurry for some sightseeing before he had to leave for Paris.

He was shown to the backseat and Mike took the shotgun position. The ASAC and the rest of the detail would follow in the NIS temp G-Car. With the Principal safely aboard, Agent Lewis, the driver was ready to roll and shouted to the police, "Andiamo Adesso!" Translated in Italian it meant "Let's go now!"

With blue lights flashing and sirens blaring, the motorcade was off. Since they had a police escort, in no time at all they pulled into the hotel main entrance area. It was definitely different driving in Rome – drivers actually obeyed the police. Mike was out like a flash and opened the back door to allow the Admiral to quickly exit.

It would be a quick stop at the hotel while he changed into civilian attire. He was anxious to get to his first stop at St. Peter's Basilica and the Vatican Museum. The ASAC decided that no police escort was required. The loud siren and flashing blue lights brought unwanted attention

Parking the car near St. Peters, while Jack watched the cars, Mike, Ned and the ASAC played tour guide for the Admiral. Joining a tour group, informally of course, conducted by a guide, their little group cruised right through into the Basilica. Mike was fascinated to hear all the history of the place narrated by the guide. Mike hoped someday he would be able to return as a simple tourist.

The tour guide pointed out the statue of St. Peter where one must kiss his right foot for good luck. Mike tried to guess how many times it had been kissed over the centuries but had not a clue – perhaps in the millions.

Last stop in St. Peter's was to visit the Sistine Chapel in the Vatican Museum. Their luck still held as they bypassed the two hour waiting crowd and went straight in. How Michelangelo was able to paint the scenes over years of work was hard to imagine. Since only 10-15 minutes were allowed in the Chapel, they were soon back outside and headed to the car.

As daylight faded, it was time to hurry to the hotel in order for the Admiral to get dressed to attend a dinner party in his honor at the oldest restaurant in Rome – the 500-year-old La Campana. While Dave and Ned kept watch on the Principal, Mike and Jack made a quick reconnaissance of the restaurant. It was to be a very low key affair with less than 10 people in attendance and the Admiral would be dressed in a suit.

The selected eatery was small and cozy which allowed the agents to keep a close eye on the Principal. The ASAC made the call that only one agent would be inside with the Principal. They matched coins to see who got to eat inside – Jack Lewis would dine on traditional Roman cuisine while the rest ate pizza delivered from a shop next door.

Dinner concluded. It was time to head for the hotel. The three-star had other ideas. He wanted to visit the magnificent Trevi Fountain and toss his two coins. One was for a wish to come true and the other was a hope to return some day as legend had it. Mike had read the history of the fountain and was astounded that it was still functioning since it dated to the 1700's.

Up early the next day, the agents had their man back to

the airport, no worse for wear. All agents and their Italian counterparts were gathered for a photo op. The VCNO thanked all involved with his security and boarded the plane. He would make a stop at the Italian Aviano Air Base for a working luncheon before continuing on to Paris. This would give the team plenty of time to catch their flight and meet the Admiral when he arrived in France.

The rental car was returned and they checked in their bags, including the aluminum weapon case. The four tourists boarded their flight to Paris. Before Mike had time to dig into his travel guide, the plane's PA system announced it was time to fasten passenger seat belts for the landing at Charles de Gaulle Airport.

The agents exited the aircraft and hurried to the baggage claim area. They were anxious to meet the embassy representative and get out of the airport. As they approached the baggage carousel, Mike became a little concerned; he saw no one looking official; no sign and no paging from the airport PA system - nothing! What to do?

While Mike and the others stood at the carousel and looked forlornly for some official person to show up, a loud buzzer sounded. Baggage started to move and passengers pushed and shoved to get closer to the carousel. OK by the agents, they were in no hurry to pick up the luggage especially the incriminating aluminum case. All too soon their bags appeared and moved along the conveyor belt. Deciding the best plan was to let them enjoy a circular ride; the agents moved away. It wasn't long before the only bags left belonged to the agents.

The ASAC got the ball rolling and suggested, "OK, here's

the plan. We pick up our personal luggage and put it on a trolley cart. We leave the aluminum suitcase to continue its journey around the carousel." Not much of a plan but it did give them time to think.

Mike expressed a plausible explanation for their predicament. "Maybe there was a mix up and he's waiting for us at customs and passport control." The troublesome suitcase made its appearance and it was now or never!

Approaching the clearance area, they all said a silent appeal to see someone - anyone but it was not to be. No official was waiting. What the hell to do now? It was too late to retreat so the agents opted for the only course of action left to them – bluff! With their blue tourist passports out, they reluctantly joined the line for customs. It was unanimously decided showing their maroon official passports would be a very bad idea under the present circumstances with the incriminating aluminum suitcase.

"Venez Ici" from the uniformed official followed by a cheery "Bon Jour." The foursome moved ahead to greet him. Seeing their blue American passports, the official gave them a pleasant greeting. "Welcome to the City of Lights and passports please" in his halting English. As he examined them, he asked, "Business or pleasure and do you have anything to declare?" Quickly they responded in unison, "We're here on holiday and have nothing to declare." With that declaration, the official stamped their passports and bid them to enjoy their stay in Paris.

The next stop for our men from Naples would be to rent a car. While they walked to the rental agency, Jack Lewis played the 'what if game?' "Hey guys, imagine the look on the custom official's face had he opened the aluminum case. It would have been: open the case – close the case – open the case – close the case. Not believing what he was seeing, it would have looked like a skit from the old Here's Lucy TV program. You know where Lucy pulled some crazy stunt and her husband Ricky called her on it with, Lucy, you got some 'splain-in' to do." Ned laughed and responded, "You know Jack, as the saying goes in the sports world, no harm - no foul."

With a collective sigh of relief, it was all aboard their rented very cool looking silver BMW 4-door. It would be their G-Car for the next few days. Throwing the luggage in the trunk, they sped off to the hotel. Already checked into their room, there was just enough time to go over last minute details. Much like details in Naples, both agents and Principal would be staying in the same hotel. Ned would remain at the hotel for security.

It was time for the Principal to be picked up at Orly Airport, located about 13 km from Paris. No excitement at the airport and with him safely deposited in the backseat of their temporary G-Car; it was onward to the hotel. The rest of his staff followed in separate vehicles. Once the Admiral was safe in his hotel suite at the Hotel de Crillon, the agents met with the Principal's Chief of Staff. Precise details of the VCNO's visit were presented. They included formal meetings as well as tourist type activities.

Official visits would include the U.S. Embassy and the French Naval Academy, to name just two. The most exciting visit would be to Norte-Dame Cathedral. Of course, the Admiral would have to eat, so the agents would be dining in some of the finest

Parisian restaurants on the government's tab.

First scheduled stop the next morning was the U.S. Embassy. As the agents stood around the car, the VCNO's COS, a full naval captain, approached the BMW along with the Admiral. The Principal got in the back seat along with the ASAC. While Ned took his seat behind the wheel, the Captain waited at the passenger door for Mike to enter the vehicle.

The Captain assumed since he was a senior naval officer and the Chief of Staff, he would be offered the preferred seat next to the front passenger window. Mike explained he would be seated next to the window and the four striper would have to ride in the middle or the hump. The BMW was equipped with only bench seats. Not happy with this perceived slight, he reluctantly slid into the middle and Mike followed.

The team safely arrived at the American Embassy. Since it was a secured area; not much for the agents to do while the Admiral visited with the Ambassador. Mike had noticed the embassy retail store and gift shop and purchased a pretty cool key chain with the emblem of royalist France embossed on it. The courtesy call was short and they drove to their next destination, the French Naval Academy. The VCNO had a scheduled meeting with French Navy's CNO.

The agent's car passed through a guarded gate post and the VCNO was met by the French Admiral's aide. The Academy, much like the U.S. Embassy, was located in a secure compound. It was close to lunch time. The agents were invited to dine in the officer's mess located in a basement area. The Principal and his COS would of course be served upstairs in the executive dining room. The NIS agents were escorted to the basement dining room and were introduced to several junior members of the Academy staff.

Once seated, menus were produced but to the dismay of the agents, they were written in French. What a surprise! Eating at a French military installation and the menu was only in French – go figure?

Mike along with the other agents stared at the menu in silence. The silence was maddening. A very polite English speaking young lieutenant approached, "You do not read or speak French?" "No, we don't." He helped the agents order and recommended the 'la viande de cheval' which the agents gladly accepted. They assumed it must be some type of beef.

The meal was served and of course accompanied with generous amounts of wine. Since the agents were on duty they politely abstained. Mike, was curious and wanted to know what they had just eaten. He inquired, "Monsieur, what exactly did we eat? It was quite delicious."

The French officer was at a loss for the English word and demonstrated with unique sounds and gestures. As the Americans sat with astonished looks, he made whinnying sounds accompanied by riding gestures and slapped his thigh. Oh my god, it suddenly dawned on the team - they had just eaten horse!

While the meal was quite good, it was the image of Sea Biscuit consumed with much gusto which was a little unsettling. With a very fine dessert served and port for the French, it was time to rejoin the Admiral for the return trip to the hotel. Not much activity back at the hotel, except to setup watch responsibilities which would include spot checks of the hallways and lobby areas.

Dinner was next on the agenda but first the Principal needed a short nap. Mike was certainly looking forward to dining in the City of Lights. Paris at night was purported to be spectacular and the all agents were ready. Departing the hotel and yes, the Captain still rode the hump; it was off to the restaurant. Agent Hommes would be on duty at the hotel. The chosen eatery, the Taillevent, a Michelin three-star, was located across from the Champs-Elysees. At the restaurant, the standard detail procedures were executed with one agent and the COS entering the restaurant for a quick security check. S/A Lewis would remain outside.

Mike's radio crackled with, "Ok, Mike, all secure and bring in the Admiral." Mike who was already standing by the VCNO's door, opened it and escorted him inside where he joined the French CNO. The ASAC and Mike found a table which provided a clear view of the front entrance. The American and French Admirals were seated in a nice corner table with a view of the River Seine with the Champs-Elysees in the background. The portly owner with his chef, Claud Disoode, introduced themselves.

It had been a long day and lunch was hours ago. Mike was hungry. European dining habits dictated dinner sometime after 9:00 PM. Menus were promptly brought to Mike's team. The VCNO would not need one, he was to dine on a specially prepared meal.

Not surprisingly the menu was in French and the restaurant provided no English translations. Mike found the word for horsemeat and the two agents settled on bifteck (steak) and poulet (chicken).

The inside agents would check from time to time with Lewis. It was more from being bored than any perceived or actual threat. The usual European dining time of two hours came to a conclusion. It was time to return to the hotel.

Exit protocol would be the reverse of the aforementioned entering procedure. Mike checked the outside, radioed the all clear and the Admiral's party departed the restaurant. Their Principal requested a leisurely drive down the boulevard of lights before he retired for the evening. Upon returning to the hotel, security watches were set up for the remainder of the evening.

The next day would be the Admiral's last and it would be to visit Notre-Dame Cathedral. Mike had some free time so he decided to do a little research and used his guide book on the Cathedral.

The construction began over 800 years ago when Maurice de Sully was elected as the first bishop of Paris. The first stone was placed by Pope Alexander III. Over the succeeding years, it was completed with numerous improvements, additions and modifications. The history of Notre-Dame would be filled with glorious proceedings and important gatherings throughout its long and storied history.

The French Revolution was pointed out as a particular bleak time in its history. One result was the 13th century spire was disassembled and 28 statures in the Gallery of the Kings destroyed. Mike thought this was a pity but apparently respect for religion was not at the top of revolutionaries' agenda.

In the modern era, a most noteworthy event occurred when Charles de Gaulle's funeral was held at the Cathedral

Mike was assigned the midnight to 4:00 AM watch and made his rounds. As he checked the hallways and stairwells, he found all was in order. Mike maintained security outside the VCNO's room and none too soon, 4:00 AM rolled around. He was relieved and had time to catch a few winks.

At around 8:00 AM, it was time to depart. Mike checked the VIP's exit from the hotel to the car. Radioing back to the ASAC, the all secure code, the Admiral was hurried into his official vehicle. For this trip, the Embassy provided a staff car and driver for his use. The ASAC, Dave Albright and the COS would ride in the Principal's staff car. The rest of the detail followed in their BMW G-Car. With a Parisian metro police car to lead the way, the motorcade sped toward the Cathedral.

Arriving at a prearranged private entrance, Mike ran to the staff car. With all in order, Mike opened the Admiral's door and he, the Principal entered Notre-Dame. Mike accompanied him and the other members of the team maintained security at the cars.

The tour was pretty impressive with the Admiral making positive comments as he walked. Leaving the inside, he was shown the entrance to the Crypte Archeologique by the tour guide. The Crypt was opened to the public in 1980. The only way in was going down a flight of stairs. Mike was most impressed by the carvings on the walls dating back to Roman times. He thought the place was a little spooky and was relieved to see daylight again.

The next morning a tired detail safely delivered the Vice

Chief of Naval Operations and his staff to his aircraft. A new Naples' detail would pick him up once he landed in Germany.

Returning their well-used BMW to the rental agency and checking in their luggage, including the aluminum weapon suitcase, it was time to board and head for Rome and then on to Naples. Another safe protective detail was now concluded and in the NIS Naples' journal.

Back at the office Mike was concerned about the Paris portion of their last detail. He needed to find an answer so he asked the ASAC.

"Dave, I know we have permits here in Italy that covers us with our weapons but in France how were we covered in case we had to use them to protect the VCNO?"

"Mike, sometimes we just have to do what is necessary to get the job done and worry about the consequences later."

CHAPTER 9
ROMANCE IN BELLA NAPOLI

What would working and living in Bella Napoli be without a little romance? Yes, Mike did have time to join the single dating scene. It would prove more difficult than he could have imagined compared to dating back in the states. Apparently, Mike working as a NIS Special Agent was not the best credential for attracting a single lady. The stigma attached would be due to Mike's job; to apprehend service members involved in illicit activities. A comment he would become all too familiar with; "We don't do NIS agents." While this attitude was disappointing, he did meet with some success.

One day in June, Blackstone had a routine medical appointment at the base hospital. Parking his G-Car and entering the hospital, he was met by a perky young female working at the front desk. Never one to miss an opportunity to chat, he met Sandy, who was working as a civilian nurse. While waiting to see the doctor, Mike tried a couple of his tried and true lines on her; she wasn't buying any of them. Thinking similar lines had worked in the past, he decided to try a different approach – honesty. What a concept! Just when he was coming straight to the point to ask her out for dinner, the doctor showed up. Sandy left and continued her duties.

"Damn it, Doc! Your timing could not have been worse."
"What's the problem, Mike?" Explaining his dilemma, Doc Watson set his mind at ease. "Sandy is single and will still be at the front

desk when we're finished." Mike had a plan to put into action – he would march right up to her and ask her out. It wasn't much of a plan but that was all he had.

Sure enough as Blackstone headed for the main exit, she was standing at the desk. He got the distinct impression she was trying really hard not to notice him. Navy blood ran in his veins, it was 'damn the torpedoes, full speed ahead.' In his best devil may care look, he approached her. To his surprise the direct approach actually worked and a dinner date was set for Saturday night. The trip up the hill made it worthwhile. It was time for him to get back to work.

Time moved quickly with his heavy case load and before he knew it, Saturday had arrived and it was time to pick Sandy up at her Parco. A Parco was similar to a small subdivision back in the states where many people stationed in Naples liked to live. Mostly, only military officers and civilians could afford to live in such a place.

Since he did not have much time for background gathering on Sandy at the hospital, he was surprised to see a different woman who answered the door. She was as good looking as Sandy but younger. It turned out that she was Sandy's roommate and an enlisted hospital corpsman.

A very nice evening was spent dining at Mike's favorite pizza place, Bagnoli Jo. Sandy was delightful and he could definitely see the possibility of more nights with her. Alas, it was not to be.

Figuring that their first date went pretty well, Mike was

hoping for more but was confused by Sandy's avoidance of him. After many attempts to contact her including visits to the hospital with no luck; it was always one excuse after another why she wasn't available.

At this point, he was getting a little paranoid. Phoning her at her apartment was not an option; she was in the same boat as Mike – no phone. Perseverance finally paid off. One afternoon, he ran into her at the base exchange and she agreed to a cup of coffee.

Not much talk as she came straight to the point. Her enlisted roommate was partaking in recreational drugs just like many of her junior enlisted contemporaries. She went on to explain while she enjoyed Mike's company, it was only a matter of time before her roommate or her friends were busted by NIS. Sandy felt her roommate might think she had 'ratted' on them. Not much he could do to combat her logic so like a gentleman; he would bow out graciously.

Strike One and hopefully, Sandy would be the exception and there would be no Strike Two or heaven forbid Strike Three. Trying hard not to get depressed, he began to think being a NIS S/A might put a damper on his social life. Always Mr. Positive, he wasn't about to give up and would keep pressing ahead with his efforts.

With Blackstone's attitude that the glass was always half full as opposed to half empty, it wasn't long before opportunity knocked again. Oddly enough, his second attempt at dating would be due to the fact that he was a NIS Special Agent and his new possibility thought that it was pretty cool.

Mike had developed the habit of stopping by the Officer's Club on AFSOUTH after work for a drink or a light meal. On one of those nights he was introduced to Mary Gandersen, a good looking tall red headed U.S. Navy Ensign.

After only a few minutes of talking it was apparent she had a good sense of humor with a bit of wild adventure thrown in for good measure. A date was set with Mike picking her up at her apartment the next evening. Bidding her a good night, Mike left and headed to his apartment.

On date night and driving up to her place, Mike was amused to see a bright red Triumph sitting in the driveway. Since he owned a Triumph, only bronze in color, he felt a match made in heaven was a possibility.

This first date was a rousing success and plans were made to do it again. More dates followed and it wasn't long before Mike was spending some nights at her place. She did have one quirk; she loved to have his .357 S&W hanging in its shoulder holster on the headboard. She even came up with a nickname for him: Dirty Harry; you know the famous character played by Clint Eastwood. Returning the favor, he would call her, Crazy Mary. Ensign Mary shortened Dirty Harry to DH and Crazy Mary became CM. It was her idea of secret code words. He was having a good time so whatever floated her boat was OK by him.

There was more to the relationship than some pretty good sex. Italy had many wonderful and exotic places to explore. On their days off, she and Mike would travel to local beautiful and interesting sites. With seven days of vacation time, it was decided to travel outside the Naples area. Plans were made to visit Mount Vesuvius, Pompeii, the island of Capri with its Blue Grotto and finish up in Rome with a visit to St. Peter's and the Vatican. A lot to see and not much time.

First on their list was a visit to Mount Vesuvius, an active volcano, located outside Naples. It would be an easy drive.

The volcano had a long and painful history with numerous eruptions since the fateful day in 79 AD. Without warning, it erupted and destroyed the city of Pompeii. The latest one occurred almost 40 years ago in 1944. For Mike and Mary, knowing it was still an active volcano made the trip all the more exciting.

Arriving at the volcano, Mike was happy to see there was a chair lift to the 4,000-foot summit. The day of their visit some areas were placed off-limits. They could, however, go pretty much anywhere else on the lava mountain with a guide

Reaching the desolate and lunar-like peak, the couple were rewarded with a spectacular view of the Bay of Naples with the ancient city of Pompeii in the foreground. As they looked down into the crater, it was unsettling to see rocks shake loose and feel the earth move ever so slightly. Mike figured it was just the old girl letting them know she was still alive and kicking.

The hired guide took them on a little path sloping down towards the bottom. It was scary but at the same time exhilarating. As they continued their stroll, Sulphur gases escaped from the cracked lava. Their guide put on quite a show. He would bend down and light his cigarette from the cracks. This demonstrated that extreme heat was still present. Pretty cool! Heading back up to the chair lift, it was time to leave and continue their drive to Pompeii. This would be Mike's second visit and Mary's first.

According to Mike's trusty guide book, when the volcano erupted in 79 AD, Pompeii, a commercial port of some 20,000 souls was destroyed and buried under 20 feet of hot mud and volcanic ash. The ancient city was first rediscovered in the 17th century, with attempts to unearth it around 1700. Since then, massive amounts of restoration projects have been completed.

Parking the car, Mike and Mary paid the admission charge and began their exploration of the sites. Even though much restoration work had been going on for years, the couple could see the destruction and felt the panic the residents faced. As the couple walked this trading city; an eerie feeling was present. It was like the pulse of past shoppers was still beating.

Continuing the tour, Mary noticed the street had a single or double stone imbedded. "DH, what do you make of these stones?" Consulting his reliable guide book, "Well, CM, it says that one stone meant the street was a one-way for chariots and if there were two stones; it was a two way."

Among the most interesting sights were the plaster cast molds of actual citizens who perished and were covered with ash. The molds showed the exact position these unfortunate people were found the moment they died. The most disturbing mold was a mother clutching a baby under her to save the child. Nothing would have worked. The extreme heat and ash engulfing Pompeii would have been horrific.

The visitor to Pompeii would still see the remains of shops, food stalls and even public lavatories. The citizens had running water and a sewage system. One ancient building was marked with a symbol indicating it was a bordello. Mike was amused by the erotic mosaics and figured they were there to set the mood for the patrons.

Mary also found these 'pleasure palaces' interesting but was more intrigued by the stone beds. Looking at the beds, she figured they could not have been all that comfortable. Mike guessed, "Those beds must have been where the term 'rough sex' originated."

Next door was one of the public lavatories that was a 10-holer. Hard to believe that well into the 20th century, some Americans still used a pump to bring water into their houses and were relegated to outhouses to do their business. "Mike, do you have any idea how these 'johns' worked?"

Breaking out his well worn guide book, he researched for an answer. It seemed that around the birth of Christ, their system was pretty simple. Sewage would run into the gutters and running water from numerous flowing fountains would take it out to the sea. Never missing a detail, the engineers of this system installed large stones bisecting the streets to allow pedestrians to cross without getting their sandals filled with 'unpleasant stuff.'

Mike had pretty much experienced enough of this ancient strolling and his feet were talking to him. It was time to head back to Naples and home; tomorrow would be another day.

Up bright and early the next morning, the day's schedule

235

would be a drive to the port and catch a hydrofoil to Capri, located just off the coast. While Mike had previously been to the island on a protective service detail, he was looking forward to just being a tourist for the day.

Parking Mary's Triumph close to the port, Mike strode over to purchase their tickets. The line was long and he was used to standing in a queue so he proceeded to locate the end and joined his fellow tourists. As the line was moving, he was shocked to see four male Italians march straight to the head of the line and purchase tickets. Apparently in Naples, the attitude was, 'lines are for others but not for me - I am the only important one.' Mike experienced this same attitude many times during his tour with NIS. It seemed Naples was unique with this attitude. He never experienced this phenomenon anywhere else he traveled in Italy.

Finally reaching the ticket booth and buying his tickets, he collected his girl and boarded. Time to sit back, relax and enjoy the boat ride. Breaking out his guide book, Mike discovered Capri, in ancient times, was famous as a getaway for Roman emperors such as Augustus and Tiberius. Many movies have been made on the island, featuring movie stars such as Sophia Loren - a native of Naples.

Arriving at the port of Marina Grande, the couple were anxious to catch the funicular from Capri Town to Anacapri at the top. Mike really enjoyed the ride up, he remembered the last time he was on Capri, while he was on detail, it was one hell of a car ride. A 360-degree view awaited and on a clear day one could see Naples and Vesuvius. The flowers and gardens were exceptional.

While Anacapri was lined with unique but expensive shops and diversions, Mary was anxious to see the world famous Blue Grotto.

Down from the top of the island, DH and CM made their way to the ferry that would deliver them to the entrance to the Blue Grotto. The ferry would be too large to enter the cavern. Tourists including our duo would have to transfer to very small two passenger row boats to enter the Grotto.

Their tiny boat was a little tricky. The captain grabbed a fixed rope and pulled the boat toward the entrance shouting, "Sdeaiarsi" to our couple, which meant "Lie Down" in Italian. A very big problem arose as the couple had never heard the word so they sat upright as the boat raced toward the entrance. Just when the couple were about to be decapitated, the captain shoved their heads down.

The clearance into the cavern was only about three feet in height, just enough room for the boat to enter. Once the boat was inside, the eerie blue sunlight reflected off the water and gave it a deep blue sapphire color. While the analogy of a blue sapphire stone might be a good barometer to measure the color; Mike estimated it needed to be tripled to do the color justice.

Rome, the Eternal City, with its glorious past was a must on Mike and Mary's bucket list.

The couple dedicated two days and nights for sightseeing and planned to visit the Coliseum, the Roman Forum, St. Peters and the Vatican. Mike had seen St. Peter's and the Vatican on a protective service detail and he hoped to see more. Of course the food was not to be missed.

Mike decided driving to Rome in either Mary's or his car wasn't a great idea. Flying was the quickest and fastest way so the couple were off to Cappodichino Airport to catch their flight to Rome. Checking in at the Aero Transporti Italiani ticket counter and requesting a non-smoking section, it was time to board. The flight was at full capacity, luckily Mike and Mary found two seats together in the front on the left side. The cabin door shut and the stewardess welcomed all in Italian. Mike was waiting for the English but since it was a domestic carrier; none was forthcoming.

As the flight began to taxi the fellow to Mike's right lit up the foulest smelling cigarette. He was not alone with at least 10 more passengers who followed suit. Mary who was also a non-smoker motioned for the stewardess to complain.

With their limited Italian they tried to explain they requested non-smoking and this fellow not two feet across the aisle was smoking.

"Signore e Signorina lei sei in non fumare." and proceeded to point to their side of the aircraft. Mike quickly checked his Italian dictionary to see what the hell the cabin attendant was talking about.

"Mary, I think I have it. We assumed just like U.S. airlines the smoking section was in the back of the plane. Only the Italians would divide the aircraft down the middle to separate smokers from non-smokers." The plane quickly filled with tobacco smoke and it seemed Mike and Mary were the only ones having a problem with the arrangement. None too soon the flight landed in Rome and they made their way to the hotel.

The Hotel Aberdeen was not cheap at 200,000 lira (1,500 = $1.00) for a double but it did have many luxuries and Mike felt like splurging. It was centrally located with only a three-minute walk to the metro and 12 minutes to Trevi Fountain. Dinner was at a nearby small trattoria and an early night to bed.

The first site on their list was the Coliseum which was built around 72 AD. Climbing to the top Mary was amazed at its size. At the top tier of the stadium, Mike could imagine scenes from the movie 'Ben Hur' staring Charlton Heston with gladiators fighting each other to the death.

In its day, it could hold over 40,000 spectators taking in the blood orgies for what the masses considered a fun day at the ball park. The Coliseum could even be thought as the prototype of the modern day sports complex. Alas, the structure of today was only a shadow of its former glory. In the 5th century AD, it was made into a quarry for use in building other marvels of Rome. This explained its cheese like appearance.

Next stop on their Roman adventure would be the Roman Forum. Not too much time was spent there by our traveling duo because there was not much to see. Only a few columns remained of this once magnificent structure. Historically, the Forum operated as the center of public life into 400 AD, when Caesar decided he had to build his own palace. Before he abandoned the Forum, he held a banquet for over 20,000 of his closest friends.

In the same century, those pesky raiding Barbarians practically destroyed it and by the Middle Ages it was pretty much only fit for cows munching on the grasses. It was not until the late

19th century that archeologists began to excavate the site.

If the visitor had only a short amount of time to spend in Rome, St Peter's and the Vatican would have been right at the top of any list. Of all the great churches in the world, St. Peter's was the big guy on the block. According to the Guinness Book of Records, it ranked first as the largest church in the world and had the world's largest dome.

The couple planned to visit both St. Peter's and the Vatican the next and last full day of their visit.

Mike and Mary thoroughly enjoyed their previous night's dinner and they decided to return. The Ristorante da Giovanni was only a short walk from their hotel. What the couple liked best about the restaurant was the absence of patrons speaking English. It was a local's place which suited our couple just fine.

The next morning after a full breakfast buffet provided by the hotel, Mike and Mary were anxious to reach their first stop – St. Peter's and the Vatican.

No matter what a person's faith, entering the Basilica would be a moving experience. Once inside, Mike thought it was even more impressive than the outside. The altar, where a daily Mass was held, was so beautiful that Mike and Mary stood transfixed at the sight of it. They walked from one ancient part to the next ending with the mandatory stop at the statue of Saint Peter.

Once the small crowd gathered in front of it moved on, Mike noticed the Peter's foot had practically been rubbed bare by visitors. On his one and only previous visit, he had noted the same phenomenon. Never missing an opportunity for some good fortune, both gave it their best polish job. Finishing with St. Peter's, it was time to find the Vatican Museum and more importantly the Sistine Chapel.

Once outside our travelers headed in the direction provided by a church guide for the entrance to the Museum. As our duo rounded a corner of St. Peter's Square, it was not hard to see where the entrance to the Vatican Museum was located. A crowd, no a mass of humanity, numbering in the hundreds was standing in an orderly line for the entrance.

Approaching the crowd, Mike remembered there was not much indicating this was the entrance. There were no signs- no church representative – no nothing. Mike would have no 'head of the line' privilege this time. Taking their place at the end of the line, Blackstone thought Romans had courtesies of line waiting Naples did not. How refreshing!

After two hours of waiting, our tired, hot and intrepid couple were finally at the front and headed inside. Moving along a long corridor filled with priceless paintings and tapestries, they reached the Sistine Chapel entrance.

In 1508, Pope Julius II commissioned Michelangelo to paint the Sistine Chapel. It took him over five long painful years. He later regretted ever taking that commission. It did not stop him from returning 12 years later to paint the world's masterpiece - The Last Judgement. Since only minutes were allowed for each group to spend time in the Chapel, they left and went to lunch.

With Mike looking through his travel book for a restaurant, Mary mentioned one she had heard much about. Mike's Lira

Pistol was running low so a visit to Pasticceria Dagnino was in order. According to his guide book they served an inexpensive buffet and the place was a hit with locals.

Instead of flying back to Naples, the couple decided to rent a car. On the two-hour drive back it gave them time to think about their relationship. While they both enjoyed each other's company, the romantic aurora was wearing off. Mike and Mary decided it was best to end their relationship. Neither one was interested in a serious long term commitment. Mary found out she was being transferred back to San Diego, California in two weeks.

As the old saying goes, when one door closes, another opens, however, he was in no hurry to see what was behind the door. It was weeks later when he met Judy, a very attractive dentist working as a civilian at the clinic. Surprised by her forward attitude, Mike decided to give it a shot and asked her out. Reluctantly, even though Mike was a NIS agent, she agreed to a date.

This first date lead to a few more but it happened again. She was advised by one of her friends she should not be dating a NIS S/A. It was not a good idea. Oh my, Mike seemed to remember that tune being played before and he didn't like the ending. Judy asked her friend why she shouldn't continue to see Mike? "They told me to tell you that we don't do NIS agents."

Judy would not accept this simple explanation and urged her friend to continue. "Judy, you know some of our social group 'smoke' a little and if we got busted, you might be blamed." Sadly, this was probably true, not that she, was a source, but her friends might assume it. Judy told Mike she would think it over and let him know what her decision would be. Mike hoped he would not get another strikeout.

Weeks passed, Mike pretty much thought his relationship with Judy was at a dead end. To his relief, she contacted him. She had told her friends to go to hell and she would date a person of her choosing and not theirs. Mike was happy he had found a woman with some grit. Wow, some girl, not only did she have guts, she was some kind of drop dead gorgeous.

Judy was a statuesque 5'9" blonde with big blue eyes and a figure to die for. Prior to graduating from dental school and joining the navy, she had been a professional dancer. In fact, in her off duty hours she would teach dancing at the base theater.

Since his new love had a thirst for travel, Mike would let her be his tour guide; opening mysteries of Italy and Europe. After a few months of dating, they decided to spread their wings and go on vacation together outside of Italy.

The first planned trip would be skiing in Germany. There was however one major and one minor problem. The big one was Mike had no idea how to ski and the other was he did not have any ski equipment. No problem as downtown Naples was one big marketplace filled with shopping alleys. The alleys would be known for the products sold: shoe alley, electronics alley and so on. They agreed to go shopping the next Saturday to ski alley. Judy liked to sleep late on weekends so they would start at noon.

With so much work on his schedule, the week went by quickly and at the appointed time Mike picked her up from her apartment in his TR-7. Mike had been in Naples long enough to drive like a local and with the pedal to the metal, the couple soon arrived at their destination. Finding a parking place would be a tad difficult. Mike decided to do the Italian thing and pulled his car up on the sidewalk. As they walked away from the car, Mike thought it was kind of crazy but he remembered an Italian saying. A parking spot was in the eye of the beholder. If one wasn't available - make your own.

With Judy leading the way, they went in search of some primo ski equipment. As they walked, Mike thought to himself, *was this trip really necessary? Was it really a good idea to go traipsing down some alley in search of skis?* Of course in his duties as a NIS agent, he had been down some pretty seedy areas such as the Gut.

As they passed numerous stalls where brand name items were displayed, Judy advised they were looking for a certain stall. Not long after the start of their quest, she pointed out Luigi's which was her favorite. Entering she received the traditional Italian greeting: a kiss on both her cheeks.

It was time to see how much this sport was going to cost. Deferring to his girl, she began the negotiating process. In Naples, it was common practice, in fact, encouraged to haggle over the asking price of items.

Judy started the process with 50% off the sticker prices. Of course, Luigi was offended by this low offer. While she negotiated, Mike looked around. The names on the ski equipment might as well been advertising Italian sports cars as far as he was concerned. A price was agreed upon and Mike was the proud owner of a set of Rossignol skis, poles, boots and goggles.

Mike pulled Judy aside, "What is all this stuff going to cost me?" Remembering back home, a friend of Mike's had paid over $200.00 just for skis. Mike was prepared for the bad news but didn't want to disappoint Judy so he pulled out his wallet. Happily, surprised and definitely relieved, the entire bill was only 100,000 lira or about $65.00 U.S. – what a deal!

Figuring their shopping was finished, he was ready to head back to the car but it was not to be. Instead of heading in the direction of the car the couple continued down the alley.

"Where are we headed now?" "Really Mike, you can't go skiing in ordinary clothes." It would appear they were in search of a suitable wardrobe for this novice skier. Finding the right stall, Mike was soon outfitted in a pretty cool blue bib overall ski suit, ski hat and gloves. Once again, when time to pay, the total cost was a measly $25.00 U.S. Now he was really finished and ready to head to the car.

Mike felt like an overloaded pack mule as he carried the skis, poles and boots back to the car. Judy carried the light load of clothes.

After a six block walk with Mike huffing and puffing, they reached his car. To Mike's surprise, the car was still where he'd left it and was missing no tires or anything else. This was Naples and theft was a way of life.

Putting down the top, the skis and poles were loaded next to Judy's seat with the poles sticking up like some directional signal.

245

The boots and clothes went into the trunk: time to roll.

As has been previously discovered, driving in Naples was an exercise in a type of demolition derby but now it became quite the comical sight. Judy held on for dear life and still tried to control the flight characteristic of the skis and poles. Mike thought the whole affair reminded him of Jed Clampett and the family from the TV show, The Beverley Hillbillies, tooling along in that flatbed truck with Granny sitting on her sofa. The difference was Granny wasn't holding ski poles.

Of course the sight of two crazy Americans drew no attention from the locals they passed. Naples' drivers were used to weird ways of traveling in the city: six people squeezed into a Fiat 500, about the size of a Chevy Chevette; three people jammed on a Moped scooter designed for two; a bicycle with Italians riding on the seat, rear fender frame and handle bars – the list could go on and on. With no traffic problems except several funny looks from drivers, the couple pulled up to Judy's apartment.

Unloading Mike's treasures in the apartment; time for a well-earned repast. Tony's was the best known pizzeria near Judy's apartment. It was obvious she was a repeat customer and she was readily recognized; the two were seated at a primo table.

Mike had fallen in love with real Italian wood fired pizza. The fresh ingredients would make anyone's mouth water. Mike always ordered his pizza with fresh made sauce, mozzarella di bufala cheese and fresh basil herbs. After being seated, their meal was ordered with red wine. Judy could not wait to show Mike a brochure on skiing in Germany.

Their destination would be the General Walker Hotel located in Garmish, Germany. During WWII, the hotel and facilities were taken over by the Nazis and used for rest and relaxation by high ranking SS officers. After the war, the U.S. military assumed control and turned it into a recreation complex.

Mike scanned the brochure and found some very interesting facts about the hotel. Besides world class skiing, there would be opportunities to tour bunkers, tunnels, a movie theater and even an underground bowling alley. Mike thought, *Hmmm, maybe this skiing thing won't be so bad after all.* Plans were made and a date was set.

A month later with reports of good snowfall in the Bavarian Alps, Mike and Judy boarded the train for the day and night journey to Garmish. At the Garmish station they hired a cab that would take them to the hotel. Mike thought Naples' drivers were crazy and speed demons but the cab driver's hair raising 10-minute ride would have put many Neapolitans to shame. Thankfully, they reached the entrance safely and checked in to their room.

The next morning, when Mike walked outside the hotel, he was so overcome with the beauty and he shouted to the world, "Que Bella!" The five story hotel surrounded by so much snow inspired Mike that he could hardly wait to hit the slopes. Caught up in his euphoria of the moment, he remembered he didn't have a clue on how to put on skis much less use them. Ski instruction would be held on the bunny slope. The slope was for beginners and would commence the following morning.

Up bright and early with breakfast out of the way, he was

off to the bunny slope for instruction while Judy planned to hit the big people's slope. She would be skiing down the Black Diamond runs. Agreeing to meet for lunch, she left Mike and was off to the chair lifts. Ready or not, Mike joined a group of a dozen school aged children.

Walking up to the group was a very Nordic looking blonde fellow who introduced himself as Hans. He would be their instructor for the day. Surprisingly, he spoke fairly understandable English but with a thick guttural accent.

Dressed in his cool blue ski overalls and with his skis, poles, goggles, hat and boots, he was ready to be taught the finer art of skiing. For the novice ski buffs, the bunny slope was on a slight rise that would lead to the top of a very small hill. Our beginners would reach the summit by holding onto a slow moving tow rope.

Now that Mike had mastered the art of 'tow-rope skiing,' it was time for the real thing. With visions of flying down the toughest slopes, which would impress the hell out of Judy, Mike was brought back to reality by Hans. Before anyone, much less Mike, was turned loose to ski down the bunny slope, Hans gave a demonstration on how to stay upright on skis.

Several dry runs were needed which showed them the 'snow plow' method or as he pronounced it 'Schno-plow.' Snow plowing would be accomplished by pointing one's ski tips inward but not touching. Figuring Mike and the children had the basics down, it was time to go skiing.

Hans lead the way much like a modern day Pied Piper only on skis. Mike and the others went zooming down the bunny slope.

No, zooming would not quite be the operative word to use as they moved at the speed of a fast turtle or slow bunny rabbit. It didn't matter; he had been skiing – Yahoo!

The real story Mike planned to tell back at the office was he was flying – creeping just wouldn't hack it. If anyone asked, "Boy, you should have seen me – I was zigging and zagging down those slopes; more like some Olympic skier." Mike figured he qualified to use the adage, "It was my story and I'm sticking to it."

After about three hours of alternating between 'Schno-plowing' and falling down, Mike was ready for lunch and met Judy at the restaurant. Even if he wasn't a big league skier, he still looked pretty impressive or so he thought.

After lunch it was back to Hans; happily, Mike and the others were informed the bunny slope instruction was finished. The afternoon was spent riding the chair lift up and alternating between skiing and falling down a beginner's slope and back up again. It was much like trial and error for Mike and on his last fall, he had enough. He just wasn't cut out to be a skier.

Maybe he should have rented his equipment, instead of buying the stuff. No, he never did anything half way – it was all the way or no way at all. The next day he planned to the tour the complex and check out the WWII features.

Up the next morning and with Judy heading for the slopes, Mike was ready to begin his guided tour. First on the list was a trip downstairs to see the two lane bowling alley. Sitting in a seat in the private movie theater was next on the list. Mike imagined top SS staff officers relaxing with a game or two or watching a movie that was either approved or most likely not approved by the Fuhrer. A series of bunkers fascinated Mike; the hotel was connected to these by tunnels which led to other areas of the complex. Our couple used the bowling alley and caught a movie while they stayed at the hotel. At the conclusion of his tour, Mike headed back to their room to wait for Judy's return.

Dinner was not at the hotel but at a nearby mom and pop restaurant serving local dishes. This little hole in the wall reminded Mike of eating at some of his favorite trattorias back in Naples. The evening was finished off with an Irish Coffee at the hotel bar.

The next morning was another beautiful day in the Alps but instead of a day of skiing it was time to head to the train station for the return trip to Naples. Back home, Mike left Judy at her apartment while he checked in at the office.

Mike kept busy with work and Judy did the same. Weeks passed with more dates and adventurous outings. They were having fun.

One afternoon while Mike was duty agent, the ASAC came into his office and asked if he had any vacation plans coming up? If not would he and Judy be up for a visit back to Germany? Mike could not think of any and was always ready for some R&R. "No, nothing planned," answered Mike. "Good, because we've put together a group of wives and agents to go to Munich for Carnival or as the Germans call it, Fasching. We would like you and Judy to join us for a couple of days. For the fancy balls, we would be dressed in costumes, much like costumed balls at Mardi Gras in New Orleans."

The ASAC went on to explain that the group would be comprised of six couples. They would take the overnight train from Rome and each compartment held six people. He named the agents with their wives: The Jones, the Trailors, the Tosgoods and the Hommes. "With you and Judy that would make our sixth couple." Mike said he would check with Judy and get back to him.

The appointed day arrived and everyone met at the office to begin their big adventure. Their baggage was loaded into two cabs for the short trip to the train station. The group boarded the train and got settled in their respective six-person compartments. Dave's wife called a short meeting to go over activities planned for Munich. After the meeting, Mike, Judy and their compartment mates returned to their compartment to relax. As the train sped toward Rome; some read books on Fasching while others drank some good old red vino di tavola.

As the hours passed and the wine flowed, the train soon approached Rome. Mike's compartment supply of wine had run dry and tried to borrow some from the next compartment. Bad plan, he was advised that for some strange reason they were almost out as well. Whoever had been nominated as the commissary officer had certainly failed in his job. A new plan was hatched with Mike and Ned being volunteered to buy more wine at the Rome train station.

With a thirty-minute stopover scheduled, Mike convinced all he was a track star and that he and Ned would be back in a flash with the wine. As the train screeched to a halt, Mike and Ned were off in search of some good Italian wine while the rest of the group headed for the connecting train to Munich.

Huffing and puffing the duo found a wine store. Evidently Mike had forgotten 20 years had passed since he ran the ½ mile race in high school. Purchasing two cases there would be no sprinting back to the train – a slow walk would be more to the point. True to his word, the official wine buyers got back to the train just before it pulled out of the station.

Everyone tried to sleep but it just wouldn't happen for most. Various attempts at catching some 'shut eye' were tried with limited success. The answer to the sleep problem was solved by most of the agents. Mike would call them 'sea stories' or exaggerated stories that passed back and forth. The more wine consumed the taller the stories rose. Getting bored with the drinking and storytelling, he broke out a brochure on the German Carnival.

Fasching was celebrated from January 6th to February 9th with the wildest days at the end of festivities. The spectrum of balls could be as low key as impromptu office parties to spectacular balls sponsored by such corporations as beer king Lowenbrau.

The next morning a bleary eyed group departed the train in Munich. Immediately, it was obvious the party was in full swing with costumed groups everywhere. Some of the costumed revelers would have found their costumes in expensive specialty shops while others were content with homemade ones. Grabbing a couple of cabs, it was off to their hotel to unpack and get dressed for Fasching!

With the group's arrival at the Hotel Hamer Hof, a 23-room family owned hotel, it was time to make group plans as well as individual activities. It was time to hit the streets.

Mike hurriedly dressed in his Count Dracula costume and Judy in her clown outfit. They left the hotel for the city center with Dave and his wife in tow. The tram ride to downtown was really something. Mike noted at least 50% of the riders were costumed: both young and old. The costumes ranged from simple masks to elaborate affairs.

The tram stopped at the Marienplatz, located in the city center. The foursome exited and were ready to party. At any time of the year, it was a busy tourist attraction with shops, beer halls and food emporiums. During the festival, it was especially alive with all the music and costumed individuals celebrating.

One of the most visited attractions was the Rathaus-Glockenspiel, a clock tower dating back to the early 1900's. At 11:00 AM each day a show was presented lasting around twelve minutes, depending on the tune played. Various characters which represented ancient figures in history, rotated on a carousel ending with a tiny golden rooster that would chirp three times ending the show. On the day the foursome saw the show, Mike estimated over 200 costumed people gathered. Mike along with Judy was glad they arrived in time. He took some good photos especially of the golden rooster.

Mike's group joined the throngs of costumed festival goers and made their way to various stalls which sold many Bavarian treats. Of course, they stopped from time to time to sample large steins of German beer. The smells from the food stalls and the roasting of chestnuts was an assault to the senses albeit in a very satisfying manner.

Sadly, even in the 1980's fast food chains were making their appearance in Europe. Even in the historic and beautiful setting of the Marienplatz, located right smack in the middle was the home of Ronald McDonald. Yes, hard to believe but the Big Mac was alive and well in Munich. To make sure no one could miss it, the restaurant even had the signature Golden Arches displayed on the roof. The place was packed but would definitely not include our intrepid party goers.

The four had spotted a small bistro next door that served authentic regional cuisine. Mike told Judy, "I didn't travel all the way to Germany to eat at a Mickey D's." Once seated in the bistro, a fantastic lunch was enjoyed, washed down with a very fine Pilsner. With it getting late, the group rode the tram back to the hotel to rest and get ready for the night's dinner and festivities.

Refreshed and dressed in their costumes it was time to meet the others in the hotel lobby. With all assembled and after comparing each costume, it was time for dinner and dancing at one of the beer halls sponsored by Lowenbrau. Once inside the hall they were shown to their reserved table by a waiter dressed as an elderly brewery worker. The ASAC leaned over to Mike, "Say, maybe that old guy wasn't wearing a costume; could he be some old pensioner from the brewery moonlighting?"

As if by magic another two waiters appeared at the table, each holding six huge glass beer mugs. Along with the beers, menus were produced. The Naples' contingent scanned the extensive menu and by unanimous decision; it was the Sauerbraten. Looking around the room, Mike guessed the ballroom had over 500 costumed revelers in attendance and would hold 200 - 300 more when filled. Mike along with the rest of his group of partiers, 'prosted' the night away with their beer steins held high.

The band struck up the popular song, simply called The Chicken Song. Mike and Judy joined the dancers on the floor and gave it their best shot; clapping their hands, flapping their arms and squatting with the best of them. While some people thought the German people were regimented and lacked a sense of humor – not this crowd - they came to party.

After great quantities of food and drink were consumed, awards were handed out for the best costumed participants. This would be the conclusion of the night's festivities. The twelve party goers from Naples left and returned to the hotel. Tomorrow would be another day of sightseeing and partying at another beer hall.

While the others were still in bed, Mike and Judy were up and out to return to the Marienplatz. They had noticed a pastry shop near the McDonalds and wanted to try a German pastry for breakfast and a good cup of coffee. Mike loved his coffee but at the hotel, it tasted more like tea. As they entered the shop, the display cases were filled with tasty delights. Mike and Judy decided on the German apple strudel and coffee. Mike led Judy to a table with a wonderful view of the square.

He dove into his strudel filled with chucks of apple the size of walnuts and washed it down with some of the best tasting coffee.

Finished with their strudels and coffees, it was time to pay the check. The bill shocked Mike to say the least. The two pastries were $2.00 each and the coffees were $3.00 apiece. For the 1980's their breakfast was pretty costly. Mike had read in his guide book Germany had no coffee growing regions thus had to import all coffee beans.

As they left, Mike thought that back in Naples for the same $10.00, he and Judy would have shared a great Neapolitan pizza and a bottle of wine. Who cared? They were in love and on holiday. With a little more sightseeing it was back to the hotel to meet with the others to see what group plans were in store.

On the way to the tram stop, fast food restaurants were packed with breakfast patrons. Mike just couldn't buy into it. Some local folks obviously wanted to try something different from their local fare but tourists always searched for a known taste of home, no matter what country they visited. *Oh well, let them,* Mike thought.

The group's last night in Munich would be spent celebrating at the Augustiner Keller. This Muchen landmark opened in the 1800's. Its claim to fame was their own brand of beer that came straight from the aging wood barrels to your beer mug. Since it was winter, the group would be down in the cellar but had it been summer they could have joined 5,000 of their closest friends for a beer in the garden. The night was festive and the beer flowed.

All too soon it was all aboard for the return trip to Naples. Unlike the trip to Germany the return trip was a little more subdued. The party fever had worn off and now time was spent reliving various adventures and drinking a lot less wine. Reaching the Naples' train station all caught separate cabs and headed for their respective homes.

Even though, Mike and Judy's relationship continued to blossom in the ensuing months, it was apparent their time together was coming to an end. Judy was due to be rotated back to the states for a new duty assignment, while Mike was also to end his tour in Naples with NIS. It seemed appropriate their last night together would be on New Year's Eve. Plans were made for the upcoming last date.

New Year's Eve arrived and they would spend it at the five-star Hotel Excelsior in downtown Naples. Mike recalled how impressed he was with the hotel when two VIP's had stayed there during two details. After they checked into the hotel, it was time to start the night with a few drinks at the bar. The couple, dressed in their best attire, tuxedo for Mike and a beautiful blue gown for Judy, walked arm in arm to the dining room. Dinner was a four-course meal accompanied with copious amounts of champagne. They would certainly be going out with some style.

With the hotel's band playing Glenn Miller tunes, the night was probably the most romantic they had shared together. Maybe knowing the end was near made it more special. Sooner than they wished, it was midnight and the band rang in the New Year with the favorite song: Auld Lang Syne. For Mike, the most romantic moment was the one last kiss on the dance floor he gave Judy. They both agreed to remember the lyrics of the song; their good times would not be forgotten.

The next morning a much subdued couple made their way back to her apartment. At the apartment, Mike walked Judy to the front door and with a tearful goodbye left. He had moved out of the apartment he shared with Lt. Richards. His temporary quarters were in the same hotel he had stayed when he first reported to Naples.

The rest of the day, Mike spent quietly at the hotel. He had already shipped his car and household goods home. Instead of moping around his hotel room, Mike decided to catch a cab to travel one more time through the streets of Naples. It did not matter to him that most businesses were closed; he just wanted to take it all in one more time.

Taking a chance, he stopped by the Anti-Drug office to say goodbye. It was his lucky day. The Major and a few of the CARBS were in the office celebrating the New Year. He joined them in a round of toasts and since it was their party he started to say his goodbyes.

Mike was caught by surprise when he was presented with some mementos of his time working with them. They included a military calendar with Italian paintings; four Italian military posters and a most prized miniature pewter military officer in full formal dress uniform. More important than these wonderful gifts was the bear hug Mike received from Sergio. Mike thought he saw a small tear in the big guy's eye.

He caught a cab back to the hotel and reflected back on his time in Naples. Unbeknownst to Mike, he had really become attached to Bella Napoli and would miss it. In his hotel room, it was time to pack for tomorrow's charter flight back to the states.

The next day, Mike was off to the NIS office for the last time. He had to turn in his last remaining equipment, his well-worn

NIS Credentials, his Porto d' Armi permit, the Ruger .357 and ship his personal S & W revolver back to the states.

He met with the SAC and told him he hoped he had done a good job for NIS. Caught off guard, the SAC informed him that if he ever wanted to come onboard as a civilian S/A, he would be proud to be his sponsor. "Mike, speaking for myself and the rest of my agents, we never thought of you as an officer agent - you were just one of us."

Mike joined his former NIS agents in the briefing room for a last goodbye. As a parting gift, Mike received a bronze NIS plaque showing his dates of service to go along with his Operation Red Blanket banner. Since he was a bachelor and maybe not such a great cook, the wives of the agents gave him the Official Naval Investigative Service Manual for K-P Organization/Admin./Systems (NIS-8) to help with meal preparations.

As the old saying goes, all good things must come to an end and for Mike so true. Mike not only ended his relationship with Judy, he was no longer a NIS S/A and he had decided to resign his navy commission and re-enter the civilian world.

As chance would have it, an old friend of his, a retired Virginia State Bureau of Investigations Special Agent had contacted him. He had started his own Private Investigator business in Virginia and wanted Mike to join him as a partner. The next chapter in the life of Mike Blackstone former NIS Special Agent would begin as Mike Blackstone Virginia Private Investigator.